To Lizzie,
Happy reading ♡

K. C. Carmine

To Lizzie,
Happy reading ♡
V.C. Cosmine

Stitch
ME

K.C. CARMINE

QUEER ROMANCE
WITH HEAT

Copyright © 2023 by K.C. Carmine

All rights reserved.

No portion of this book may be reproduced in any form without written permission from the publisher or author, except as permitted by copyright law.

The author does not own any copyrights to the brands mentioned in the novel. Most places in Bristol and Chicago are real, but modifications had been made to fit the story.

Cover design by Joe Satoria

The people on the images are models and should not be connected to the characters in the book. Any resemblance is incidental.

Edited by: Colin, Jennifer, Rebekah

Beta read by: Ellie, Kate

Blurb and Warnings

Blurb:

His career a mess and the excitement of his sex life fading, Rod is ready for a change. He needs someone who can fit into his world as a true partner, but also feed his dominant and sadistic sides. Impossible? Maybe, but he needs to try. He signs up for a new dating app, just as a feisty young man catches his eye.

Desperate to escape his dead-end existence in the US, Caleb flees to England in search of a different life. Along comes a trusted friend, a new dating app, and a chance to find a cuddly bear to submit to, but without a proper job, he might be forced to return home.

Consumed by his white-hot passion, Rod refuses to let his perfect sub slip from his grasp. He's determined to do whatever it takes to earn Caleb's love before they run out of time.

A high-heat MM romance.

Trigger and content warnings: discussions of past abuse and child neglect, death of a family member, suicide, overdose, grief, recollection of a kidnapping, homophobia, fighting, D/S dynamics, consensual punishment, insertion of objects, medical kink, morally grey characters.

Please do not use any work of fiction as your guide to BDSM lifestyle. Do extensive research, practice SSC/RACK/PRICK, and/or reach out to people in the community for information.

Chapter One

Caleb

It had been three months and Caleb still found it weird to ride on the upper deck of a bus. It was one of many things that made him feel completely uprooted from his beloved Chicago when he moved to Bristol.

Nearing downtown, or rather, the city center, he pressed the button for the bus to stop. Hefting up his backpack with a folder full of his sketches, he patted his pocket to make sure he hadn't lost the thumb drive before he bounced down the bus's stairs. The commotion in the center reminded him of his home city, even more so as he approached a rusty bridge he kept forgetting the name of. Brunel's Swivel Bridge—yeah, that was it.

Much like Chicago's downtown, Bristol had lively areas, as well as some seriously seedy ones. Walking under the wrought iron marked by age and weather, he headed towards a row of brick houses that had been built during the reign of some monarch three kings or queens back and were probably full of mold. He had spent little time in the UK, but he was certain by now that the smell of old damp buildings would be stuck in his nostrils forever.

Caleb knocked on a white door that had a little glass window with a rose on it. Weird fucking choice, considering who lived there.

The heavy footsteps contradicted the slim frame that appeared on the other side of the panel.

"What do you want?" Kris cracked the door open, showing his unkempt mustache.

"It's Caleb. I brought some drawings."

Kris pushed the panel open wearing a worn robe over a t-shirt and pajama bottoms, a joint hanging off the side of his lips.

"I hope these are better than the previous ones," Kris grunted as he tightened the sash around his waist.

"What's that supposed to mean?" Caleb paused with his hand closing over the thumb drive in his pocket.

"The designs from last month didn't sell."

"Like fuck they didn't."

"I'm telling you."

"Then you have shit advertising or whatever 'cause they were killer." Scanning them then digitally fixing them on the slow computer at the local library was no small feat either.

"I pay you for designs, not business opinions. Last I checked you didn't run one of your own, so your expertise means shit here."

Fucking asshole. Caleb had found him through an online forum after delicately asking around if there were places that would pay cash for his art. Kris uploaded them to a website with stock designs and Caleb had a feeling he was not the only one being paid shit for their art.

"Fine. Just gimme the money." Caleb sighed, handing over the thumb drive into Kris's sweaty palm.

"I have a check for you." Kris fumbled in the pocket of his robe.

"Can't you do a transfer or fucking PayPal like people do in this century? Who the fuck uses checks anymore?"

"I do. Do you want to be paid or not?" Kris waved the paper with his chicken scratch on it.

Caleb had spent ages fucking around trying to find proof of address last month just to open a basic bank account. Still, if that allowed him to use the money from Kris, it had been worth the hassle. He snatched the paper and frowned.

"This is half of what you paid me last time!"

"You didn't deliver so I can't take a risk anymore. Now, bugger off."

"Piece of shit," Caleb mumbled.

"What did you say?"

"It's lovely," he chirped in his best fake-English accent.

"See you next week, boy!"

"Don't call me that."

"And you better deliver," Kris smirked. "Boy."

Caleb caught the bus back home, to a tiny flat his friend let him crash in. He'd met Sandra nearly two years before on Twitter. He'd followed her after reading her extensive thread about David Bowie's impact on music fashion. Liking each other's posts and glamrock discussion quickly turned into DMs, and they'd hit it off pretty quickly over music and general life rants.

When Caleb had told her he was moving to Bristol, the place where his recently-deceased grandpa had been born, Sandra invited him to stay with her. It was an offer Caleb couldn't refuse. The money Grandpa had left hidden in an envelope under the bedroom rug was enough for the ticket to the UK and an unexpected expense, courtesy of his mom. Within days, Caleb had packed Grandpa's old suitcase and bought a plane ticket to Bristol.

It had been his first flight and he'd been scared shitless. O'Hare International was huge, and he'd felt like a three-year-old at a shopping mall who'd lost his parents. Once he'd sat in the plane, he'd thought the worst was over. Then he'd re-lived that huge-ass rollercoaster ride at Six Flags that he'd gone on once. At sixteen, he'd sold his bike to afford the ticket. It had been money well spent, but unlike the rollercoaster, the plane hadn't been anchored safely to the ground during turbulence. Thankfully, he'd survived the nine-hour flight and stepped on UK soil on wobbly legs.

Since he was little, he'd loved his grandpa's stories about his childhood in England. After Caleb had moved in with the man, he'd told him that if Caleb ever wanted a new beginning, he could go to the UK and apply for citizenship based on his mother being born on the British Isles.

Once in Bristol, Caleb had filled out all the paperwork to confirm his automatic citizenship. He'd presented his mom's birth certificate, and attended the UK Visa and Citizenship Application Services office to give his fingerprints and photo. As bureaucracy goes, they'd told him he'd have to wait up to six months for the approval. Which meant he was stuck on a tourist visa with no way to work. Well, not legally...

He'd known that starting from scratch in a new country wouldn't be an easy ride but he was beginning to think that it had been a bad idea altogether. The streets of South Side Chicago raised him not to be a quitter, but having never gone further than Indiana or Wisconsin, he hadn't been prepared for the realities of becoming an immigrant with no right to work. If not for Sandra, he'd be in even deeper shit. No wonder so many Americans didn't emigrate. Thankfully, he'd found a few places where he could get some money under the table to cover his expenses until he could get a UK passport and he could look for legal work.

The bus stop was just a few minutes' walk from Sandra's Southville flat and Caleb sent his roommate a text asking if she wanted something from the local Tesco Express. Three dots appeared before a message came through.

'Nope. Cause we're going to a pub to celebrate. I got my boobs appointment.'

Sandra's excitement was so infectious Caleb could feel it traveling through the phone line, filling him with happiness for her.

'Awesome! Be there in 5.' He shot the text back, grinning all the way to the apartment.

Sandra was a year into her transition and was waiting for an appointment with a doctor to see about breast implants. For some reason, the clinic couldn't send a text or an email—it had to come by fucking letter, making the process much longer than necessary.

After reaching the long, four-story building, he bounded up both flights of stairs two at a time.

"Congrats, Sandy!" he yelled, the moment he set foot on the apartment's blue carpet.

"Thanks, babe!" Sandra threw herself into Caleb's open arms, squeezing him so tight his ribs nearly cracked. "I'm stressed but feel so much better already."

"You'll have a beautiful big rack in no time," he said. With Sandra plastered against his body, he felt her laughter erupt before he even heard it.

"Silly." She pushed him away. "It's going to be a moderate B, thank you very much." Her long brown hair fell around her shoulders as she twirled, sending her flowery skirt flying above her knees. "So, I'm thinking The Lion's Mane for a drink?"

"Is that the one with the pulled lamb sandwich?"

"Yup," Sandra grinned, reaching for her light jacket. Despite it being late May, the typical English evening chill had long outstayed its welcome.

"I'm in. Just gimme a sec." Caleb stepped into his room to toss his backpack and the folder with his art on the bed. He sniffed his t-shirt and decided on reapplying deodorant and changing clothes. His worn black jeans would have to do, but he spiced up his outfit with a badass black t-shirt before re-entering the living room.

"Oh, Lady Gaga. Fancy." Sandra pointed at his chest.

"Perfect to celebrate." He smirked, grabbing his leather jacket off the hanger by the door. The weight of it was like home on his back. He'd put care to make it look like new after he found it in a Goodwill store back home. It had been just his size, so he'd deemed it fate and spent all the cash in his wallet on it.

After a short walk, Sandra and Caleb entered the old-English pub, with wooden floors, a long bar, and a huge-ass TV reserved for soccer—or rather *football*—evenings. Caleb ordered the pulled lamb sandwich for himself, fries for Sandra, and two beers. Their tiny table in the corner overlooked the patio with more tables and a few potted plants.

"I'm glad I broke up with Peter, but it still hurts that he didn't want to stay friends. As if fucking was the only thing keeping us together." Sandra wrapped her hands around the cold glass in front of her.

"Fuck that douchebag." Caleb nudged the fries towards Sandra to encourage her to eat. "He hasn't texted back in two weeks now. He's probably still crying into a pillow and it's too hard for him to contact you. Or he's just an asshole."

"Yeah, well." Sandra took a sip of her beer. "I think I need a break from relationships. You on the other hand..."

"Oh no, I'm not looking for a relationship. I can't imagine trying to find someone decent with all the other shit I'm dealing with right now. Besides, relationships are not my strong suit. I mean, Natasha was great but we never clicked as a couple. And every guy I've been with just lays there to be serviced. I need someone who'd take some fucking initiative, but people like that don't just fall into my lap."

"But maybe you could find someone to cuddle," Sandra sing-songed, waving her finger at him.

"Eat your fries." Caleb pushed the plate again.

"These are chips, you filthy American."

"Filthy, huh?" Caleb laughed. They'd had a running joke of him using Americanisms on purpose, even if he knew things had different names in the UK.

"I'm serious, Caleb. Have you heard of this new dating app?" Sandra asked, dipping a fry in ketchup.

Caleb sighed, looking towards the bar to see if his sandwich was ready. "Not again with the dating apps. I need to get citizenship, then a stable job. I can't waste time on dating."

"Oh, come on, you can date and do the rest at the same time. Martin said this one was good for those who like bigger guys. Sure, he may not have clicked with the bloke on the first date, but he said it was still nice." She cheekily pointed a fry at him. "How about *you* try it with a daddy?"

"Fuck you, Sandy. That's the last thing I need. Someone to boss me around. Fuck that shit."

"But you do like big, cuddly bears, right?"

"That's beside the point. I haven't found one who wouldn't pull his macho shit on me. I'm not gonna cater to their every whim in exchange for some decent fucking."

"Yes, your pride and your muscles wouldn't let you do that." Sandy waved a hand, indicating Caleb's entire body. "Which is great."

"How's that great?" he mumbled around a stolen fry.

"Maybe you could find yourself a teddy bear daddy. And well, this Bears-4-U app—"

"That's the stupidest name I've ever heard."

"Shut up and let me finish."

"Fine." Caleb stole a thick fry from Sandra's plate and tossed it into his mouth.

She glared at him and continued. "This app allows you to sort of build your own bear and then depending on the info you put, it searches for people on the app to match with you. Let me show you." She extended a hand. "Gimme your phone."

Caleb grunted but fished his phone out of his pocket and handed it over. "If you see my porn folder, you're welcome."

Sandra snorted and started tapping. "Ok, got it downloaded. Now, some basic information about what you need."

"What I need? Show me that," Caleb protested with his mouth full.

"No, cause you'll ruin it all. Promise me you won't look at what I put in your profile." Sandra was typing furiously, a grin on her face.

"Why would I promise that?"

"Cause you trust me and you know I want you to be happy."

"Pffft. Fine." Caleb sat back and reached for his beer.

"Done. Now a picture." She pointed the phone at Caleb.

Caleb smacked a hand on his face to cover it up. "That's stupid."

"You're grinning, despite not showing your face. So cute," she squeaked.

"I'm not cute."

"Course you're not, you grump." Her thumbs worked overtime. "Now, we can pick a bear or a teddy bear for you. Then if someone has the characteristics and needs I put for your profile, you'll match. It might take a while."

"What do you mean by 'my needs'?" Caleb narrowed his eyes. This was getting out of hand.

"Let me handle this. You're a switch, right?"

"Yeah," Caleb sighed, burying his face in his hands. This was going to be a disaster.

If he ever connected with people, it was beyond gender and looks, so an app devoted to a body type wouldn't work for him. Then again, it wouldn't hurt giving it a shot either.

He liked girls, always had, even though his attraction to men was a lot stronger. His latest girlfriend, Natasha, was into mixed martial arts, and worked at a gym she'd opened with her friends where women kicking ass wouldn't be snickered at. He'd been the first man to sign up for her classes and learned her tough love pretty quickly. She was as commanding and strict in the gym as she was dominant in the bedroom.

They hadn't worked as a couple, but she'd taught him how to throw a punch better than the average street fighter, and they'd remained friends.

Caleb shot to his feet as Simon, the barman, waved at him to pick up his sandwich. Simon handed it over, but his gaze stayed on something behind Caleb. A fist landed on the bar with a thud, drawing Caleb's attention. On its wrist a black, tattooed 88 stood out against the pale skin.

"You're not welcome here, I told you that before," Simon said, his voice calm but clearly on edge.

Caleb eyed the muscled guy next to him, easily a head taller than Caleb, with close-cropped hair.

"Don't be a tosser and do your job. I need a beer. We all do," the asshole said, nudging the two lackeys at his sides.

"That's not my problem. Now please leave." Simon enunciated slowly.

"You know this dick?" Caleb asked, putting his sandwich away.

"He's about to go, right Leo?" Simon replied, looking pointedly at the trio.

"What did you call me?" Leo asked, smacking Caleb's arm.

Caleb braced for a punch but Leo pushed his sandwich off the bar. Like a fucking angry cat. Aware of the diversion, Caleb didn't move, only heard the flop of his food on the floor.

He looked up to meet the dude's gaze and smiled. "I called you a dick cause you're not very nice. But I was mistaken."

"Damn right you were," Leo snarled, looking Caleb up and down.

"I meant to say small dick." Caleb held his smile as he saw Leo's fist tighten in the corner of his eye.

Caleb ducked the blow and sighed, straightening back up.

He didn't want to do this.

Oh, who was he kidding? Of course he did.

He grinned before his fist flew to connect with Leo's jaw.

Leo's head snapped back as pain exploded in Caleb's hand. Oops, Leo didn't fall. Well, then.

Caleb ducked when the meaty fist swung his way and aimed a shot at his opponent's side.

Sliding on the filthy floor of the pub, he bumped into someone behind him. "Sorry," he shot as he bounced off the guy and back into the makeshift ring in the middle. There were no ropes, just people. It was all the same to Caleb.

At 5'8, he wasn't a giant but he'd learned how to use his size to his advantage in a fight.

"Toss him into the river!" someone yelled and a cheer erupted.

Caleb ducked and landed another punch.

"Caleb, watch out!"

Sandra's voice made him turn her way. Was she OK?

Pain exploded in his head, and his vision got blurry. He swayed but caught himself on the edge of the table.

"Oi! That's enough! Get the fuck out of my pub!" A yell sounded behind him.

Caleb gave Sandra an apologetic look and hauled ass before security dragged him out.

"He started it—" Leo whined, but Simon stopped him, a baseball bat in his hand.

"I said bugger off. And I don't give a rat's arse who started it, I'm not your mother."

A wave of laughter erupted as Caleb followed the asshole.

"I'll see you around!" Leo pointed a finger at him, his lackeys flanking him as they walked away.

Caleb sat on the sidewalk, his back to the cold brick wall of the pub.

"Caleb, you idiot! Are you alright?" Sandra's footsteps echoed close before she squatted next to him, his jacket safe in her hands.

"I'm fine," he said, despite his swelling eye. "Are you?"

"Yeah, I got your jacket. You cross the street when you see those guys, not start a fight with them, you know?"

"Fucking Nazis. That fucker owes me a sandwich, too," Caleb mumbled, trying to rein in his anger.

Sandra laughed then sucked in air, crouching closer. "Oh, hell, you're bleeding."

Caleb blinked and swiped his hand over his eye. Red. "I'll be fine."

"That needs stitches." A low voice sounded from the direction of the pub, the rumble sending a warm shiver through Caleb.

"I said, I'll be fine," Caleb snapped, then followed the sound of footsteps until they stopped in front of him. He looked from black combat boots, up thick thighs, to a wide chest and bearded face.

Who the fuck is this guy? He glanced at Sandy but she shrugged, clearly not knowing the dude either.

"Of course, you will. But if this won't stop bleeding, you'll end up with a five-hour wait in A&E. I can save you the trip if you just let me look at your head." The guy kneeled in front of Caleb, right there on the wet pavement. His deep brown, kind eyes were a contrast to his huge frame and the vicious burn scar above his left eye that partially deformed his eyebrow.

A hot bear dude wanted to inspect him. *Who am I to say no?*

"Sure. Are you a doctor or something?" Caleb followed the movement of the man's thick arm as he lifted it up to Caleb's face. *Well, I'll be damned.*

"Nah. I just had a bunch of accident-prone siblings growing up. I'm Rod, by the way." He tilted his head, brushing the hair off Caleb's forehead with gentle fingers.

"Caleb." He nodded. "And that's Sandra."

"Hi," Sandra said, standing out of Caleb's field of vision.

"Pleasure to meet you," Rod rumbled, breaking away to look at Sandra, then back.

Caleb stilled when Rod used his other hand to keep his chin steady. Heat flooded his abdomen at the decisive, yet gentle touch.

The movement opened Rod's bomber jacket to reveal a black t-shirt with a colorful picture. "Are those unicorns fucking?" Caleb snorted, pointing at Rod's chest.

"That they are," Rod smirked. "I need to bring some water to clean this. And paper towels. And sanitizer." He started to get up, but Sandra stopped him.

"I'll get it all. You just..." She waved her hand between the two of them. "Yeah." She darted off. The minx. It was as if she knew Caleb's heartbeat quickened with every second Rod's fingers touched his face.

Chapter Two

Rod

Rod welcomed the roar of the crowded pub as he entered. His hulking figure, black attire, and a scar above his left brow made it easy for him to pass through the partying crowd to get to his mates already waiting for him. Patrick and Geordie sat at their regular table in the corner, a round of beers decorating it.

As he headed towards them, however, a fight broke out and a bloke half his size but feisty as fuck bounced off his flank.

Rod watched the fight and the subsequent hassle as the smaller guy walked out with dignity while the bigger one argued with the staff.

A trace of worry flashed through Rod's mind, as he realized it'd be all too easy for the big bastard to carry on the brawl with the smaller guy outside. Indicating to his friends that he'd be right back, Rod ran out the door in hot pursuit.

It was none of his business. And yet, he followed them out to see the nasty bloke walking into the distance with his mates.

Mr Feisty was sitting on the pavement outside, talking to his friend. She looked worried, clutching a leather jacket in her hands as she stepped closer.

The next moment, Rod was kneeling in front of the guy, inspecting his split eyebrow and trying not to get lost in those big eyes that looked black in the dim light of the pub behind them. They exchanged names, and Caleb's smooth American accent made Rod desperately crave cold water for his face. And for Caleb's wound.

When Caleb's friend offered to get supplies for the cleanup, they were alone, bar a stranger passing on the other side of the road.

That left him with his hand on Caleb's chin, the other holding the man's short, black hair back off his cut, and trying not to lean in for a kiss. *What is wrong with you?* But Rod Galicki had left the building. It was Rod the Horny who was in charge, now. No, no, he needed his sane side back.

"Do you always bounce off strangers to beat up guys bigger than you?" Rod asked, dropping the hand that was on Caleb's chin. Caleb's gaze followed it, as if he wanted it back. *Oh, God.*

"Oh, that was you. Sorry for barging into you, man, but that shit-for-brains deserved it. Simon asked him to leave." Caleb gritted his teeth and the fire coursing through the man's body was palpable.

That voice. That accent. Silky with a rasp.

"He's been in and out of jail for race crimes, but the charges were dropped every time. For some reason, he keeps harassing the pub. Good thing you gave him hell." With his right hand, Rod inspected the split skin where blood was still trickling.

"Not nearly enough—" Caleb hissed but didn't flinch away.

"I'm just pinching the wound closed." Rod leaned in for a closer look and his nose filled with Caleb's scent. Sweat and blood. The fingers of his left hand drifted under Caleb's chin to tilt his head up towards the light from a street lamp. His naturally tanned skin accentuated the perfect imperfections of his face: the thick black eyebrows, a slightly crooked nose as if it had been broken before, and a sharp jawline.

One moment he was looking at a split eyebrow, the next his eyes glazed over as soft lips met his own.

Caleb's kiss began as gentle, but the man's hand on Rod's pec burned like a hot poker as it slid up to his nape. A rumble rose in Rod's chest as he opened his mouth to welcome Caleb's tongue. It was as feisty as the man himself, exploring with sensual haste. Rod didn't question his instincts despite knowing nothing about the stranger who set him on fire within seconds. His left hand slid from Caleb's chin to gently wrap around the man's throat. The deep moan coming from Caleb suggested he approved of the touch, and he gripped the hair at Rod's nape tighter.

Rod's cock swelled, and he went from wanting to help a stranger to wishing he could fuck him right there, face to the pavement, arse up, or against the wall with legs around Rod's waist.

"I have the water—Oh!" Sandra's voice broke the magical moment.

But Rod wasn't done.

He placed a hard kiss on Caleb's lips before he completely pulled away, letting his hand unhurriedly slide from Caleb's neck.

"Thank you, dear," Rod said, reaching for the bottled water Sandra brought. He refused to pretend that the kiss hadn't happened, but he wanted to give Caleb the space to make of it whatever he wished.

It was Caleb who had initiated it, after all. His cheeks were flushed and his deep brown eyes blazed with heat, never leaving Rod's face. They burned with their intensity and Rod took a moment to bask in the stare.

Only a moment.

Popping the small sanitizer bottle open, Rod slathered it on his hands thoroughly, before rinsing with water. He didn't want the alcohol in Caleb's wound. With a finger under Caleb's chin, he tilted his head back.

"Close your eyes," he instructed and Caleb obeyed, the simple action giving Rod a buzz of delight. He poured water over the split skin, wetting Caleb's face and the collar of his t-shirt where a sliver of a tattoo peaked out. "It's not as bad as it looks." Rod wiped the water off Caleb's cheek with his palm. It might have been his imagination, but he saw Caleb lean into his touch. His eyes still closed, he let out a slow exhale— and didn't that just made Rod's heart beat faster.

"Stay still." Rod's voice dipped lower. He reached for the paper towels Sandra was clutching in her hand, her face bright red, her wide eyes taking in the scene as if something magical was happening before her. Maybe she was onto something.

Rod patted the skin around the split with the towel, careful not to let any remnants get into the wound. Caleb was unmoving but he had opened his eyes, which were now boring into Rod with unbridled intensity. Rod straightened on his knees to pull out his wallet and retrieve a packet of steri-strips.

"You always carry these around?" Caleb asked, a smirk playing on his face.

"A habit, I guess." Rod shrugged, recalling the many times he patched up his brother and sister at home to avoid going to A&E, risking social services being up in his mom's face again.

Peeling apart the backing, he inspected the wound, thinking about how to position the strips strategically so they would hold.

Caleb didn't so much as flinch when Rod pinched the skin on Caleb's brow. It took all five strips to keep the wound closed properly.

"Take the rest home, these are bound to pop, but try not to get them wet for a day or so."

"Sure, thanks." Caleb nodded but didn't accept the strips until Rod shoved them in his hand.

"How's your head otherwise?"

"Good." Caleb stood up and shrugged into his well-worn leather jacket, so befitting his bad-boy looks with the split eyebrow and strong, if not tall, frame.

Rod was still on his knees, looking up at Caleb. He opened his mouth to ask the guy's shoe size or the number to his tattoo artist, anything to make him talk, to make him stay.

"Thanks," Caleb said, extending his hand for Rod to shake. "We'd better get going. It's been a long day."

"Anytime." Rod released his hand with reluctance and shook Sandra's before the two turned to leave.

"Why didn't you ask for his number, you knob?" Sandra elbowed Caleb, whispering loudly enough for Rod to catch it.

"Shh! He just helped me. Jumping his dick is not my idea of a thank you."

"Why not?" Sandra laughed.

Rod stared after them as they made their way down the street, overwhelmed with disappointment. The rest of their conversation quickly became too distant for him to hear, but his heart lit up when he saw Caleb glance over his shoulder with a look that Rod was sure mirrored his own.

Then just like that, after one kiss, Caleb was gone like some fucking Cinderella.

If only Rod had so much as a shoe to help him find the guy again.

Aida would be proud of his reference. His younger sister was a woman now, but in his heart, she'd always be the little girl who'd made him watch all the Disney movies with her. His mom was wonderful, but back then as a single parent working two jobs, she hadn't had the energy to spend quality time with them. She'd tried. But she'd tended to fall asleep from exhaustion when making soup or playing board games with them. Those moments had made Rod's teenage ass snap back to reality and take some of the burden from her shoulders. He'd taken the self-imposed role of his siblings' carer until they'd become old enough to take care of themselves, and only then had he gone away to uni. When he had returned, he'd found Flynt and Aida in relationships, living their lives. They still needed Rod's help from time to time, but he'd never felt truly needed again.

Rod slumped on the pavement, letting his head rest against the cool brick of the pub.

The gaping hole in his chest was becoming harder to bear every year.

Between his mom and siblings, he had a wonderful family, but he didn't have anyone who was solely his. His to cherish, to hug, to fuck, to love so hard that he'd leave bruises. He wanted someone to take care of, someone who'd rely on him. A partner.

Now, more than ever, the emptiness in his life intensified. A hole that only a life partner could fill. Unfortunately, he'd never found someone matching his needs in and out of the bedroom within the kink community. Subs were fantastic, but many of them wanted sex only, some fun play and release, then go on living their vanilla lives. He craved finding someone independent, but also dedicated to a relationship and BDSM.

He looked down at the unicorns fucking on his t-shirt and sighed as he pulled himself to his feet. He better return to his friends inside. His beer was getting warm.

The pub was back to normal. Drunken fights were too common to disrupt the pub's atmosphere.

Rod parked his arse in the booth across from Patrick and Geordie and reached for his beer. He took a healthy gulp, then another one, before wiping a hand over his mouth and beard.

"What was that about?" Patrick asked, dipping his chip in the pool of vinegar on his plate.

"The white supremacist arsehole was being rude to the barman and this bloke stepped in."

"The cute twunk?" Geordie asked. He tilted his head, thinking. "A bit too muscly for me, but those tats and his face? Mmm." He rumbled appreciatively. "Did you go to sniff him out?"

Did I?

"Nah, just put a few strips on his brow."

"The biggest goodie-two-shoes sadist this world has ever seen." Patrick snorted, fixing the bun on top of his head.

"Nah, he's just a Daddy Bear through and through. A caregiver and a sadist all rolled into one." Geordie twirled a finger in Rod's direction.

"Oh, shut up, both of you." Rod chuckled but didn't deny their words. Besides, he might have mellowed out when it came to his sadistic streak. Perhaps he'd just lost interest. He hadn't had a decent connection with anyone in a while and it had dimmed his enthusiasm. "I lost my edge with kink. Although I had a nice session last weekend."

"Do tell." Geordie leaned forward, his hands under his chin, looking adorable despite his near-cruelly handsome face and bushy beard.

"I went to London, as you know, to visit a few friends and the club." Both his friends knew he was referring to The Golden Handcuffs, so he didn't have to spell it out.

"Blah, blah, fast forward to the scene." Geordie wiggled his otter arse on the bench.

"You're shameless."

"Me? I just need to find myself a daddy who'll like all my fur." He pouted, smoothing a hand down his clothed chest. "Meanwhile, I can live vicariously through my friends."

"Or just wax," Patrick deadpanned, earning a glare from Geordie.

"That shit hurts."

"I thought you were a sub."

"Yeah, but not a pain slut, fuck you very much. Besides, it's not that kind of pain, you should know."

"OK, enough of the banter, ladies." Rod sighed then motioned to the bartender for another round of beers. "So, last weekend in London I was supposed to just go to the club to mingle, right? I was getting ready to leave when my uni roommate texted me that he needed me to fill in for him."

"Oh? Was it E? Was he ok?" Geordie leaned forward.

"Yeah, he had a great date apparently and didn't want to bail in favor of the club. I ended up doing a flogging session he was supposed to do that night."

"Sounds fun." Patrick clapped his hands loud enough to get the attention of the booth behind him.

"It was. I should take up more shifts at Blackbeard's parties again."

"I wish we had our own club, not that renting space shit." Patrick slumped into his seat.

"Yeah, so we can mingle more." Geordie nodded. "For now, the after parties at Blackbeard's house have to be enough. But you wouldn't know. You haven't been to any since you closed your practice."

Rod stiffened, and Patrick gave Geordie a stern look.

"What? He was a great therapist." Geordie's whisper wasn't quiet in the slightest.

"But you know what happened," Rod said, suddenly feeling sick.

"That wasn't your fault."

"I just don't want to talk about it, OK?" Rod sighed. "Besides that, scenes are great, but I need a connection."

"That moment when their eyes roll back, they float into subspace, and you know they do that only with you," Patrick mused, a conflicted expression on his face. He'd found his someone, but his boy had moved back to Germany and didn't ask Patrick to go with him. It had broken the man, but he seemed to be able to talk about it again. It had been three years, after all.

"So," Geordie drummed his fingers on the table, breaking the awkward silence. "Pat and I signed up for this app where you can customize a bear you want." Geordie radiated excitement.

"I don't know if a bear is who I'm looking for," Rod said, although body type had never changed the way he looked at subs.

"But *you* are one, silly." Geordie gave him an exasperated look. "Let your match find you instead."

"Right, OK. Go on."

Geordie continued explaining the app as Rod downloaded it and started filling out the information. His height, build, the intensity of his body hair... OK, that was specific. Who was he looking for? That was more difficult than he'd expected. Thinking he wanted a partner was quite different from typing out characteristics like he was shopping for a sex doll. He needed someone compatible with him in terms of sex. Yes, a submissive, a bottom or a switch, someone who'd let him take care of them, at least a little. Body type didn't matter. He wasn't intimidated by guys bigger than him, although he was generally one of the tallest in the room wherever he went.

Finished, he placed his phone on the table, face up, and pulled to his feet. "More beers?"

"Yeah, and get a jacket potato for me. They make good ones here."

"Sure." Rod walked towards the bar, bustling through the thickening Friday crowd that had gathered in anticipation of the upcoming live band. He glanced at the poster by the door and, sure enough, a concert was scheduled for today.

After placing his order, he slid back into the booth with three beers and a promise of the food coming soon.

The moment his gaze landed on Geordie's sparkling eyes and eager smile, he knew something was up.

"What is it?"

"You matched!" Geordie squeaked.

"We didn't look but your phone is right there and it lit up," Patrick said apologetically.

"Yes, three times." Geordie raised three fingers to drive the point across.

"Go on, tell us who picked you."

"Wow, either you're very good friends invested in my sex life or you need to find more excitement in your own," Rod mumbled, having a swig just to make them wait longer.

"Ouch. Bitch, we're both," Geordie said and waved a hand at Rod's phone. "Come on."

"Let's see." Rod unlocked the device and opened the first notification from the app.

"Is there a picture?" Patrick craned his neck to see.

Rod angled his phone to the guys to show the cute blond boy.

"Is he even eighteen?" Patrick squinted at the screen. "Says twenty-one, but hmm."

Rod turned his gaze to the profile. "Looking for Daddy Dom to take care of me and cater to my needs."

"Sounds like a pillow princess," Geordie said.

"You would know." Patrick elbowed him in the side.

"Piss off. Let the man read." Geordie crossed his arms and sat back.

Rod smiled at the banter and continued inspecting the profile. "'I love a good spanking but being bratty is my true nature. Open to 24/7,'" Rod read. "I have a bad feeling about this one." Rod had been into the scene for over a decade, since his uni days, and he'd learned to go with his gut feeling when it came to people in the community. He knew right away that he wouldn't click with this guy.

"OK, show us the next one." Geordie clapped his hands with excitement when Rod presented the profile pic of the second match. "Oh wow, that's a pretty face."

"Not into BDSM," Rod read underneath the photo.

"Oh, boo." The guys deflated.

"OK, one more left," Rod said, clicking on the third profile he matched with. "No picture of the face. He's hiding behind his hand but..." Rod's voice trailed off when he saw the leather jacket and a tattoo on the side of the guy's neck, barely visible in the blurry picture.

Caleb?

His heart sped up as he read the minimalistic information.

"Looking for a gentle Dom with a firm hand."

Was it possible it was Caleb? Rod had to find out. His thumbs flew over the keyboard but he deleted the message three times before he finally settled on sending a simple 'Hi.'

"Did you just text him right away?" Patrick gasped, covering his mouth with his hand as he exchanged looks with Geordie.

"Yeah." Rod put his phone away and sipped his beer.

They all jumped like teenage girls watching a rom-com when a message lit Rod's screen.

"What does it say?" Geordie's voice climbed in pitch with excitement.

"'I'll be at the Bear Picnic. Next Friday at 7 pm at The Lion's Mane. I'll be wearing a purple hoodie.'" Rod read the text aloud.

OK, that was quick and to the point.

"No chit-chat, huh?" Geordie frowned.

"I guess not." *Not now at least.* Rod shot a quick message agreeing to the meeting and put his phone away. He had to find out if it was Caleb soon or he'd burst.

Chapter Three

Caleb

"Ok, that's done now." Caleb closed the browser and sat back on the chair until it creaked. "Thanks for letting me use your laptop."

"What's done?" Sandy asked. "And you know you can take it whenever you want."

Caleb had checked his account balance online and had breathed with relief that Kris's meager check had cleared. He didn't trust the man.

He'd had to go to the bank every few days to deposit the cash he earned from fights in small increments or they'd ask him to fill out a form explaining where it was from. Fucking annoying. At one point, he had to ask Sandra to deposit the money into her account saying that it was some cash from her grandma, then wire the money to Caleb. It was a pain in the ass, but he couldn't send cash to the US.

"I sent money to cover mom's bills, but I put the cash for rent and expenses in an envelope in the kitchen."

"You know you don't have to do that." Sandra rolled her eyes. "You're my guest."

Caleb kept it a secret that he was also setting aside a sum to chip in to Sandra's surgery.

"What? I'm not your roomie? Why would you hurt me so?" Caleb clutched the imaginary pearls on his neck.

"Shut up." Sandra laughed, throwing half of the croissant she'd been eating at Caleb.

Caleb caught the croissant and took a bite of it. "I won't," he said around the pastry. "And yes, I have to pay for my upkeep, even if you're my friend. That's not up for debate." Caleb crossed his arms and watched Sandra bring the envelope back to him. Caleb ignored it. He would just stuff it into the savings cookie can later.

"Stubborn," Sandra sighed, collapsing onto a chair next to him, her hand smoothing one of the old photo albums on the table.

They were amongst the very few sentimental items Caleb had brought with him to the UK. Both albums had belonged to his grandpa. One contained Grandpa's childhood and family photographs, most in black and white, glued to the thick pages. Further into the album there were pictures of teenage Pops with his best friend, up to the time he met Grandma and they'd gotten married and had Mom.

The other had plastic slots, so popular in the 90s, filled with chosen pictures of family life after they'd moved to the USA in the mid-60s: Caleb's mom when she was little and growing up, his brother Timmy being born, then Caleb, until the pictures stopped after a family tragedy, leaving several slots empty at the end.

"Did you have any luck finding your grandpa's friend?" Sandra asked, opening the old album at a page with a black-and-white picture of Grandpa at around twenty standing next to his childhood friend, arm around his shoulder, both boys smiling from ear to ear.

"No, not yet," Caleb said, his eyes lingering on the picture. "I haven't done enough research, and honestly, I don't even know where to start. How many Henry Smiths are there in the UK?"

"Probably thousands." Sandra grimaced. "But we'll figure something out."

Caleb sighed. He'd have to go through the postcards and try to remember any sliver of detail his grandpa told him. Grandpa Fred often mentioned his friend from childhood, and Caleb knew they'd never reconnected in person after Grandpa had moved to the USA with his family. Caleb thought it would be cool to meet the guy or his family and tell them that his grandpa's fond memories of Bristol and his friend were partially what had brought him here.

He smiled at the albums and placed them on a shelf in the corner, far from direct sunlight.

"Two days until your appointment. How do you feel?" Caleb asked, sitting back on the chair.

"Excited and scared at the same time," she said, releasing a slow breath. "I've waited for it for so long…"

"I'm coming with you and after the appointment we'll get that wine you like and watch The Office."

"The original one." She narrowed her eyes.

"Yeah, yeah, that one." He watched Sandra bite the inside of her cheek in thought. "Listen, whatever the doctor says, we'll figure something out. There are private clinics." He offered his hand, palm up on the table.

Sandra took it, shooting him a small smile. "I know." She squeezed his hand. "Are you ready for your date today?"

"I guess." He reached for his phone on the edge of the table. "I texted him in case he didn't recognize me from the profile picture."

"And?"

"He did, and he still wants to meet." Caleb fiddled with the cover of his phone before he shoved it back into his pocket.

"Of course. He looked at you like he wanted to eat you up." Sandra was grinning, her eyes sparkling. Caleb was more skeptical.

"Nah, he was just concerned." Caleb had been overanalyzing his first meeting with Rod and the coincidence of matching on the Bear-4-U app and was trying not to put too much hope into a man he didn't know.

"Concerned about his inability to stop touching you." Sandra smirked. "And remind me again, how did that kiss go?"

"Shut up. It was fucking hot."

"Trust me, you're going to have a blast. And I want all the dirt once you're back." She batted her lashes with an innocence that Caleb wasn't buying.

"We'll see about that." Caleb pushed to his feet and shrugged into his purple hoodie. "I'm packed for the fight later on. It will give me two hours with the guy, which is too long if I don't like him."

"And not enough if you do."

"Meh." Caleb shrugged, his stomach twisting with both anticipation and dread at his crammed evening schedule.

"You're sure you can't skip the fight?" Sandra's smile fell, her expression turning into a worried frown.

"Yes, I'm sure." Caleb picked up his backpack from the floor and slung it over his shoulder.

Caleb had seen the way Sandra looked at him when he returned from the fights beaten and bruised. She'd expressed her disapproval but there wasn't much she could do to prevent him from going. She'd even played the 'don't bring food to my house you've bought with blood money' card but Caleb hadn't listened. Even if the fight was illegal, it was still honest money. It wasn't like he had many alternatives.

"You look good, by the way," Sandra said, smiling, but the concern never left her face.

"Thanks." He didn't agree. He should wear nicer clothes for the picnic date but he refused to spend money on unnecessary items. He pulled his leather jacket over the hoodie, straightened the pockets of his tight black jeans and slid his feet into his classic three-striped sneakers. "Don't wait up. I'll be late."

Several bus stops later, Caleb entered the pub, hoping the barman wouldn't recognize him from the fight the week before. But this evening, the place looked different. A man at the door scanned something off people's phones before letting them in. That must be the confirmation to attend the bear picnic. Caleb pulled the Bear-4-U app and found the barcode under the "matched" tab.

All scanned, he entered the pub. The dimmed light inside created a cozy atmosphere and the rock music was set at a medium volume to allow for conversation. Caleb looked around and saw people dressed casually at first glance, but a keen eye could spot a spiked-leather collar here, a discreet piece of latex there, and a bit more leather than on a Friday brunch with the family.

It was a bear picnic all right, as nearly half the clientele sported bellies, chest hair, and muscle. People mingled, some chatting as if they were old friends, others looking quite tense. Caleb was trying not to be in the latter category, but who was he kidding—he was not immune to first-date jitters.

A smile overtook his face when he spotted Rod, sitting in a corner booth with two beers in front of him. The moment Rod saw him, he shot to his feet, then parked his ass back down, raking a hand through his short, thick hair.

"*CuddlySadist*, huh?" Caleb smirked, waving his phone.

"Yeah." Rod released a chuckle. "I hoped that it was you in that picture, but I'm glad you texted to confirm. You're not gonna stir any trouble tonight, are you, Mr. *Howling4Pain*?"

"I didn't last time. That fucker asked for it," Caleb grunted.

"That's right. I see your cut has closed nicely." Rod reached out as if to touch Caleb's forehead then snatched it back. "It might leave a scar."

"I'm fine with that." Caleb's eyes went immediately to the burn scar above Rod's left eyebrow and he wondered what the story was behind it.

"I got you a beer." Rod slid the glass towards Caleb. "I wasn't sure what you like."

"Beer is perfect, thanks." Caleb's eyes caught several nods to kink in the temporary decor of the pub: stuffed teddy bears in leather gear decorating the tables, phallic-shaped candles on the bar, and spiked dog-collars hanging in corners. His gaze focused on his date; on Rod's neatly trimmed beard and kissable lips with a trace of beer foam on them. "I like that the place is closed to the public for the bear picnic."

"It's to ensure privacy for everyone involved. Although it's still a casual picnic." Rod added the last part hastily, as if he wanted to assure Caleb he hadn't planned for them to fuck on the table. Not that Caleb would mind that. "I like this place, but the music could be better."

Caleb nodded. "The 80s had much better pop."

"That's true. And the 90s had better rock," Rod said and Caleb clinked his glass to Rod's in agreement. "The art they have here is quite unique. Not something you'd expect in a pub."

Caleb took in the watercolor paintings of beautiful landscapes, meadows and lakes, with the odd bouquet thrown in. "Yeah." He'd noticed them before, but the first time he came here he'd got shit-faced drunk, and the second time, he ended up in a fight. The paintings hadn't left a lasting impression then, but he wanted to see them up close now.

"They're amateur but very good." He stood up, beer in hand and approached the first frame.

"According to the plaque next to the bar, they were by the original owner's wife but because of her lower class status and no influential contacts, she wasn't able to have them in a gallery, so he displayed them here."

"That's dope."

They walked from painting to painting, reading on plaques how the owner took in Jewish families fleeing from Europe on their way to America during the second world war. He even repurposed his cellar and built a shelter with lots of food. Then more locals hid there during bomb threats as well.

Caleb remembered his grandpa telling him about his family fleeing from Germany, his mom pregnant with Caleb's grandpa who had eventually been born in Bristol. He kept the story to himself and commented on the brushstrokes and the artist's obvious passion for the process, before stopping suddenly as he realized Rod was watching him with intent.

"You know about paintings?" Rod asked, finishing his beer.

"Nah. Not much. I just like art. I try to visit any gallery I can." Or he had when he was young, if they were free. "I sketch a bit, but I'm self-taught so—" He shrugged, not willing to draw attention to his art. "How about you?"

"I like looking at it. I can't draw for shit." Rod shook his head with a laugh. "Even my writing is chicken scratch."

Caleb chuckled, then ordered another round of beers before they returned to their table, their easy conversation jumping from topic to topic.

Rod was so easy to talk to that Caleb completely lost track of time. It wasn't till Rod excused himself to go to the bathroom that he glanced at the clock behind the bar.

Shit. The spot for the fight should be announced by now.

The organizers of the underground fight ring mixed the locations each event took place to avoid getting caught, and everyone who signed up got a text two hours before the fight. That would give anyone in the Bristol area enough time to get there, but not enough for the cops to figure out what was going on.

Fishing his phone out of his pocket, he checked his texts as Rod was returning from the bathroom. It was at the factory again, like it had been three weeks prior. Thankfully, it wasn't far, so he still had time to wrap up this date. With great reluctance, though.

"Checking if you matched with someone else already, huh?" Rod squeezed Caleb's shoulder before sitting.

"Fuck, no," Caleb laughed. He could tell Rod was just ribbing him, but the relief on his face was clear, too. In the little time they'd spent together, Caleb felt at ease around him. "But I'll have to run soon."

"Right." Rod's smile fell. "I hope we can repeat this sometime. You can message me on the app. Anytime."

"Will do. You know, it was Sandra who set it up for me, so I haven't used it beyond texting you."

"Did she fill in the profile info, too?" Rod asked, and Caleb nodded. "So you're not looking for someone to keep you in check?" Rod quirked a brow.

"What the fuck are you on about?"

"It was in your profile."

"No, I'm not. Fucking Sandra," he muttered, shaking his head as a smile formed on his lips. "She told me to trust her."

"I see."

"Don't you 'I see' me. It's true. And you're a *Cuddly Sadist* then, huh?"

"Yup." Rod's smile never faltered.

Holy shit.

"So you like hurting people?" Caleb asked, wishing he didn't have to leave the moment their conversation was taking an interesting turn.

"Yes, but only when they ask me to. Begging is preferable." Rod's delivery was so calm and matter-of-fact that it threw Caleb off.

He swallowed, then released a laugh. *Is he for real?* "And then what? You cuddle?"

"Precisely. I like to see anyone who's hurt well taken care of after."

That explained their first encounter. Then again... "Is it sexual?"

"Can be, but doesn't have to. It's definitely different from getting into a bar brawl." Rod pointed at Caleb's healing brow.

"I'm sure." Caleb's mouth went dry. He wanted to know more. Fucking hell. Scheduling the fight after the date had ensured he had a way out if it was a bust. It hadn't been. "I really gotta go now and catch a bus before I'm late."

"Oh, you're pulling that Cinderella shit on me again," Rod smirked.

"The what?" Caleb frowned as he stood up to put his jacket on. "I have some business to take care of. But I'll—" Caleb's words got stuck in his throat when Rod's hand gently wrapped around his wrist. He looked into the deep brown eyes then down to Rod's lips. "But I'll text you, OK?" He slung his backpack over his shoulder.

"Let me walk you out."

They stepped outside the pub, the light of the lanterns and the establishment behind them.

Caleb danced his fingers up Rod's arm and to his beard, feeling cheeky. Rod didn't seem to mind as he looked down at Caleb, his eyes searching, his head bowing lower. Caleb stood on his tiptoes, his free hand on Rod's chest for balance. They closed the gap between them to let their lips meet for a soft peck.

But Caleb couldn't pull away.

The next thing he knew, he was marched backwards until his shoulder blades hit the wall, his backpack sliding to the ground.

Air left his lungs and his body surrendered to the delicious entrapment of Rod's body. He was his cage and Caleb didn't want to leave it. Rod's tongue prodded for entrance and they kissed with a ferocious need. His hands gripped Rod's jacket in fistfuls at his back as Rod pinned Caleb hard to the wall. Caleb moaned as he felt Rod's erection pressing against his abdomen.

He wanted to see it. Lick it. Suck it. Moan around it.

But he had to go.

Caleb broke the kiss on a moan soaked with regret.

Panting, they let their gazes lock.

"Go, before I do something indecent to you in public." Rod breathed hard, his voice husky and dripping with sex.

"I hope you will. But not tonight." With one last peck to Rod's lips, Caleb ducked under his arm and snatched his backpack off the ground.

His bus was on its way to the stop so he jogged to catch it just in time.

As he climbed up the stairs, he caught a glimpse of Rod still standing where he'd left him, gazing up at the cloudless sky.

Chapter Four

Caleb

Caleb lay sprawled on the couch, watching the weird, round plaster patterns on the ceiling, clutching his phone to his chest.

Should I text him? It's not too early, right?

"Oh, for fucks' sake, just text him," Sandra said as she passed by on her way to the kitchen.

"How the fuck do you know what I was thinking about?"

"You have that adorable puppy look on your face." She poked his nose with a finger, then snatched her hand back when Caleb tried to grab it.

"I do not!" Caleb sat up abruptly, sending his phone flying and scrambling to catch it on its way down.

"You said the date went great, so just text him! You don't have to confess your undying love just yet," she threw over her shoulder.

"You're so mean."

"Mmmhmm. I'll make tea."

Caleb couldn't stop thinking about Rod. He had been so pumped by the date and the kiss, he'd utilized that energy in the fight right after and he'd won. Of course, he had. With a huge-ass grin on his face.

Since that night, he'd been mulling over Rod's casual remark about making someone hurt in a sexual setting. Caleb had seen porn that included pain play and BDSM elements, but meeting someone who was actually into that stuff was different. Not that it would scare him away. Quite the opposite, in fact. He found the idea even more fascinating now that it felt real, not just a porn fantasy. He needed to do more research.

But first, he had to get to know Rod more.

He didn't have Rod's number, but he fired up the Bear-4-U app and texted *CuddlySadist* from there.

'Hi'

Delete. That's so lame.

'How's life?'

OMG, no. Delete.

'I've been thinking about our kiss goodbye...'

Nope. Too soon.

Caleb squeaked when three dots waved in the chat.

Rod was typing. *Holy shit.*

'I have an idea for our next date. If you still want to meet again.'

'YES'

Caleb clicked send before he realized he had caps on. Fuck. Now he looked desperate.

'Excellent. How's Saturday?'

'Sounds great.' Caleb's cheeks flushed with blood, and he smiled, leaning back on the couch.

'I saw a movie that I thought you might like.'

'Oh really? What was it?'

They continued chatting and Sandra gave Caleb a knowing smirk as she passed by again, seeing the stupid grin on Caleb's face as he typed away. He flipped her the bird and continued texting.

'So this Saturday. How about a walk?' Rod suggested, taking Caleb aback.

'A walk? Sure. Sounds like something guys in frilly coats would do in those movies with dukes and shit.'

'Period dramas?'

Sounded like the horror Caleb's ex-girlfriend went through once a month. 'Yeah, the stuff you have here on BBC.'

'Well, at least if we're in public I can keep my hands off you.'

'Who said that's what I want?' Caleb's stomach flip-flopped as he waited nearly thirty seconds for a reply.

'Tempting. Meet me at Bristol Museum at 3 pm.'

The museum was rather grand, Caleb noted, with its majestic columns above the arched entrance—though not nearly as grand as the man leaning casually against its facade.

Caleb's face split into a smile when he saw the mountain called Rod. His heavy leather boots shone to perfection and his dark beard gleamed in the meek afternoon sun. He had one hand buried in his jacket pocket, scrolling his phone with the other. Even relaxed, his big body looked powerful. But also, like he could lie on top of Caleb and squish him, hug him so hard he would feel enveloped.

Rod lifted his gaze, and the moment he saw Caleb his eyes brightened, his entire face transforming from focus to unbridled joy.

Wow. Did I do that to him?

Caleb looked behind himself to make sure but there was no one there.

"Caleb," Rod said, patting his own cheek with a finger.

Oh.

Caleb stood on tiptoes and touched his lips where Rod had pointed, melting at the tenderness and the clear way Rod expressed what he wanted from Caleb.

"Nice t-shirt," Rod commented, pointing to the two cartoon-like people with nondescript features holding hands on one side and plaques with their pronouns on the other.

"Thanks. It's my design. Sandra printed it for my birthday last month."

"That's yours? You're good! I love this." Rod reached to touch the design and Caleb held his breath when the man's fingers brushed his chest.

"Not good enough."

"Says who?"

Caleb shrugged. "I don't know. Everyone." Well, that was a lie, but it felt like no one liked his art.

Rod shook his head, his brows furrowing as if he didn't like the answer. "Whoever said it doesn't know art." Rod took his hand away, but not before he let it slide down the shirt. "I'm sorry I missed your birthday."

"You didn't know me yet."

"That's just another reason for being sorry."

Caleb smiled, bumping his shoulder to Rod's. The words Rod said sometimes struck Caleb as so raw and honest, he wasn't sure if Rod meant them.

The past two weeks had been filled with texting, flirting and exchanging pictures. A hint of Caleb's hip for a snap of Rod's hairy chest. Caleb's lips sucking on his finger for a shot of Rod's erection in tight boxer briefs. Each time Caleb had ended up with a fist around his cock and a finger up his ass, moaning Rod's name as he came while thinking of the man's touch.

Now, seeing him in the flesh, he had to shove his hands in the pockets of his leather jacket to prevent himself from brushing his arm by 'accident.'

Rod led them into the building, and Caleb noted with relief that entrance was free. Caleb took in the grand staircase and the high ceiling, thinking that he would have visited all the museums in Chicago if they were free like this one. But having never seen cash for more than a moment before he spent it on food and bills—even as a teen—he wouldn't spend his hard-earned dollars on a museum.

"It's like the Wright Brothers' flyer isn't it?" Caleb looked up at the wooden biplane suspended above his head.

Rod followed Caleb's gaze upwards. "I don't know much about planes, only what I read from the plaques. But that's the Bristol Boxkite. It's much smaller than the flyer and a bit different." He met Caleb's eyes again and gestured towards the balcony. "The best view of it is from up there. There's also an art gallery on the second floor you might like, but we can make a day out of it next time. I have other plans for today."

"Next time, huh?" Caleb smirked as warmth spread to his cheeks. "Lead the way, then."

"Here." Rod turned Caleb to the right.

"Whoa. This looks like it doesn't belong here." Caleb frowned at the small statue of an angel on a pedestal with a can over its head and pink paint spilling down its body. The juxtaposition of the classic-style statue and its modern defacement pulled on Caleb's art heartstrings. He read the plaque under it and frowned. "I thought Banksy was a graffiti artist."

"Yeah, but that's one of his creations, too. He collabed with the museum for a takeover in 2009 that they called 'Banksy Versus Bristol Museum' and this piece has stayed here since then. I remember the insane queues to see the event. He's a native and we have a lot of his works around the city."

"No shit," Caleb said with excitement. He knew that a few of Banksy's statement-laden murals were in LA and New York, and lately even in Ukraine, but he'd never looked much further into it. Researching art he could never travel to see would be depressing, but now he regretted his ignorance.

"That's what we're going to see today." Rod's lips twitched in a smile as he clapped a hand on Caleb's shoulder. "Come on."

Caleb felt a sudden urge to grab that hand and intertwine their fingers, but it was gone in a second as Rod headed for the exit.

Well, OK, that idea of a silly stroll in the city had become much better now.

They walked along Park Street, which Caleb was vaguely familiar with by now, passing groups of students chatting and teens on skateboards like it was the 80s all over again. The crisp afternoon air mixed with the whiff of the harbor and car exhaust, but Caleb took a lungful anyway, enjoying the thrum of the city around him.

Rod stopped him with a hand on his arm. Right there on a side wall, a mural portrayed a window from which a man looked, as if trying to spot someone in the distance. Next to him stood a scantily-clad woman, and at the very corner of the windowsill hung a naked man, covering his bits with his free hand.

It had been shot with paintball, which Caleb assumed was not the artist's doing.

"This one's called Well-Hung Lover," Rod said, crossing his arms as he gazed at the art. "Considering this building used to be a sexual health clinic, this is pretty on point."

Caleb snickered, thoroughly amused, but in awe of the resourcefulness. It couldn't have been easy to organize a graffiti session so high from the ground. "I love this. And the play on words, too." It was simple, yet meaningful.

Caleb glanced at Rod to see the man looking at him instead of the art. He didn't smile with his lips, but his eyes twinkled in an inquisitive assessment of Caleb's reaction. The fact that Rod had put so much thought and planning into a date with a man he barely knew spoke volumes to Caleb. Rod was clearly a man who wasn't afraid to take action.

"This is great." Caleb grinned, resisting the urge to kiss Rod over and over again. The day was already a hit and they'd only just begun. The weather was perfect. Not too warm, just cool enough to be tempered by Caleb's jacket and open hoodie.

"The next stop is not a mural, but a pub," Rod said. "Claiming to be the oldest pub in Bristol, actually. It's just over there." He folded his arm so that his elbow created a loop and looked at Caleb with a glint in his eye. "Come on."

Laughing, Caleb threaded his hand through Rod's arm and they continued along Frogmore Street like Victorian gentlemen. They reached a white house-like structure with black wooden planks criss-crossed over the facade. It screamed 'old,' and the 'Licensed 1606' next to the name, The Hatchet Inn, confirmed it.

"I passed this place before but never thought much of it. There are so many old buildings around, you never know which are the important ones. I like this one, though." Caleb looked up at the old wood.

"It's Tudor-style, but now they organize rock and heavy metal nights in the upstairs bar." Rod reached for the handle of the studded oak door. "Supposedly, these doors are lined with human skin from the bodies of executed criminals," he said in a half-whisper, with a smirk on his face. "Some sort of custom back then. I say it's a great marketing ploy, but you never know." He opened the allegedly creepy door, waving Caleb in.

Rod's Bristolian r's were a lot easier on Caleb's American ears than some British pronunciations he'd heard before, and he listened to Rod talking about the pub as they walked through it. Supposedly, the famous pirate Blackbeard had been a regular client since he was a Bristolian, and, later, the place hosted various events, from cock-fighting rings to bare-knuckle boxing.

"Bare-knuckle boxing?" Caleb perked up. "I'd love to see that."

"Yeah, some victories are commemorated on the plaque right there. One fighter is even said to haunt the building occasionally," Rod whispered in a spooky, low tone right into Caleb's ear.

Caleb found himself leaning in involuntarily, wanting Rod even closer.

"Want a beer?" Rod asked, ghosting fingers over Caleb's hip.

"Sure."

"Two pints please," Rod said to the bartender. "And a portion of chips."

"Paying separately." Caleb sat on the stool next to Rod.

"Come on, let me woo you." Rod nudged Caleb's shoulder with his own.

Caleb's independent nature howled at him to protest but the smile on Rod's beautiful lips broke his resolve. "You already are. But OK." Caleb shook his head. "Wooing me with a walk. Who would have thought?"

"When you live in a city that is a gallery itself, then why not treat it as such?"

"True. Have you ever been to Chicago?" Caleb asked, thanking the barman for the beer he slid into Caleb's hand.

"No. I've been to New York and San Francisco on business, but never got to see Chicago." Rod took a sip of his lager then wiped the foam off his upper lip.

Caleb wished he could lick it off instead. He recalled with clarity how Rod's full beard scratched his face when they'd kissed, how his skin was tender for hours after. He realized he was staring when Rod's lips quirked into a smile.

Caleb cleared his throat. "I grew up and spent the entirety of my life there. I haven't seen much beyond it, but I love Chicago. And hate it a bit too."

"What do you love about it?"

"The people, the laid back culture, the mix of backgrounds and nationalities, but also, the city itself, with tall buildings and neat downtown with an enormous lake." He sighed wistfully, "Ohmygod, the best thing though: food! The last few weeks, I've been waking up wanting to drive by Dog Stop, Portillos, or even that Polish deli on Milwaukee Avenue. There's not a day I don't miss the taste of an Italian beef sandwich." Caleb added drama to his deep sigh and grinned as he saw Rod smile as well.

"They're not available anywhere around here? I mean, I've never heard of those but maybe if you checked?"

"Trust me, I googled and asked around. Nope."

Rod chuckled. "Well, it sounds like a great place to live. And yet, you still left."

"I grew up in Chicago's South Side, which is the shittiest neighborhood, to put it mildly. And my family... Well, I don't keep in touch with them for a reason." Caleb shrugged then scrambled to move on from the topic. "I wish I could show you Chicago like you're showing me around now." Oh shit. That came out a bit more serious than it had sounded in his head. "I mean, you know, if you ever have a business trip and I happen to be there or something."

"I'd love that, too. But I closed my practice and I don't go to conferences on business anymore." Rod looked straight ahead, his expression drained of the joy it had just moments before.

"Practice?" Caleb's interest piqued.

"I thought you were planning to stay in Bristol, or in the UK at least." Rod changed the subject quickly but Caleb made a note to ask about the practice he'd mentioned.

"Yeah, well." Caleb wiped the droplets on the outside of his glass. "If I can't find myself here, then I'll go back to the place I know. There's always work to catch here and there. I did roofing for a while. They're always eager for me to haul heavy shit up and down a ladder. Especially in the summer. There are other odd jobs in winter, too. Plenty of snow to shovel around." He shrugged. He didn't want to leave. It would mean he'd failed, but he had to be realistic.

"Right. So you're not set to stay here..." Rod's voice trailed off.

"I'd love to but I'm still waiting for my paperwork. I'll decide once I have it and see if I can settle properly with a job and all."

"Of course."

"I thought I'd move to England and it would sort of work. But it's been much harder than I planned. The bureaucracy, the job market. It seems I don't fit here and I don't know if I ever will, you know?" He'd never said that but now that it was past his lips, he realized the truth of his statement. It was so easy to talk to Rod, he was afraid soon he'd say too much and become a rambling bore, or worse, a burden.

"You might leave any day then?"

"Well, no. I'm giving it a shot first. Then I'd probably do some sightseeing before I go. See London, at least." He shrugged. He'd had vain hopes he would travel to get familiar with the country, not to say goodbye.

Rod nodded, not meeting his gaze, looking at the bottles that lined the back wall of the bar and downing the rest of his beer.

They'd met mere weeks ago, but Caleb already knew he'd hate to leave Rod if it came to that. He wanted to explore this connection, but he wasn't sure he was ready to jump with both feet into a relationship. Especially while he was on such rocky ground.

"I'll enjoy every moment with you until I know for sure," Caleb said, placing a tentative hand on Rod's arm.

"Me, too." Rod finally looked at Caleb, then at his empty glass. "Ready to go?"

Rod opened the heavy door to let Caleb out. They remained quiet for a long moment as they walked, Caleb's head filled with negative scenarios of Rod telling him not to contact him again, that he was too much, and that they wouldn't work.

"I have to say this up front, Caleb." Rod's low voice made Caleb brace for the worst. "I like openness, I like having all the cards on the table. So as much as I hate the idea of you leaving, I'm glad you told me about it."

Caleb was used to talking a mile a minute, sometimes even oversharing, but he noticed it was not a very English custom. He liked that Rod appreciated that, rather than his eyes glossing over with boredom.

"I, ummm—" Caleb cleared his throat. "I hope to stay here, but if I'm not able to get a decent job, I'll have to go back."

"That's understandable. You have family there, and—"

"It's more about the fact that I know Chicago and what I can do there. I actually don't keep in touch with my family. It's one of the reasons why I came here where Pops was born. Sort of searching for a connection to him, to family roots, I don't know. Even though Grandma and Mom were born here too, I've never had a strong bond with them." Was he saying too much? "How about your family?"

"I have two brothers and a sister. All younger." Rod smiled, sliding his hands into the pockets of his jacket. "We try to meet once a month and, of course, on all holidays. I visit mum most Sundays."

"One parent, then?"

"It's been like that since Aida, the youngest, was born. Dad just disappeared. Mum didn't have anyone until I left for college. She's now happily married to Mariella."

The tension of their earlier conversation eased as they reached a museum with a big 'M' on it, which stood to the side of old train tracks and industrial cranes. Bristol was so full of gritty surprises, much like the tracks of Chicago's L train spanning throughout the city.

Once they entered the museum, Rod led them to a haunting mural of a grim reaper with a scythe. It was enclosed in plexiglass, looking eerily out of place.

"It was originally painted on the side of a boat that was converted into a bar and restaurant. To prevent the decay of the harbor getting the best of it, the city moved it here," Rod said, his hand resting comfortably on Caleb's lower back.

A walk along the river brought them to an enormous ship Caleb could see in the distance, but Rod said that would be an attraction for another day if he wanted. With Sandra's apartment being quite close to the harbor, Caleb had seen the M Shed and Burnel's SS Great Britain ship before, but Rod added fond memories with their chat, casual touches, and the air between them crackling with the need for more physical contact. After turning left, they meandered through the marina and behind old buildings that reminded Caleb of the back alleys of Chicago's neighborhoods. There, they reached a mural that looked like Vermeer's Girl with a Pearl Earring, except her ear was decorated with an outdoor security alarm. Rod told him that the piece's name was a Girl with a Pierced Eardrum.

A longer walk back to the other side of the river brought them to a red brick wall. On it was a simple block quote in the shape of a smiling face: "You don't need planning permission to build castles in the sky." It was simple, yet, like all the other pieces, meaningful. Their chat turned to lighter topics, and soon they passed Bristol Cathedral, just as the sky darkened with the promise of rain. When they reached Bristol Museum where they'd initially met, the drizzle turned into rain and they hid in the museum's foyer.

"That was awesome," Caleb said and pecked Rods's cheek above his beard. "Thank you." He checked his phone and his shoulder slumped, knowing he'd have to end the date. "But I have to go."

"I can drop you off wherever you need."

Caleb's stomach turned at the thought of Rod finding out his plans. "I don't think that's a good idea."

Rod's thick eyebrows formed a frown. "It's pouring rain outside."

"Yeah, but you probably don't want to see where I'm going." Caleb winced as the words slipped out. He was sure Rod would hate the fights by the way he acted so caring over a stupid eyebrow cut.

Rod took a step back, searching Caleb's face. "I don't like the way that sounds." His voice grew serious, a tone that sent shivers through Caleb. As much as he liked Rod's protective demeanor, he didn't appreciate the judgment.

"Easy, man. I just don't want you to get into trouble in case shit goes down." OK, maybe he sounded a bit more condescending than he'd thought. Rod could definitely take care of himself if needed.

"What?" Rod stiffened, his body, so much bigger than Caleb's, looking ready to fight for him. "Are you in trouble?" Worry tinged Rod's voice.

"No." Caleb wiped a hand down his face. "Fuck, no, I'm not."

"Does it have anything to do with the bruises on your arm and your scraped knuckles?" Rod asked, his fingers reaching for Caleb's hand. "I didn't want to ask before but I'm pretty sure any damage from that bar fight should have healed by now. Did you get into another one?" Rod's voice softened. "It's not prying, I'm just..." Rod took Caleb's hand in both of his. "You can trust me, OK?"

Caleb wasn't sure if he wanted to cry, apologize, or bolt. "Oh, for shit's sake, you can drop me off at the abandoned factory in the city center."

"Great." Rod's brows smoothed, and he dangled his car keys. "Let's go then."

Rod led them to a black Honda SUV parked by the street nearby. It looked big next to a Beetle but would be considered a medium-sized car in the US. Caleb slid his ass into the passenger seat, then startled when he saw the steering wheel in front of him.

"Shit." He jumped out of the car and rounded it, having completely forgotten that UK drivers sat on the wrong damn side.

"I wouldn't let you drive her even if you asked, so that was a cheeky move." Rod chuckled as he slid the key in and buckled his belt.

"No, fuck, I just..." Caleb shook his head, buckling up too.

"I get it. Everyone new to the UK does that."

"I haven't been in a car since I came here so this is new, yeah." Caleb relaxed into the seat, his backpack on his lap.

"The factory, then, huh?"

"Yeah."

Rod parked a street over, in a seedy residential area. He remained in the car, eyeing the people walking in the direction of the abandoned building. Most of them hid their faces under hoods, with duffel bags over their shoulders; others walked with umbrellas and watches so shiny they were visible in the rain that was slowing to a drizzle.

Caleb got out of the car. He wasn't sure if Rod was going to follow him, but he emerged a moment later and locked the doors. "Whatever this is, it's not legal, I assume."

"You're not a cop, are you?" Caleb nudged Rod to the side with his elbow.

"No, I'm not." Rod snorted but there was no amusement in his tone. He sounded worried. "But what exactly will you be doing here?"

Caleb shrugged his backpack higher on his shoulder. "Fighting."

Rod stiffened, cursing under his breath. Caleb could see he was onto him. "Are you doing it for the money?" Rod asked, as they walked towards the brick building.

"What if I am?"

"I can lend you some and you'll pay me back when you can."

Caleb's hackles rose immediately. "Fuck you. I don't need your charity. Or anyone else's." He knew pre-fight jitters were getting to him, but he didn't need a reminder that he was in deep shit financially.

"You'd rather get your face smashed while beating others?" Rod was talking through gritted teeth, but he remained at Caleb's side, his boots hitting the puddles with a splash.

"Damn right, I would."

"I'm coming in with you."

"You can't stop me." Caleb kept his voice down to avoid attracting attention as he stepped in front of Rod.

"I know," Rod growled, sidestepping Caleb. "But you also can't forbid me from going as a spectator." He leveled a pointed look at Caleb.

Caleb cursed under his breath. "Just don't pull any shit."

"I'll just watch." Rod paused, holding Caleb's gaze, his finger under Caleb's chin. "Maybe stitch you up after."

"Dude, you're seriously something," Caleb scoffed.

"I'll take it as a compliment."

Chapter Five

Rod

Rod followed Caleb inside the old iron doors, held open by guys even larger than him. And that was saying something.

He didn't miss the fact that Caleb introduced him as a 'trusted friend' to get him in. Rod's back stiffened at the moniker. Frankly, he'd rather be called his boyfriend. Of course, it was way too early for that, but every second he spent with Caleb made him want it more and more.

The smell of damp and ancient brick invaded Rod's nose. Low murmurs grew louder as more people flooded the derelict building, mixing with the hum of generators that powered the large LED floor lamps situated in corners of the open area.

The middle of the concrete space was laden with mats, much like in a Karate dojo. A single piece of rope was secured around them all in a square attached to waist-high standing poles. Needless to say, if anyone from the makeshift ring lost balance, they'd be hurling themselves into the waiting crowd. That was probably why the front row was visibly vibrating with excitement.

Caleb patted Rod's arm and looked up at him with eyes full of determination. His shoulders were back and his muscles tense, clearly in the fighting headspace already. "I'll meet you after?"

It was a question. Was he doubting that Rod would stay?

"I'll be waiting." Rod squeezed Caleb's forearm.

He didn't get a chance to see Caleb's reaction as he snatched his hand away and turned to head in the opposite direction. He disappeared into an alcove behind makeshift poster stands and a pop-up changing station.

Rod followed the spectators, opting to stand at the back to avoid the bloodthirsty first rows, buzzing like bees. It was a mixed-gender crowd, like the fighters on the other side, dressed in joggers or shorts, with their knuckles taped and mouth guards ready. No gear, no professional equipment.

Worry stirring his gut, Rod looked around. With the bare brick, battered columns, and illumination coming only from the floor lamps surrounding the ring, it was easy to deduce that there was no running water or sterile spot in this building. Hopefully, the guy holding a first aid kit knew what he was doing, but Rod doubted anyone here wasn't aware of the risks.

The first fight was between two women, one with hair pinned up, the other with a shaved head. Both in sports bras, shorts, and bare feet. It took five gruesome minutes of punching, kicking, and spitting blood before one of them was declared the winner.

"What a fantastic fight!" A middle-aged guy with a handlebar mustache announced through a microphone. He stood at the side of the ring entrance and lifted the looped rope off the pole to let the fighters out.

"Next up, the one and only Mean Machine! He's been with us for over a year with many fights won and only a handful lost! How will it go today?"

The crowd erupted in cheers.

"This newcomer has proven to be a worthy opponent since he joined us only a few weeks ago," the man continued, raising his free hand. "Make some noise for the Angry Wolf."

Rod's heartbeat accelerated when his eyes landed on Caleb emerging in shorts and nothing else. A myriad of tiny tattoos were scattered on his body but Rod's eyes locked on the detailed depiction of a kneeling male angel with folded wings on the left side of Caleb's ribs. Caleb grinned, turning to his opponent. Thank fuck he put a mouth guard in.

Oh God, that beautiful face is going to be beaten and bruised.

Rod had faith in Caleb's fighting skills but the Machine Man, or whatever his name was, was twice Caleb's size with muscles that seemed to grow on top of other muscles like a cartoon character.

Even from afar, Rod could see a glint in Caleb's eyes. At first, he couldn't pinpoint what it was. A mix of eagerness and excitement? Bouncing on the balls of his feet, there was no fear in his gaze, but anticipation.

When Caleb smiled a devilish grin, it hit Rod straight in the chest.

Caleb was looking forward to being hurt.

Breath hitched in Rod's lungs at the realization. Was it possible?

His eyes locked on Caleb as the man ducked his opponent's blow. The other guy was heavy and slow, and Rod realized it might be his downfall. No, he hoped it would be.

Caleb was quick on his feet, his fists jabbing the big man in his midsection before he landed a nice hook under the guy's jaw.

Machine Man stumbled only to turn on Caleb with eyes like a raging bull, spitting blood into his face. He landed one, then two angry blows to Caleb's side, then face before he shielded it with his forearm.

Rod held his breath, then panted. He couldn't remember the last time he'd been so overwhelmingly stressed. If he died of a heart attack at the age of thirty-five, he'd be royally pissed.

"Come on, Caleb," Rod whispered. "Finish him already."

As if on cue, Caleb landed a kick to the other man's side then, when the Machine guy folded in half, Caleb punched his face.

Down.

Fuck, yeah.

Rod exhaled with relief as the ringing stress in his ears mingled with the roar of the crowd. He shook his head to clear it as he nearly swayed on his feet. That was insane. And so fucking hot.

Eyes glued to Caleb's brilliant, yet bloody, smile, Rod watched as he extended a hand to help his opponent stand up. Handlebar Stache announced Caleb as the winner, lifting his hand in victory. Caleb turned around, showing the huge howling wolf tattoo on his back before everyone exited the ring.

Caleb approached a guy in a blue tracksuit and accepted a roll of cash. They exchanged several sentences and Caleb nodded before he slung his backpack over his shoulder and disappeared into the crowd.

Rod's eyes scanned every head to catch Caleb, hoping he wouldn't assume Rod had left already.

He felt a tap on his forearm. "You're still here!"

Rod turned to see Caleb, shirtless and with blood smeared on his face and knuckles.

"I said I'd be waiting." Rod raised his voice over the ruckus of the next fight being announced.

No one had even bothered to clean the blood off the mats.

Instead of yelling in reply, Caleb motioned for them to move away.

They walked deeper into the building in near complete darkness, then up the stairs. Moonlight streamed through the glassless windows, illuminating the empty concrete floor and brick.

"It's quieter here," Caleb said, standing in front of the window, casting an eerie shadow behind him. His features were relaxed, and not like he'd been in a bloody fight. He looked like he had had sex, but still wanted more. "So, did you enjoy it?" Caleb asked.

"I—" Rod puffed his cheeks on an exhale. "I have mixed feelings about it."

"You didn't like how I fought?"

"Oh, that part was great."

"So, what part wasn't?" He turned to Rod, inspecting his reaction.

"When you got hit."

"Pft. I'll heal."

"How are your ribs?" Rod reached out but didn't dare touch Caleb's bare skin.

"They'll be fine."

"Can I see?" Rod hesitated.

Caleb spread his arms wide. "Sure."

With gentle fingers, Rod traced the spot under Caleb's pectoral covered with a tattoo of a warrior angel, kneeling, holding a sword.

Caleb hissed but didn't flinch otherwise.

"Might be bruised. How's your face?" Rod lifted his hands and Caleb caught them by the wrists.

Their gazes met and Caleb's smile was tired. "I said I'm fine."

"You look exhausted," Rod rumbled, letting Caleb guide his palms to his hips.

"Nah, I'm just calm."

"That calmed you down?" Rod nearly squeaked, waving a hand in the general direction of the chaos below.

"Yeah. The fight, but mostly the pain. It makes me feel alive."

Rod's heart pounded faster. *Pain.*

"I'm all pumped up and excited, too." Caleb's hands traveled up Rod's chest over his polo shirt in a bold move.

But it was dangerous. Reckless.

"It was scary to watch." *Because I felt every blow on my skin.*

"Why? You don't like seeing me in pain?" Caleb smirked, his thumbs brushing over Rod's nipples.

"No, that would be fine, if it was safe. That shit wasn't."

Rod could give Caleb pain in a much better way. Watching Caleb fight had been a rollercoaster ride and Rod was aware that he'd gotten off on it. Now he was completely discombobulated, his legs wobbly, his head still spinning.

He was happy Caleb was alive, but also furious that he did that to himself. He was so full of conflicting emotions. Too much.

Rod's eyes locked on Caleb's and he let his body guide him.

He grabbed Caleb by the throat and marched him until his back hit a wall.

Caleb's gaze was defiant, his eyes filled with fire.

"You were reckless, stepping into that ring." Rod exhaled a shaky breath. "But you were so fucking hot, too. I'm mad and turned on at the same time." Rod growled, putting his face an inch from Caleb's. "Damn you."

"I can tell," Caleb smirked, his hands playing with the waistband of his joggers as if there wasn't a hand wrapped around his throat. Right then, he thrust his chin up, giving Rod more access to his neck. His eyes hooded as Rod tightened his hold.

Fuck.

Rod dropped his hand, then raked his fingers through his hair. He was about to apologize when Caleb gripped him by the shirt to pull him closer.

Rod's breathing was heavy as he took in Caleb's honed chest splattered with blood, his joggers pulled low to reveal a white waistband. Rod left it to Caleb to close the gap between them. The man didn't waste a second and fused their lips together.

Rod's hand drifted to Caleb's back, then down, underneath the waistband of his joggers and... *Fuck. Is he wearing a jockstrap?*

Growling into the kiss, Rod squeezed the firm ass cheeks.

Caleb released a pleased grunt and gyrated his hips, rubbing his erection hard against the taller man's thigh.

Caleb's blunt nails dug into Rod's back and nape, as if the man wanted more, wanted to crawl under his skin and devour him. Rod was afraid that he might let him.

Rod's fingers slid inside Caleb's crack, coming to rest on his pucker. Not prodding, only testing the waters.

Caleb thrust his arse back in a blatant plea, moaning into their kiss.

They were in an isolated alcove of the building, but if someone were to wander upstairs, they'd see them. Rod didn't care. And Caleb didn't seem to care either.

"I want to fuck you through this wall," Rod whispered against Caleb's lips, his need stronger than propriety, stronger than the voice in his head telling him not to rush their relationship.

"Promises, promises," Caleb smirked.

Rod snarled and yanked Caleb's joggers down to his knees.

The white lines of the jockstrap accentuated Caleb's honed physique and naturally tanned skin, but the front pouch was barely holding its contents. Rod wanted to see Caleb's cock, taste it on his tongue, then fuck the man bare and deep.

No. He had to stay smart, even in the face of lust.

Rod watched Caleb's expression, hooded eyes, confident angle of his jaw and lips parting on a gasp when Rod squeezed Caleb's scantily-clad bulge.

Grinding into Rod's hand, Caleb fumbled to open Rod's jeans. With hasty movements, he fought the button, the zipper, and Rod's boxer briefs to pull out Rod's cock.

"Fuck," Caleb breathed, squeezing Rod's shaft before he slid the foreskin down to reveal the crown.

Rod grunted as Caleb stroked him several times then looked up to Rod's face, his hand gliding up Rod's chest. Rod thought he wanted a kiss but instead, Caleb spoke against Rod's lips. "Condoms are in my backpack."

Caleb thrust into Rod's touch with a groan before he slid his joggers off, only to slip his feet back into his trainers.

"Good," Rod said and reached into the inside pocket of his bomber jacket to fish out a packet.

Caleb grinned.

It looks like we both came prepared. Then again...
"Lube?" Rod asked, cursing his earlier assumption that they wouldn't go that far and not stacking on those lube packets Geordie recommended so often.

"I think I ran out. But I'll check."

With utter reluctance, Rod released Caleb's bulge to reveal the wet spot on the white fabric. God, how he wanted to bury his face there. Caleb squeezed Rod's cock one more time before he let go to reach for his backpack on the floor.

He unzipped the front pocket and rummaged in it. Sure enough, past the strip of condoms, there was a tiny bottle of lube. Caleb lifted it to the moonlight. Definitely empty.

Had Caleb used it to fuck or be fucked, Rod wondered. Maybe it was only for masturbating? But if that was the case, he wouldn't have it in his backpack when he left the house. Unless he was counting on someone fucking him tonight. Maybe that was what he always did—pick out a person from the crowd to fuck after a fight. Rod didn't want to know. It was none of his business.

Caleb left the backpack in disarray and Rod noticed a toothbrush and a pair of socks in it. Quite bizarre, but he filed that thought to ponder later.

"I'm fine without lube," Caleb said, straightening up, his finger tracing the vein on Rod's cock.

"I'll settle for sucking you off." Rod took Caleb's chin in his thumb and forefinger, making their eyes meet.

"I won't. I want that tree stump inside me now." Caleb's gaze didn't waver.

Rod chuckled. Fuck. He was so gone.

"Spit will do, come on, Rod." Caleb flicked his tongue over Rod's lips. "Oh, you think I can't take you?" He smirked. "Clearly, you haven't seen my ex-girlfriend's collection of dildos."

"Are you telling me you're loose?" Rod lifted a brow, wondering if Caleb got riled up easily.

Caleb shrugged, seemingly unfazed. "I do my kegel exercises, but I sure as fuck want to feel your cock slide inside me tonight."

He was getting dirty. Must be adrenaline from the fight. Or was he always like that?

"You certain you won't regret this later?"

"Are you going to fuck me or not? Jesus, Rod." Caleb reached for the hem of Rod's shirt to slide his hand under. His fingers glided over the hair on Rod's chest and he moaned as Rod cupped his junk again.

"You're so fucking hot when you're needy." Rod stopped Caleb from turning around and gripped his buttocks. "Jump."

Caleb frowned for a second, then grinned and jumped up, wrapping his legs around Rod's waist, his arms around Rod's neck.

"I want to see your eyes well with tears when you stretch around my cock," Rod murmured, watching Caleb's expression.

Caleb sucked in a breath but Rod wasn't sure if it was at his statement or his hands squeezing his buttocks hard as he stepped forward to let Caleb's back rest against the wall. "These are so firm and round. I'd love to see them red from a belt or a cane."

"Sweet-talker." Caleb ground his hips. "Now shut up and fuck me."

Rod chuckled. He was unable to figure out this man but trying to do it was proving to be a lot of fun.

Rod leaned in for a kiss. It was sloppy, messy, and exactly what he wanted. His heart pounded and all the blood went to his erection.

"Now spit." Rod lifted a hand to Caleb's lips and the man spat on it with the mixed saliva of their kiss.

Rod reached between them and slid a slicked finger into Caleb who groaned, his body sucking in the digit eagerly.

"So good. Can't wait for my cock to be in there," Rod rumbled.

"Then do it." Caleb rolled his hips then hissed when Rod added another finger until his knuckles met Caleb's ass.

"Ah!" Caleb's eyes bore into Rod, his kiss-swollen lips parted.

"Are you okay?" Rod asked.

"Of course I'm not."

Rod froze at the words but Caleb continued.

"I want you to fuck me already. Ah, fuck!" he yelped when Rod crooked his fingers to put pressure on the sweet spot inside him.

"Don't bullshit me, I want to rail you, not hurt you."

Caleb smirked. "Fine, I'll tell you to stop when it hurts too much. Happy?"

"Yes." Rod leaned in to kiss Caleb's neck, tasting the sweat from the fight that gleamed on his body. He licked and sucked on the spot while massaging Caleb's prostate with his fingertips. "Take the condom out of my inner jacket pocket and rip it open," Rod instructed.

With one hand still around Rod's neck, Caleb reached for the packet and ripped it open with his teeth. "Now, hurry up." He held the condom up in his fingers.

"Brat," Rod mumbled and hoisted Caleb higher to reach under and sheath his cock in latex. He stroked once then brought his hand up to spit on it.

Spreading it over the condom, he teased Caleb's hole.

Caleb pushed down and the head of Rod's erection popped in.

"Oh, fucking hell!" Caleb barked through gritted teeth, tightening his hold on Rod's shoulders. Then he exhaled and bore down, letting more of Rod's cock in.

Rod pulled out nearly all the way, looked down between them and added more spit before he slid back in. He wanted to ask Caleb if he was OK, but there was no need.

"Yes, goddammit, more!" Caleb panted between Rod's thrusts.

Bloody hell, so responsive and vocal. It would be so lovely to have him submit, so easy to read all his reactions and judge what he liked and what he didn't. Rod could definitely give Caleb a different form of pain.

He was close, his orgasm building as his entire body became in tune with Caleb's ragged breaths. Rod groaned at the tightness around his erection, and he leaned in again to press a kiss to Caleb's cheek. "Stroke yourself," he gasped, needing Caleb as close to release as he was.

Caleb pulled his cock out of the jockstrap and squeezed, his thumb spreading the pre-come around the head.

Rod slowed down, pulling out halfway to watch Caleb's hand working his erection. It was medium-length and slimmer than Rod's. But fuck, was it a gorgeous cock. He could fit it in his mouth, deep throat it too. Lick and suck until he tasted Caleb's come.

"That's right." Rod started moving again.

"I'm close," Caleb panted, his eyes fluttering closed only to open again and focus on Rod. "Fuck me faster. Harder."

Oh, yes.

Rod repositioned his hands on Caleb's hips for a better grip and pounded into his new lover with ferocious need.

"Fuck, Rod, yes!" Caleb shouted, clearly not caring if anyone heard them.

Rod's balls drew up as fire coursed through his veins. He buried his face in Caleb's neck, sucking on the skin there until he closed his teeth on Caleb's flesh.

Caleb yelled his release, his blunt nails marking Rod's upper back. The pulsing squeeze of Caleb's asshole and the lovely sound of his wail undid Rod completely and he came so hard, he wasn't sure if it was him holding Caleb or the other way around.

A moment passed as both of them caught their breath, before Caleb murmured something unintelligible and braced his arms on Rod's shoulders to lift himself off. He winced as Rod's cock left his abused hole, but the sated look on his face spoke volumes.

Rod had to fight the urge to wrap Caleb into a hug, feel their bodies close, and share a moment of comfort. But Caleb was already moving on.

"Holy shit, I needed that," Caleb said, picking up his joggers to pull them on.

Rod took off and tied the condom before putting it in his pocket and tucking his flaccid cock into his trousers. He watched Caleb's round buttocks disappear under the fabric like it was a sexy ad before his gaze moved up.

"Oh, God, your back!" Rod reached out but stopped his hand before he touched the scraped skin over bruises already forming from the fight. "I did this to you." The gorgeous tattoo of a howling wolf between Caleb's shoulderblades was speckled with blood.

Caleb shrugged and turned to face Rod. "I'll feel the scrapes when I fall asleep and it will be like you're there—" Caleb's face fell as his eyes filled with shock at what he'd just said. Releasing a dry chuckle, he looked away and crouched by his rucksack.

Can I be there when you sleep? Rod's thoughts were loud in his head. "I'm sorry," he said instead.

"It was a good fuck, don't sweat it."

Ouch. Was that all it was to Caleb? Why was he avoiding Rod's gaze?

Caleb pulled on a t-shirt and his purple hoodie and tilted his chin in a goodbye gesture. He was leaving.

"Your back needs to be cleaned."

"I'll just take a shower," Caleb said over his shoulder.

"Let me drive you home."

"It's fine, I'll catch a bus."

"Caleb," Rod said with urgency.

He stopped with his back to Rod.

Rod circled him and lifted Caleb's chin with his finger. His face was tired and the bruise forming under his eye would look nasty tomorrow, yet his gaze was sharp, alert, and maybe a bit confused.

"Let me take you home." Rod could see the conflict playing on Caleb's face, but he didn't want to give up yet. "Please."

Like a wild animal coaxed out of his lair, Caleb released a breath and nodded. "Yeah, OK. It's raining outside." Caleb shrugged but led the way out, looking over his shoulder for Rod to follow.

CHAPTER SIX

Caleb

Caleb directed them across the open space of the derelict building. That way they could leave without walking through the crowd cheering downstairs as people fought on, adding their blood to the mats.

Rod's heavy footsteps let him know the man was right next to him as they walked in the near darkness. With every step, the soreness of Caleb's used hole remind him of the thorough fucking he'd just received.

He tried to tell himself it was just that; he needed the release and clearly, so had Rod. But the way they bounced off each other, and their easy push-and-pull made it more than a rough fuck against the wall in search of a quick release. But more of what? Caleb didn't know. Once he'd stepped away from Rod, he immediately wanted to return, to feel the man's arms around him, squeezing him hard. So he'd quickly dressed and planned to bolt, not wanting to stay in Rod's proximity and fight the needy urges he had.

Rod's talk about giving Caleb the good kind of pain had made Caleb even hornier. Had Rod just said that to rile Caleb? Or had he been serious?

Rod had fucked into him hard, the rough wall behind Caleb scraping his back. He hadn't cared then; the aching stretch in his hole and the all-round pain of his muscles had let his mind fly free. In that moment, he was completely consumed by Rod's scent in his nose, his breath on his neck and his cock deep inside. At that moment in time, his body was owned by Rod, and Caleb rode that wave all the way to their earth-shattering climax.

"I still feel bad about your back," Rod said as they descended the stairs in darkness.

"It's nothing." Caleb rolled his shoulders, feeling the skin pull.

He could tell that Rod wanted to say something more, but they had reached the floor where the fighting was taking place and Rod would have to yell over the crowd for Caleb to hear him.

By the exit, Caleb exchanged a few words with the bouncer twins and headed out, promising to return for the next event on Wednesday. The drizzle motivated them to walk briskly to Rod's car.

"You said you like the pain of the fight," Rod said, zipping up his bomber jacket.

"Yeah. I know you're gonna say it's fucked up or some shit." It was good to feel the muscle burn, and the bruises for a day. What was wrong with him for wanting to hurt?

"No, I won't say that." Rod opened the passenger door to his SUV and motioned Caleb in.

A bit taken aback by the gesture, Caleb slid onto the leather seat. The dark interior screamed practical rather than posh despite being high quality. Much like Rod, actually...

"But I would tell you that there are other ways to feel pain," Rod continued as he took a seat and slid the key into the ignition.

"What, like BDSM?" Caleb scoffed, buckling up as Rod nodded. "Yeah, I thought about it, but I'm not gonna lick anyone's boots or some shit to get my ass spanked."

"It doesn't have to be like that." Rod looked at him for a second before he turned to the road as the engine rumbled to life.

"Oh, really? And you're an expert, huh?" Caleb's amusement sparked as he recalled Rod's screen name on the app.

"I wouldn't say an expert..."

"Next thing you'll tell me that you're one of those people who have a dungeon in their basement." Caleb buckled in, turning halfway to look at Rod's profile.

"It's in the loft, actually." Rod's lip twitched into a smile but he remained focused on the road.

"You're shitting me." *A kinky dungeon in the attic! How fucking cool.*

"It's no dungeon, more of a playroom. Couldn't find a decent piece of property with a nice basement. Besides, it's quite cozy there." Rod smiled, turning on the wipers and blinker.

Caleb snorted. "A cozy dungeon. It must be hot there in the summer."

"Not the kind of hot you're worried about. I installed AC, I'm not a barbarian."

Caleb lifted an eyebrow. He wouldn't mind if Rod was one in bed. "I'd love to see it," he said, then tried to backtrack. "I mean I'm not inviting myse—"

"I can take you now. Just so you can look around," Rod added quickly.

Why are we suddenly awkward?

"Yeah, that." Caleb shifted in his seat, knowing he'd feel the soreness in his asshole for days. He wouldn't be opposed to fooling around otherwise, but he was dead tired and Rod had sated all his other needs to the point he was ready to to burrow himself under the covers. Still, his curiosity to see a loft-turned-dungeon was greater than his need to tend to his sore ass.

"Don't worry, I can keep my hands to myself when needed."

"I'm glad you didn't today." Caleb wanted Rod to know that there had been no misunderstanding. Caleb had wanted his cock then and there. Fuck, he'd *needed* it.

"Good. Because I might have died tonight if I couldn't have my hands all over you."

Whoa. "You know how to sweet talk," Caleb snorted.

"I'm serious." Rod's grip tightened on the steering wheel until the leather creaked. "I haven't been turned on like that for—" He hesitated, frowning. "For a long time. You were so fucking hot in that ring. But I also wanted to get in there and drag you off those mats by the scruff of your neck so you wouldn't get beaten."

Is the heating on? Caleb hated when people forbade him to do stuff, and his first reaction was to break all the rules. Yet he felt that Rod's primal instinct came from deep within. Came from care for him - a person he hardly knew.

"I won in the end, though."

"I know. But your eye... your ribs." Rod puffed his cheeks on a long exhale.

"Meh, I've had worse." And he'd been much younger, too. He could swear Rod growled next to him, before pulling into a slanted driveway. "Oh, is this your place?" Caleb asked as Rod parked and turned off the engine.

"Yeah, welcome to my humble abode," Rod said, ducking out of the car.

Caleb jumped out, grabbed his backpack and took in the red-brick house with a small green front lawn. From his short stay in the UK, Caleb had learned that free-standing houses half the size of a regular house in the USA were a lot rarer in bigger cities, but just as expensive.

"You live here alone?" Caleb asked, approaching the sturdy door with ball-shaped plants hanging off hooks to the sides of it.

"Yup. You don't have to worry about housemates."

"Or boyfriends?"

"Yeah, no. I'm definitely single. I would have told you if I was looking for something non-exclusive."

"Doesn't hurt to make sure." Caleb felt the loyalty vibe wafting off Rod but he'd been burned before.

"You?"

"Only casual dick for me."

"Right." Rod sounded as if he didn't like the answer. Was it because of promiscuity or the fact that Caleb was not looking for a relationship? He'd already explained his situation, so it wasn't as if he was keeping Rod in the dark. Looking at Rod's wide shoulders and pert ass leading the way to his house, Caleb thought he wouldn't mind that man railing him on the regular. Once he'd set down roots in the

UK. Until then, he had to refrain from picking out a ring.

The door opened with a click of bolts, the modern frame merged with traditional style of wood. Caleb noted the doorbell with a camera on the side and more plants and flowers in the front yard.

Rod untied his boots and left them by the door, so Caleb did the same, placing his sneakers on a mat before they stepped onto a wooden floor.

The interior was modern, with a brown leather couch, sleek white sideboard and a huge TV on the wall. Minimalistic and to-the-point. Then Caleb's eyes landed on the shelf with DVDs and Blu-Rays of box-sets of TV series and movies. They looked like BBC dramas and crime shows that Caleb had heard of but never watched. Until he spotted Star Trek, the original series. Oh, he would gladly binge-watch that one with Rod. It was easy to imagine both of them curled on the couch, Rod's big arms around Caleb, holding him tight.

Caleb shook his head to clear it from a dream that shouldn't plague his brain on their second date. He didn't do cozy movie marathons. Or rather, he never had before.

"You want something to drink?" Rod's voice trailed from the kitchen on Caleb's right.

"Water would be great, thanks."

Rod arrived with a glass and Caleb downed its contents in a few gulps, realizing how parched he'd been. "So about that attic..." Caleb wiggled his eyebrows to Rod's visible amusement.

"Come, I'll show you." Rod led them up wooden stairs. "I have three rooms, but one is a storage space since I don't want to clutter the loft."

"Makes sense." Caleb chanced a glance towards a bedroom, but in the darkness, he could only see a big bed in the middle and stacks of books. He continued to follow Rod one more flight up much steeper stairs.

Caleb stepped into the attic, still bathed in darkness bar a tiny sliver of moonlight streaming through a roof window. A click sounded somewhere behind him and a soft glow illuminated the open room.

Whoa.

Caleb's eyes darted from side to side, taking in the cozy space on one side and torture chamber on the other.

A leather couch with several folded fluffy blankets sat in a corner, with a lambskin rug at the foot of it. Next to it was a shelf with books and a wicker basket of pillows on the floor.

Adjacent to the couch on the other side was a large cage with a padlock, and a collection of floggers and other steel devices hung down from a slanted roof wall. At the very back, on one of the two walls that were upright, was a huge padded-leather X with matching handcuffs on top and bottom. Several chairs, a horse-without-a-head looking thing, and some other bizarre contraptions were neatly organized. The dark side of the room ended with a bench press and a stack of weights.

Caleb took a step back and bumped into Rod's big body. A hand on his elbow steadied him and he looked over his shoulder to the man who so tenderly stitched his forehead when they first met, and fucked him deliciously rough just an hour before.

Yeah, this room definitely suited Rod.

His new lover stepped away, giving Caleb the option to go back downstairs.

Instead, Caleb surveyed the other end of the room, where by the second straight wall, the entire expanse consisted of a huge shower stall that could easily fit four people, with a toilet in the corner. Tiled floor and slanted walls encapsulated in glass made Caleb's mind recall a golden shower video he'd stumbled upon months before.

He swallowed audibly. The possibilities of this attic expanded beyond Caleb's knowledge of kinky sex. "Add a kitchenette in the corner and you can live here," he said, keeping his fascination out of his words but not his deepened tone of voice.

"I have a kettle for tea in that cupboard, if needed." Rod pointed to a closed shelving unit by the couch.

Caleb wasn't interested in tea at the moment. His eyes returned to the cage and he walked towards it. It was sturdy, with thick iron bars, reaching Caleb's waist and longer than his body. A black mat covered the entire floor space as if it was there to...

"Can a person sleep in there?" Caleb asked, tracing a finger along the top bar.

"Yeah. If they want to. The mattress is comfortable," Rod replied, his body heat close to Caleb's back.

"Oh, really?" Caleb turned around to see Rod's face, his eyes watching Caleb closely, his posture relaxed.

"I've never had anyone complain about it."

"Oh..." Caleb imagined laying down in the cage, surrounded by the bars around him. Rod would lock it and hold the key as he sat on the couch. This idea should scare Caleb, but instead he felt safe.

How many people used it for sleeping? How many used it for something else?

Those were the types of thoughts that stopped him from researching online, afraid he'd want to delve more into things he didn't know how to handle alone. His gut told him that he could ask Rod all the questions that plagued his mind and he wouldn't be judged for them.

"What about these?" Caleb pointed to the array of toys hanging from the slanted ceiling wall, and rubber and steel toys on the shelves under them.

"Do you get lots of complaints from the neighbors when you use these on someone? Assuming—"

"The walls are soundproof. So all the screams stay here. And your assumption is correct." Rod smirked, scratching his short-trimmed beard.

"So you get people here often?"

"Not as often as I used to."

"Why?"

"I don't..." Rod sighed and shook his head, crossing his arms over his massive chest. "I like a sub I can connect with. Whose needs match what I can give. So I guess I just became pickier with age and I turned to the dating app for help."

"You don't look very old, wise man." Caleb snickered, but hoped he was different from Rod's previous partners.

Rod snorted. "I'm thirty-five, and the scene has been a big part of my life for over twelve years."

The scene.

"I'm twenty-four," Caleb said. He knew there was an age gap between them, but standing in a sex attic with that information reminded him how naive he must seem to Rod. How naive he actually was when it came to knowledge of this BDSM shit.

Yet, he wanted to learn. From Rod.

"Does the age difference bother you?" Caleb asked.

"You're an adult and you act like one, so no, it doesn't. Unless that's an issue for you."

"It's not." Caleb swallowed, looking at Rod's beard, then slowly moving his gaze up to meet Rod's mahogany eyes. "You don't treat me like your inferior."

"Because you're not. And age has nothing to do with it. It's about respect." Rod leaned in to graze Caleb's ear with his teeth. "You could be my slutty wolf, crawling on your knees to sit on my cock, and I'd respect you and your choices," he whispered.

Blood rushed to Caleb's dick so fast he nearly swayed, gripping Rod's forearm to ground himself.

I want this.

Caleb could imagine himself needy and begging Rod to fuck him, knowing that the man wouldn't think less of him for it. He was ready to do it now. But his body was tired and yet he still wanted to know so much more about Rod's take on BDSM. Now, he had an opportunity he shouldn't waste.

He was starting to sweat, so he shrugged off his jacket and hoodie, then tossed them on the couch. Trying not to hiss at the pain all over his body, he returned to the display of fetish gear.

"What are the masks for? I mean, I know what they're for, but what's their purpose?"

"Depends on the mask and the person." Rod sat on the couch, crossing his legs at the ankles. He looked like he didn't mind the array of questions Caleb had, so there was no need to stop asking.

"Some are designed to hide your face in public, in a club for example, or just to feel latex or leather on your skin. Others are for sensory deprivation. If you wore that one," Rod pointed to an eerie-looking latex piece with just a mouth opening, "you wouldn't see anything. If I added ear plugs or buds with loud music, you wouldn't hear anything either." Rod's voice dropped an octave, as if the thought turned him on as much as it did Caleb. "You wouldn't know when the next strike would come at you. Or what it would be. A hand? Paddle? A cane? An electric jolt?" Rod's lips lifted in a smile tinged with evil mischief. "And some masks are just for decorative purposes."

A paddle? Oh yeah. An electric jolt? Fuck... maybe.

Caleb swallowed hard, stepping from foot to foot to reposition his erection discreetly. With his back to Rod, he traced his fingers over a pup mask that was the last in a row. It was detailed, with black pieces of leather forming a perfect snout.

"This one is gorgeous. Wow!" Caleb breathed, imagining the smell and creak of leather so close to his face.

"It was handmade. A gift from an old friend who makes them himself."

"Wow, that's some talent right there." Caleb whistled low.

"He's talented in other ways, too."

"A former lover?" Caleb turned to see if Rod wasn't annoyed with the questioning yet, but he looked chill.

"Yes and no. More of a mentor-turned-friend."

"Sounds complicated."

"It actually wasn't. Don't get me wrong, he's hot, always has been, but I wanted to know the kink ways, more than be with him. And I don't think I was his type."

"Well, he needs his eyes checked," Caleb deadpanned.

Rod snorted out a laugh.

"I know you can find kinky people online, but does anyone just agree to meet for a session?" Caleb sat on the other side of the couch, making sure to put weight on his side, trying not to wince at the ache in his ass.

"That's where munches come in. We have quite a large community in Bristol, and we communicate online and invite new people. We alternate between several restaurants or pubs for the munches, where the newbies and everyone else can come to a public location and feel safe—meet the kinksters in a vanilla setting and clothes."

"Like the bear picnic."

"Exactly. It was organized as a munch, but through the Bears-4-U app."

"I assume you can't do the scenes you mentioned before at a local pub. So where do you go? To houses with rooms like this one?"

"Sort of. My place is not spacious enough for a big party; a small group scene max, but some members with bigger houses organize those. Or rent a club once a month, but it's a regular disco on any other night, so we can't stay for the weekend and we need to take everything with us."

Caleb imagined a club full of people in leather gear, with him and Rod amongst them. Caleb would be scantily-dressed, or better yet, naked, if that was allowed. "There's no kink club around here?"

"Unfortunately, no. A man from the community, Blackbeard—"

Caleb snickered and Rod shook his head at him with a smile. It was understandable that someone would be reluctant to use their real name if they had some important job.

"He has plans to open a club," Rod continued. "Based on the one in London I attend sometimes."

"Oh?"

"It has different sections, for shows, dancing, group scenes, one-on-one BDSM presentations like flogging. But also, it has rooms for hire where you can stay the night and have access to all the equipment your kink heart desires. I was privileged enough to be invited to the opening twelve years ago when I was just learning the ropes, so to speak."

"And that was when the leather masks guy taught you?"

"Arran, yes. I met him when I was at uni in Manchester and joined a community there. I attended a few small house parties at first but quickly learned that the city had a lot more to offer. Arran guided me into the scene and to becoming a dom. A few years later he opened a club of his own in Edinburgh. I try to visit twice a year, but it's a lot further than London."

"Could you teach me like that? But not to be a dom. Just... in general, I guess." Caleb's face felt hot and he knew he was blushing. Telling someone to fuck him roughly was one thing, but what he'd just asked called for a longer arrangement.

Rod nodded. "It would be my pleasure. We can discuss details later. Would you like it non-sexual or—"

"Sexual. Rod, come on." Caleb chuckled. "We're dating, right?"

"Yes."

"So, can we just... make it a part of it? I don't want to be a hookup for a night." *Not while I'm still in the UK.*

Rod cursed under his breath and reached for Caleb, searing their lips together. It was a quick kiss, but Rod's hand on Caleb's nape and the growl leaving his chest made it feel like a seal of contract for their new relationship.

"Bloody hell, Caleb," Rod said, pulling away. "You drive me insane. Your curiosity and your very presence makes me want to rail you right where you sit." He raked a hand over his face and released a breath. "Tell me, what do you already know?"

Caleb licked his lips, his eyes on the beard that scratched them so deliciously. He repositioned to ease the pressure of his jockstrap on his hard-on and willed his brain to work again. "I watched a bit of kinky porn, but there's not much of it on free sites. I read about safewords and the traffic lights system, but I don't know what's actually useful in reality, you know? I fought my entire life to stand on my feet and to be my own person... the idea of submitting just doesn't sit well with me. And it scares me how much it turns me on when I think about it."

"Submission doesn't take your autonomy away." Rod said, placing a hand on Caleb's knee. "You have your safeword and you can wield it. But even before you need to use it, I'd be watching your reactions and expressions."

"Do you have a safeword?" Caleb asked. "Do you even need it?"

"I do. Subs are usually the receivers in a scene but that doesn't mean doms stay aloof and don't experience it second hand. I use the traffic lights system too."

"Oh. There's so much of it that makes sense once you say it, but I wouldn't think of it myself. Maybe I'd have to—" Caleb looked at Rod, licking his lips. "I'd have to try it first to know."

"And you already had my cock up your arse." Rod's smile was infectious, even with the evil glint in his eyes. He was already planning something.

And Caleb couldn't wait. He could still feel where Rod had been.

"Have you thought about your limits?"

"Uh, for now can it be: no permanent damage, and..." Caleb thought. "I don't know the possibilities much, so I guess, for now, I'm open to whatever there is."

"That's fair. We'll take it slow and I'll ask you at every step. I won't do anything you don't want and you can always tell me to stop. Communication is key."

"You told me that, but I guess it extends to sex."

"Even more important there, yes." Rod nodded.

"What if it's a—" Caleb swallowed, remembering a tag that led him down a rabbit hole on a porn site. "If it's a rape fantasy, um... *scene*, and the person would scream *no* but wouldn't mean it?"

"This is an excellent point. That's why the traffic light system and safewords are so important. Red can be replaced with a personal safeword too, something that you wouldn't scream during sex."

"So, for everyday play, 'no' could be fine?"

"Yup. And I'll always react to it until we agree beforehand that I shouldn't."

Caleb smoothed a hand over the soft upholstery he was sitting on. "The couch seems out of place here, all cozy and shit," he said flippantly, even as his mind supplied him with images of Rod railing him on that very piece of furniture.

"It's mostly for aftercare."

"That's the cuddling part."

"Yes, exactly. And anything else needed. Applying lotion, checking for damage, and comfort." Rod patted the armrest. "It pulls out to a full-size bed too."

"Nice." Caleb repositioned on the couch and winced.

"Was that butt, back, or ribs?" Rod asked, his eyes sharp and focused.

"All of the above," Caleb hissed at the pain in his ribs, unable to hold onto his composure anymore. The high of the fight had died down and the pain was seriously kicking in.

"Will you let me wash your back at least? I just want to clean the scratches."

Caleb glanced at the big-ass shower stall. "Sure." He certainly wouldn't mind Rod's hands roaming all over him, washing every inch of his body.

Chapter Seven

Caleb

Caleb stood up slowly and was thankful when Rod helped him take the t-shirt off. He winced as it got stuck on a piece of healing tissue and they had to pull on it.

Sweatpants still on, Caleb took off his socks and balled them up, watching as Rod walked into the spacious shower. He eyed the two metal stools inside the shower recess. Each one had a round cushion covered in black rubber. They reminded Caleb of the old-school ones at a doctor's office.

"Your joggers will get wet," Rod commented.

Caleb lifted a brow at Rod's look of mock innocence. "Sure they will." He smirked. Eager to be naked around his new lover, he stepped out of his sweatpants and left them on the floor. He left the jockstrap on, recalling Rod's positive reaction when he'd seen it first. "Your clothes will get wet, too."

"I wasn't planning on keeping them on. You don't mind?"

Mind? Was he insane?

"Go ahead." Caleb waved a hand casually but his cock twitched the moment Rod pulled his t-shirt over his head.

His thick arms looked like he could bench-press Caleb and wouldn't break a sweat. No tattoos or piercings in sight. The hair on his chest was thicker than the trail going down his belly and Caleb wanted to sink his fingers into it and stroke. Rod didn't have a six-pack, far from it, and Caleb was drawn to the soft middle surrounded by muscle. It was clear that Rod chose to look that way, that he honed his body to perfection and the result was absolutely mouthwatering.

Calebs's eyes snapped up to see Rod's smirk.

Busted.

Without further ado, Rod rid himself of the rest of his clothes to reveal thick thighs that Caleb wanted to squeeze when he was on his knees sucking Rod's dick.

"Fuck," he said the moment Rod unceremoniously slid his boxer briefs down.

"What? We don't have to do anything—"

"No, no, that's not it. I want to do so much with you, I'd have no idea where to start. It's just that..." Caleb hesitated, his mouth salivating at the sight of the plump head hidden in foreskin. He didn't get a chance to see it properly in the darkness before and now he couldn't pull his gaze away. "You're uncut."

Rod's chuckle was low and seductive. "It's not uncommon around here." He tossed his last garment on the pile of clothes on the couch.

"Well, I've only seen them in porn before," Caleb confessed. His mouth watered as he imagined sucking on the skin, feeling it in his mouth, and playing with it with his tongue.

"Sit." Rod waved to the chairs.

Caleb snapped to reality. Right. Rod was supposed to wash him, but it was clear that neither of them wanted it to stop there.

He entered the stall and took a seat on the chair facing the tall stylized pipes on the wall. The showerhead extended high and into the middle of the tiled space while a smaller one, on a flexible hose, hung attached next to the hot and cold taps. To the side was a tray with slim shower head attachments, one of which was shaped like the head of a penis. Caleb frowned then realized what it must be for. *Neat.*

Rod rummaged around, grabbing washcloths and a bowl that he filled with several small bottles and tubes, before placing it on the floor. Caleb was getting hard watching Rod's thighs flex with every step he took. His pecs were like pillows Caleb could see himself sleeping on, his tight nipples looked perfect for sucking, and his dick, hanging thick, was the perfect size to glide inside Caleb.

Unhooking the long shower hose with a small head, Rod turned the water on and checked the temperature with his hand. "I'll tackle the grime first," he said, cupping Caleb's cheek.

"I can wash my face by myself," Caleb scoffed, looking up.

"But would you let me do it?" Rod's thumb brushed Caleb's lips.

"Knock yourself out." Caleb shrugged, battling the confusion inside him.

Rod's gentle touch felt exquisite but foreign. He basked in the tenderness but he also wanted Rod to rail him hard, if only he wasn't so sore. He'd always liked rough, quick sex, exactly the way they had done it at the factory.

It was this slow whatever-the-fuck Rod was doing that threw Caleb completely for a loop.

Rod wet a washcloth, squeezed it and wiped Caleb's forehead, then the side of his face, coming out with blood and grime. Rinse, squeeze, repeat. This time over Caleb's neck and shoulder blades.

Caleb sat speechless, unable to decipher whether his body wanted to bolt from the utter gentleness he was so unused to, or sit entranced and see where it led.

Of course, he'd stay.

Rod remained focused on his task as he rinsed Caleb's back with a lukewarm stream before he sat on the chair behind Caleb. With a fresh washcloth, he made long strokes from Caleb's shoulders to the small of his back, all over the howling wolf tattoo covering most of his upper back.

The entire process let Caleb drift away. He didn't need to move or speak, but let Rod do his thing as his mind quietened down from processing the date in the city, the fight, and the tour of the attic.

Now it was only him, the sound of rushing water, and Rod's caressing hands.

"So you're still sore?" Rod asked, swiping a washcloth above Caleb's buttocks.

"Mmhmm." He probably would be for another day. Which was good. Every move would remind him of Rod's cock deep in him during the savage, needy fuck.

"I have an ointment that would help."

Of course, he had an ointment.

"Yeah, go for it," Caleb murmured, the thought of Rod's fingers near his arse sending heat to his abdomen.

"I promised I'd keep my hands to myself," Rod said, his sincere voice tinged with regret.

"Please don't," Caleb whispered, unable to bear the loss now.

"You sure?"

"I want you to touch me, Rod. Anywhere."

A rumble sounded behind Caleb and he realized it came from Rod.

"Scoot back."

Caleb did and half of his ass ended up hanging over the edge of the stool.

Rod turned the water off and resumed his position, his hands massaging Caleb's buttcheeks, squeezing. "Gym?"

"Yeah, but also manual labor and walking. Well, and sparring of course." Caleb's dick, chubby until now, was hardening, still trapped in the jockstrap.

"Is that how you learned to fight?"

"My ex-girlfriend was an instructor. She taught mixed martial arts and I had a free membership I refused to waste."

"Smart." Rod reached for one of the tubes in the bowl on the floor. "Hands on your thighs and don't move them."

Caleb followed the instructions without a second thought, gripping above his knees and remaining relaxed under Rod's touch.

"You're feral and beautiful when you fight," Rod said, circling Caleb's pucker.

"Ah, thanks," Caleb groaned, trying not to thrust back. "My technique is mixed with dirty tricks I learned on the streets as a scrawny kid. That's what makes me win now. Most fighters are surprised to see that in the ring. That also means I'd stand no chance in a fight with actual rules. I'd be eating the mat in seconds."

"I'm sure you'd learn quickly." Rod slid a finger in, slippery with the ointment.

Rod's movements were professional, even bordering on medical, and Caleb found this was turning him on even more.

"Do you feel bad pain, or is it just sore?" Rod asked, gently probing inside with unhurried motions, before he added another digit.

"Sore, tender." Caleb stifled a moan. "It hurts, but not in a bad way." He closed his eyes as he said it, his cheeks heating. He didn't want Rod to stop, but he wouldn't lie to him either.

"Do you like it when it hurts this way?" Rod's fingers kept swirling, slowly and gently.

Caleb's mouth went dry and he tried to swallow. "Yes." He gasped as Rod found his prostate. "Oh fuck, oh shit, ohmygod," Caleb moaned, and leaned back further.

Rod's body was right behind him, welcoming him, and his left hand wrapped itself across Caleb's upper chest, holding him in place.

"Let your voice echo." Rod put pressure on the sweet spot, massaging.

"Ah, yes!" Caleb let out a series of moans, needily circling his hips.

"But don't move."

It was easier said than done. Caleb wanted to thrust back, to fist his cock and stroke, to tweak his nipple. Anything to add just a bit more sensation so he could come quickly. Instead, he dug his fingers into his thighs, holding on tight.

"You look mouthwatering in this jockstrap, but I really hate it right now." Rod's voice was a cross between a growl and a purr.

"Then get rid of it," Caleb challenged.

He gasped when, with a sharp tug, Rod tore the front of the underwear with his other hand, letting Caleb's cock spring free, standing tall and rigid between his parted legs.

"That's better." Rod's hand slid up Caleb's left flank and chest to wrap around Caleb's throat.

Caleb tilted his head back but the grip remained loose.

"How do you feel?" Rod's rumble was a dead giveaway as to his own state of arousal.

Is Rod as hard as I am? What does his cock look like in the bright light? Is he already leaking pre-come?

"Good. Great." Caleb groaned as Rod tightened the hold on his neck. "Green."

"Perfect."

The scrape of the chair on the tiles was loud when Rod scooted closer. Caleb felt Rod's chest behind his back, his lips on his shoulder, then his cheek in a soft brush.

Caleb's hand flew to his cock to give it a stroke and he let out a moan.

"Do you want me to stop?" Rod's hold on Caleb's throat tightened.

"Fuck, no," Caleb choked out, eyed closing in pleasure.

"Then keep your hands on your thighs or I'll tie them there," Rod said, his voice a warning.

Caleb's eyes snapped open. The idea of Rod restraining him and playing with his body filled him with lust. He hadn't known the man long, but he felt safe with him and he had a feeling that he'd be able to relinquish all control with him.

In a way, he'd done that with Natasha, but her brand of fucking and pegging was rough, quick and to the point. Nothing like the sensual mix of rough and tender that was keeping Caleb on the edge.

Right now, Caleb was already strung for release, but without touching his cock, he was under a constant strain, that place so close yet not close enough. It was driving him insane.

And he fucking loved it.

"I need to stroke my dick," he groaned.

"Don't."

"But—"

"Are you safewording?" Rod growled, closing his teeth over the cartilage of Caleb's ear.

"What the fuck? Of course I'm not."

"Then wait."

Fucking sadist.

Rod increased pressure on Caleb's prostate in the most delicious torture.

A broken sob left his lips and he knew that he was giving himself bruises with how hard he was gripping his thighs to stay in place.

Rod's hold on Caleb's neck eased, his hand sliding lower to flick Caleb's nipple.

Caleb gasped and let his head fall back on Rod's shoulder right behind him.

Rod kissed his cheek as he rolled Caleb's taut bud in his fingers, pinching it, then rubbing. He did the same to the other one.

Caleb stopped analyzing the embarrassing sounds he was making. He was ready to beg. "Please," he whimpered.

"Please what?"

"Please touch my dick."

"Why?"

Caleb grunted, moaned and sighed in quick succession. "So I can come."

"I won't let you yet. Don't you like how you feel right now?"

"I do. It's fucking amazing... But I'm so close it hurts. I need to come."

"Do you enjoy this pain?"

Oh...

Rod was showing him other ways to hurt. Well, fuck.

Caleb felt a rush of pleasure, mixed with the pressure and strain in his balls and prostate. Every single one of his muscles was tight.

"Yes! Fuck, Rod. I do."

"Good. You're ready. All you have to do is ask properly."

"I just did, ah!" Caleb yelped as Rod pinched his nipple and bit his earlobe at the same time.

Right. Properly. *What the fuck does he mean?* Caleb searched his scattered brain, devoid of coherent thoughts.

"Please..." he whined. Holy shit, was his prostate connected to his soul? 'Cause, it sure as fuck felt like it. "Please, ah... Sir, uhhh Master, Lord, please let me come."

A low rumble akin to an evil chuckle came from Rod before his meaty hand wrapped around Caleb's dick.

"Oh, fuck... oh, shit. Rod, ohmygod, ah!" Caleb strained, trying to remain in place.

"Breathe," Rod rumbled. "And let go."

Caleb did and he gasped in between shouting Rod's name and curse words all mixed together. His eyes screwed shut and he couldn't see where his come landed, but it felt like he was shooting forever, each spurt draining him of physical energy and calming his head. He leaned back on Rod, riding wave after wave that overtook him.

"So beautiful and strong," Rod whispered, slowing down his stroking.

"Rod—" Caleb whimpered. "Thank you."

"Mmm. My pleasure. I wish I could taste your come," Rod breathed into Caleb's ear, making him shiver. "I wish I could fuck you bare." He retreated his fingers gently, leaving Caleb open and surprisingly less sore than before.

Caleb panted, his body coming down from the intense orgasm, his pulsing hole trying to grip something that wasn't there anymore. "I haven't been tested in a while."

"That's OK. Maybe someday. If you'll let me."

"I—"

"Shhh, no promises. Nothing you won't be able to keep."

Right. Caleb had signed up for a few dates and maybe a good fuck but each moment he'd spent with Rod made him want to shoot for more than that. He'd received more intimacy from Rod in one day than dozens of random hookups over the years combined.

He didn't usually mix sex with feelings. He wasn't sure he would know where to start with those.

He loved Sandra as his friend, he loved his Grandpa, and he even loved his mom. But he'd never loved anyone romantically. It had never been on the cards before. He and Natasha were a great team, but neither of them felt their connection went beyond friendship and physical attraction. Now, he had a big guy messing with his head, his feelings, and his unquenchable libido.

"But I can suck you off," Caleb said.

"Maybe another time. You coming on my fingers was enough of a gift."

"What if I really wanted to?" Caleb chuckled darkly. "Then asked nicely?"

He blushed as he tested the words in his head. Fuck. He ached for it, and Rod must know that, so he was fucking with his head. "Can I please suck your dick?" he said, then added louder. "Sir?"

Rod rounded the chair and lifted Caleb's chin with a finger under it.

"You can call me Roderick instead of Sir. No one calls me that and it would be more personal."

"Yes, Roderick." Caleb nodded. "Please, can I suck your dick, Roderick?"

"Yes, my Wolf. Now kneel."

Caleb slid to the cold, wet tiles, feeling the pain in his ribs and the scratches on his back, but too blissed-out to care. Rod's dick hung in his field of vision and his mouth watered at the thought of sucking it.

Rod spread Caleb's knees wide with his foot. "Back straight."

Caleb obeyed, opening his mouth in the process.

"Gorgeous. My feisty Wolf, my warrior, kneeling for me."

"Only for you."

Caleb realized how true the statement was only after it left his mouth. He'd never wanted to kneel for anyone before. Not like this, openly needy and ready to serve.

Something flashed in Rod's eyes and he traced Caleb's jaw with his fingertips before gripping it. With his other hand, he tugged his foreskin over the head, then all the way back before he guided his dick to Caleb's mouth. Caleb closed his lips around the tip and sucked delicately, swirling his tongue to feel the foreskin. He worked his mouth to get it to cover Rod's crown and he reveled in the novelty.

Rod lifted Caleb's chin higher and Caleb looked up to meet his gaze. With hooded eyes full of lust, Rod was fucking hot, his towering body magnificent.

Caleb stopped his tongue play and opened his throat, waiting.

Rod slid his dick further until it hit the back of Caleb's throat. He didn't gag, but his eyes welled with tears. Sucking, he held Rod's gaze, showing him that he wanted more.

He got it. Rod's thick cock was stretching his mouth, punching his throat, and filling him once again in one evening.

Caleb moved his hands to Rod's powerful thighs, dusted with their dark hair, and waited for Rod to protest. He didn't. He was thrusting into Caleb's mouth and didn't tell him that he wasn't allowed to touch. So it was fair game until he told Caleb otherwise.

Caleb cupped Rod's sac, rolled it then reached behind it. Rod's breathing quickened.

"Go on, Wolf," Rod said, widening his stance, still rocking his hips.

Caleb moaned around Rod's cock when he touched his lover's pucker. He pushed the tip of his finger in and heard Rod's moan echo in the shower stall.

"If you don't want to swallow, tap twice," Rod said and Caleb made sure to keep his hand steady.

He slid deeper into Rod's hole and wrenched a groan out of his lover a moment before hot spurts hit his throat.

Rod pulled away enough to shoot on Caleb's cheek, neck and chest, only to return to Caleb's mouth. Caleb sucked the last drops, moaning at the tangy taste and the fact that it was Rod's come. He had a deep urge to please Rod, but only in a way that Rod told him to.

He would be hard if he hadn't been so drained already.

Rod kneeled in front of Caleb and spread his come on Caleb's face, then kissed him lazy yet deep.

"Don't move," he whispered against Caleb's mouth.

Rod washed him; hair, armpits, and feet—all of him. His hands were gentle but quick as if he was looking forward to something. Caleb had no idea what was going to come next. He couldn't wait to find out.

Chapter Eight

Caleb

Sated and mindless, Caleb stood like a rag doll as Rod insisted on drying him. When he was done, he wrapped the towel around Caleb's shoulders and grabbed one for himself.

Once they were out of the shower, Caleb glanced at his clothes, but Rod had other plans. He unfolded the couch into a bed, spread a navy blanket over it, and replaced Caleb's wet towel with another blanket. It was the softest piece of fabric that had ever touched his skin. As if he was wrapped in a cloud or some shit.

They didn't need words when Rod reached out for Caleb and pulled him close, maneuvering them to lie down.

This was the cuddling Rod had been talking about. Caleb felt cherished, relaxed, and safe, wrapped not only in blankets but Rod, completely and utterly swaddled in warmth. There was a layer of fluff between their bodies, but Caleb could still feel Rod's flaccid dick snuggled close to his buttocks. He was sure Rod had better plans for the evening than snuggling, and self-consciousness crept its way into Caleb's brain.

"You don't have to hold me," he said. "I don't need aftercare." He tried to move away, but Rod squeezed him tighter.

"But do you mind?" Rod mumbled into his nape.

"No, I just thought—"

"This part is for me, too."

"Oh?"

"I need to feel you're OK. But as much as you deserve aftercare, physical and here," he kissed Caleb's temple, "I need it too. Closeness like this calms me down. Charges me, so to speak."

Quite a solid argument. "Well, in that case, hug me all you want."

Rod grunted with amusement and pulled Caleb even closer, making it hard to breathe for a moment, before he eased his grip.

"You're cuddly for a sadist," Caleb commented. "Your screen name is accurate."

Rod barked out a laugh. "I learned I don't have to be one or the other. The community tried to pin a daddy label on me at one point because of that. It's not too far from the truth, I guess."

"I know it doesn't mean being parental, but I don't really get it." Caleb played with Rod's fingers splayed on his chest.

"I want to take care of you. Keep you in check, make sure you eat and do things that benefit your body and your future. Be there when you're hurting, or when you need to hurt." Rod bit Caleb's earlobe then kissed the side of his neck. "Become an inseparable part of your life, if you'd let me. Or at least, that's what it means to me. Everyone's different."

It sounded too good to be true. Caleb wasn't sure he could believe a scenario where Rod accepted all his emotional baggage and embraced his needs at the same time. He'd have to tell Rod about his struggles before letting him decide. "Does it bother you that I'm not a 'little'? I couldn't be a brat either."

"I think you could be a brat." Rod chuckled. "And I was never looking for a 'little.' I want to take care of you as an adult, a partner. Instill rules and structure into our lives, and have your body for myself. If we'd ever go that far, of course."

"I like my independence. People can do what they choose, but I'm not into the master/slave shit I read about." At Rod's nod against his nape, Caleb continued. "I know the basics, I have the internet and I'm not stupid. Some rules and structure sound good though. It wouldn't be easy for me. I've been a lone wolf since my brother... since I was ten."

"What about your brother?"

"Nothing."

"You don't have to tell me. But I'm here to listen."

Caleb shrugged. He believed Rod meant it, but it was still hard to accept that he cared.

"It still hurts and..." Caleb said after a moment of silence. He had the urge to unload everything on Rod. He wasn't sure if it was some drop from the sex, the fucking blankets, or the comfort, but he wanted to bare his soul and his past to this man.

"I'm your friend and you can tell me anything." Rod nuzzled Caleb's nape, his hand still on Caleb's chest as if cradling his heart.

"Friend whose dick I've been wanting to bounce on for weeks." Caleb snorted, hiding emotions behind a joke, as was his custom.

Rod grunted in approval but didn't laugh. "You're much more than that to me. To be perfectly honest with you, I don't want to spook you away. You just should know that you can trust me. With anything."

The sincerity of Rod's words undid Caleb. *How does he know Caleb is a flight risk?* He saw Rod for what he was: big, cuddly, loving, a smidge sadistic. In short: too good to be true. Today, Caleb could enjoy the closeness while it lasted. There would come a moment, probably quite soon, when Rod would have enough of Caleb, and he'd walk away. Everyone did eventually. His friends and family. It didn't even start with Timmy, but his death changed everything.

"My brother," Caleb started and cleared his throat. "He... he died when I was ten. It broke my mom, and she never recovered."

"I'm sorry."

"It was my fault." Memories of the dark times were fresh in Caleb's mind, despite fourteen years passing.

"I find that hard to believe," Rod said, massaging Caleb's sternum as if to ease his heartache.

"But it's true." Caleb unwound himself from Rod's embrace, unable to stand the tenderness of the moment. He sat cross-legged on the couch, the blanket covering the entirety of him like a teepee. It was enough to hear the sympathy in Rod's voice, he couldn't stand feeling it in his hug too. He didn't deserve it.

Rod mirrored his position, facing him, the blanket around his waist, his chest bare. There was kind interest in his eyes and it let Caleb open up.

"I was a stupid kid. Like every ten-year-old, I wanted to fit in: wear the same clothes as everyone else, have the trendy hat, or the newest game console. But I never did. This one time, I really wanted a new pair of Jordans, more than anything. They were insanely expensive, and we didn't have a lot of money." Caleb shrugged. Looking back, he knew his childhood hadn't been bad until that day, but back then it hadn't been enough. "Timmy was 16 at the time and brought money home from

God knows where, but mom never asked when he bought groceries to fill the fridge, even smokes for her. If he had some way of getting money to help mom, I figured it was worth a shot telling him I wanted something, too." *Stupid kid.*

"So I told him about the shoes, even showed him a magazine cutout of the model. They had red laces. I hoped if I proved to him how much I wanted them, he'd help me. I said I'd chip in all of my 20 bucks I had from shoveling our neighbor's driveway that winter. Of course, Timmy agreed." The memories were too vivid for his comfort, drawing him back into that day.

"He never came home that evening. But the police did. Apparently, he'd been selling drugs under a bridge and there was a drive-by shooting." Caleb twisted the blanket in his hands, unable to look at Rod. Unwilling to see judgment on his face. "If I hadn't asked him for those Jordans..." Caleb's throat was tight as he tried to hold the floodgates closed.

"It wasn't your fault. You were just a child." Rod's baritone exuded kindness.

"Who should have known better!" Caleb snapped, tears pricking his eyes, his heart a raw wound once more.

"Not true," Rod reached out and waited, his hand in the air.

Caleb nodded and Rod found Caleb's ankle under the blanket. The touch was grounding, calming Caleb's mind which was lost in grief.

"Well, it changed everything. For me, but also for mom. She wished it was me who got shot."

"I'm sure she didn't."

"Oh, she told me." A tear spilled down Caleb's cheek. He couldn't stop it, but he swiped it quickly with his hand. "Not just once, but many times over the years. After Timmy was gone, she took up drugs as her hobby and it just spiraled down from there."

"I'm sorry. You didn't deserve that, you must know." Rod's brows furrowed at Caleb's snort and his jaw worked. He pulled Caleb's foot out, rubbing the sole with his thumbs.

Oh, that felt good. Caleb expected it to tickle but the way Rod was digging his fingers in and kneading, it was far from it.

"Thank you for telling me, Caleb. It means a lot."

"How about you? Any family drama? Or is it just me?" Caleb tried to lighten the mood but Rod remained serious.

"I was born in Bristol. The rest you already know, that I have a younger brother and a sister and mom brought us all up alone." He smiled softly. "There's not much to it, really. I had a happy childhood." He reached for Caleb's other foot, massaging the sole, the action bringing Caleb a sense of comfort.

"Can I ask, umm...about–" Caleb touched his own forehead to indicate the burn scar above Rod's eyebrow.

"Yeah. Everyone asks eventually. And no, I don't mind," he added quickly when Caleb started to backtrack. "I said I had a happy childhood, but that doesn't mean we didn't have any struggles. You see, Mom worked as a nurse, so she was in and out of the house at different times of day. Sometimes, she told me not to tell anyone when she had a night shift and we were home alone when Grandma couldn't stay with us." He touched his scar, tracing the raised tissue with his fingertips, before returning to massage Caleb's foot. "It was Aida's fourth birthday. I was about 12 and came home from rugby training that Saturday. I had Aida's present wrapped and ready, so I figured I could just take a nap on the sofa before we started celebrating. It didn't occur to me that mom needed help with the preparations. Flynt, who was six at the time, helped me hang the bunting and blow the balloons the day before so I thought we were good to go." Rod's gaze focused on Caleb's feet as if his eyes didn't really see them. He seemed mired in the past.

"Mom came back from her night shift, completely knackered, but she started baking the birthday cake. I was asleep and Aida was trying to help mom, but ended up playing with the candles. She stood next to the table by the sofa I was asleep on." Rod shook his head, squeezing his eyes shut as if the memory pained him. "I remember to this day how she poked my cheek and said 'Rod, wake up, look, look!'" Rod said it in a tiny child voice. "But I asked her to let me sleep for a few minutes more. Like any four-year-old, she didn't give up that easily. She poked my cheek again and I waved her off, batting her hand away. I didn't know she was holding a lit candle in that hand." Rod sighed. "I startled awake at that moment, and you can imagine the rest."

"Fuck. That must have been traumatic for all of you. I'm sorry." Caleb wiggled his toes and Rod squeezed them in return. It was the most natural display of comfort on both sides he'd ever experienced.

"The accident ruined Aida's birthday and she felt guilty for a long time, even though it wasn't her fault. I started helping Mom a lot more after that. She'd been overworked and I was an ungrateful shit that day," he said through gritted teeth.

"Our moms sound very different." Caleb had to bite his lip not to say 'I'd like to meet yours.' When he'd said he wanted to see the attic, Rod had driven him here straight away. He had to be careful what he wished for with this man around. He was bound to deliver.

"Is that why you left? Your mom?" Rod asked. "You mentioned that you're not close with your family anymore."

Wow, Caleb thought. Rod listened. And it was all too easy spilling everything that he hadn't shared with anyone in a long time.

"Not only. I guess I wanted a fresh start."

"What was your plan?"

"I didn't have one. Not really." Caleb snorted. "I just had to leave when Pops died, I mean my grandpa. After mom refused to even look at me when I came out, I moved in with him." Caleb felt Rod hold on as his foot tightened and his jaw worked overtime, but Caleb forged on. "Grandpa had this album with pictures from his childhood in Bristol, where he was born. He talked about the UK a lot. So when... when I came back from work one day and he wasn't breathing..." Caleb swallowed. "I knew I had no one else left."

"No other parent in the picture?"

"My brother and I had different dads. His was what mom called 'white trash' and we've never met him. Mine was a Mexican dude who was deported before mom realized she was pregnant. He found out from a mutual friend when I was born. It was clear whose I was, darker skin and all." Caleb motioned to his face.

"How did he react?"

Caleb offered a tiny smile. "I got a letter from his sister that he was overjoyed when he heard I was born. So he tried to sneak across the border and—" Caleb swallowed. "And got shot by the patrol. He..." Caleb's voice trembled. "He died trying to get to me." Caleb lacked the courage to look at Rod. "Everyone around me gets hurt. I'm the useless mutt everyone called me at school."

"No. You're a wolf. And a very brave one." Rod said it with so much conviction, Caleb almost believed him. How did he always know what to say?

"So when Pops died, mom still wasn't speaking to me." Caleb made a *duh* face at that. "Grandpa lived in a house that belonged to his sister. He poured every retirement check into mom's rehab bills, and bought food with whatever was left. I got odd jobs anywhere I could and tried to make his life as bright as he had made mine. He never judged me for being openly bi. When we were just hanging out, quiet evenings at home, he'd tell me all about his younger days..." Caleb smiled, remembering. "He told me about his best friend in Bristol. I didn't think much of their relationship at first, but as time went by, I suspected they were more than friends. Which made me think that was why he never remarried after grandma died or why they left the UK after mom was born in the first place." Caleb sighed. "He was so supportive of me when I came out. I would catch him sometimes with tears in his eyes, looking at the old photos of him and Henry, touching the picture with his fingertips. I wish I could find this guy, but I don't have enough information about him to even start."

Caleb scooted closer to Rod, sprawling his legs over his lover's lap. Rod wrapped his feet with the other blanket and patted Caleb's thigh to continue.

"Pops was like a father to me. Without him there, I just..." he shrugged, vulnerability in his tone. "Aunt Felecia, his sister, had to sell the house we lived in cause her granddaughter was getting married and she wanted to cover some expenses. Sure, I could have rented something; I had a job and didn't have to help Pops anymore with bills and all. But it felt like the best moment to start over. So, I thought I'd go where he was born and where people spoke a language I could understand, you know? He left me some money in his will and I spent it all for the ticket here and a new start."

"That sounds—"

"Desperate, I know. I wasn't expecting the citizenship paperwork to take so long. So here I am, with no money and no way to work legally until I get the fucking papers. If you snitch on me, I'm fucked."

"That's not what I wanted to say. I think it was brave. And I'll never tell anyone. Whatever you tell me stays with me, I can promise you that. But how did you even find that fighting ring? I can't imagine it was on Indeed."

Caleb snorted a laugh. "No, definitely not. I met some people online before coming here. You know Sandra. She helped me look for someone who wanted to buy my drawings, but they don't pay much."

"You haven't shown me your art, but that t-shirt is amazing." He pointed to the pile of clothes on the floor. "The detail itself." He whistled low. "Where did you learn how to draw?"

Caleb shrugged. "When you have no money but can find a pencil and a piece of paper, you learn to entertain yourself. So I got good at drawing, I guess. But it's not very lofty stuff, not fancy painting or anything. I like detailed sketches, though, and character study."

"I think our walk today proved that meaningful art doesn't need to be lofty. Does it even have to be meaningful to be beautiful?"

"No. It can be anything you feel you want to create. But you need more than being good to succeed."

Caleb saw Rod contemplate something, his brows furrowed. "And you haven't found that in Bristol yet."

"No. I realized that would be trickier than I initially thought within a week of landing in Bristol. So I texted this friend from London, Mat. I've never met him in person, but he has connections with the underground fighting community. He put in a good word for me with the Zielinski twins—the bouncers you saw at the fight. I knew I could kick ass enough to give it a shot after what Natasha taught me." He trailed off, wrapping himself tighter in the blanket. Rod didn't look bored, but Caleb wasn't sure if he signed up for the info dump. "It's so easy to talk to you. I'm sorry if this has been one huge-ass rant."

"You're easy to listen to." Rod smiled, standing up, still wrapped in a blanket. "I think tea is in order."

"That's the most English thing I've heard you say all day," Caleb laughed. "A good idea, too."

"Is Earl Grey OK?" Rod retrieved a tiny kettle from the cupboard and poured water from the sink in the shower enclosure.

"Sure, just no milk." Caleb was a coffee person, but he wouldn't turn down a cup of tea from an Englishman. He watched Rod toss teabags into two mugs and retrieve a small bottle of milk from a fridge hidden in the next cupboard, arranging it all on a tray.

"Where do you work by the way?" Caleb asked.

"At the council. A department for people struggling to get a job. I help them find courses to take and figure out what they could do from there on. Stuff like that."

"And that paid for the house?" Caleb's brows shot up. "I mean, it doesn't look cheap." They shared so much today, he was beyond rethinking every question before he asked it. For a moment he thought Rod might be offended as he fell silent, focusing on pouring water into the mugs.

"I bought it with money I earned at my previous job," Rod finally said, handing Caleb his steaming brew.

"Were you a hitman?" Caleb accepted the mug and warmed his hands against it

Rod laughed. "No, a private therapist." Rod added a splash of milk to his tea and Caleb couldn't stop watching his every move. The tea-making routine was like a calming ritual.

"Wait, you're a shrink?"

"Yes and no. It's a bit different in the UK but something like that."

"Wow. You must be analyzing the shit out of what I told you. Oh, fuck." Caleb wanted to bury his face in his hands but he had to hold onto the mug.

"I can't say I'm not, but all of what you told me only painted a more vivid picture of a man I could—" He hesitated, stirring with a loud clunk of a spoon against the mug. "Just know that you don't have to hide from me and it all stays between us."

"Spoken like a true shrink." Caleb blew on the steam from his tea, wondering what it was that had nearly slipped from Rod's lips.

"Or a friend." Rod returned to sit on the couch.

"Who made me come twice in one evening."

"A very good friend then."

Caleb laughed and angled the tea away from the blanket to avoid a potential spill.

"What made you change your job then? Tired of listening to people's issues?" Caleb winced. "Like me today."

"No, not at all. I liked my job. And you're not a client, your story is precious to me. Your voice and your accent made it even better." He winked but Caleb could sense he was avoiding something. "But my work is a story for another day." Rod nudged Caleb with his foot. "Now drink your tea so I can hold you." He repositioned in his seat. "If that's OK with you."

"It is. You say shit like that but you also like when I'm hurting," Caleb said, taking a sip of the tea and burning his tongue in the process. "Just something I noticed."

Rod shrugged. "Can't deny that."

"Fucking sadist." Caleb chuckled, nudging a grinning Rod back. "Why do you like it? Is there a reason?"

"Doesn't need to be. Sometimes you just like what you like, whether it's how you take your tea or how you like to fuck." He took a sip, the smug fucker whose beverage was cooler because of the milk. "In my case it's because I see you thrive when you're receiving it, but most importantly, I love the relief it brings you afterwards. Giving into this pain, one that you can control and stop with a safeword makes you calmer, your gaze less chaotic, your breathing even, your body more relaxed. Like now."

"I can get that when I fight," Caleb said, but his voice held no weight.

"Can you?" Rod ran his fingers under Caleb's chin, making him look up.

Caleb gritted his teeth, closing his eyes. "Fuck."

"Look at me and say it."

"You're right." Caleb's heart pounded as he opened his eyes and focused on Rod's gaze boring into him. "You're right, Roderick." He used the name as a title and the way Rod's eyes lit up sent a thrill through him.

Two can play at this game.

"How does succumbing to that need work for you?"

"It makes me feel... alive. Energized..." Caleb looked into himself to try to explain it. "Wanted."

"How so?"

"Gentle touch is fine, but only after my body is already hurting. I never liked people caressing my arm or some shit. A squeeze, a slap, or a punch meant I got some reaction out of them, some feelings, good or bad. My mom couldn't touch me after my brother died, she cringed away as if I had some disease she could catch." Caleb wrapped both hands around the mug, looking into it as if he could see his past in the leaves trapped in a bag there. "But still, when kids insulted her on the playground or at school, it gave me a good excuse to hit them so they would hit back. They cared about me enough to be mad at me and hit me, I guess? I never thought about it until now. It sounds so fucked up..."

"It's not. Like I said, you don't need a reason to want something in your sex life. But I'd love to be there for you to find a balance to what your needs are and fulfill them."

"I get what you're saying. I really do. But why do you care? I mean, I'm broken and I'm just... a nobody."

"No," Rod's stern voice made Caleb look at his face; it was full of indignation. "You're not and I don't want you to ever say that. It's not true."

Whoa.

"Right. Yeah, OK," Caleb said. He liked how that forced his bad thoughts to the back of his mind. He shifted closer and seeing Rod offer his hand, Caleb intertwined their fingers and took a deep breath.

"Caleb?"

"Yeah?"

"You're not broken, and you don't need to be fixed."

"But?"

"You might be a bit torn."

"And you want to stitch me?"

"Something like that."

Chapter Nine

Rod

A week went by and Rod woke up every day wishing Caleb was next to him. After their previous date, Caleb had gotten up and dressed early the following morning. Rod had waited patiently with eyes closed, not wanting to pressure his lover, especially after an emotional night.

Their daily texting—sharing tiny moments as well as long chats about BDSM, Caleb's limits, and pain threshold—weren't enough. Rod had the urge to storm Caleb's flat, throw him over his shoulder like a caveman and drag him back to his house. He wished to stake his claim and never let him go.

In reality, he wanted Caleb to choose a life with him. Caleb was reluctant to receive help, and asking him to move in a month after they met might be pushing his luck. Yet there was nothing Rod wanted more.

Shoving that thought aside, he turned his car off and made a break for the building he worked at. Only one more day of work and he'd see Caleb. He had special plans for him, with wrapped gifts ready for the evening.

The first several hours of work, Rod was swamped with emails and paperwork. He enjoyed working with people, but the admin side—not so much. Most days he didn't mind it, but today his phone was burning a hole in his back pocket, waiting for the break.

At 11.30 sharp, Rod headed to the staff break room, made tea and grabbed a pew by one of the round tables. He fired up the Bears-4-U app to see if Caleb was online. Of course, they'd exchanged phone numbers, but the app was fun and sexy, and they'd quickly gotten used to using it as their means of communication. Caleb was more brazen when texting, asking shameless questions about Rod's experience in the BDSM community, as well as describing new things he'd read about and wanted Rod to do to him. This on-and-off talk about Caleb's limits had become increasingly more detailed with all the online research Caleb had been doing. Rod opened their chat in the app, dying to see if Caleb had replied to his question from that morning.

'Dirty talk and sexy humiliation—yes. Degradation is a no.'

'Perfect. I can't wait for tonight.' Rod sent his reply, but noticed Caleb's profile was set to 'away.'

He opened a thread of text messages with Arran, remembering to thank him for his help.

'The mask arrived this morning. It's gorgeous.' Rod smiled to himself, anticipating Caleb's reaction to it.

Arran's message popped up within seconds. 'I'm happy to see you back in the saddle again. Bring your pup to the club sometime.'

'He's a wolf. And he's not mine.' *Not yet.*

'Edinburgh misses you.'

'I miss it too. How's the club?' Rod asked, remembering how welcoming and perfectly organized Arran's BDSM club was. His friend had a dommish way of sticking to rules, yet he instinctively knew when to bend the ones that needed to be bent to make the club a thriving reality. When a biker gang wanted to host a party now and then in exchange for a hefty sponsorship, Arran hadn't been one to refuse.

'Good, but I had a few people leave so I have a major staffing project on my hands.'

Rod remembered Arran's lilting Scottish accent and, even if his texting didn't show it, Rod could hear the words in his friend's voice. 'Who left?'

'Karol, Ivan, and Frannie.'

'Shit.'

'So yeah, I'm without lights, facilities manager, and electrician. You have anyone I could borrow?'

Rod leaned back on his chair, going over a list of people he knew. As if summoned, Silas entered the building. Rod spotted him through the glass of the break room's door, his tall and slim frame turning heads as he passed.

'TTYL, I'll let you know if I find someone.'

'OK. Have fun with your wolf.'

'Oh, I will.'

Rod pocketed his phone and waved to the young man he'd helped several weeks ago. The trick with finding a job for Silas had been that he had the skills and education to work in any IT company he wanted, but he'd come to Rod to look for a lighting tech job during events for a non-profit organization.

"Silas, fancy seeing you here. How's work treating you?" Rod clasped hands with the man and led him to his office.

"Great... until they announced yesterday they're closing." He raked a hand through his angelic blond locks, which promptly bounced back into place.

"Fuck, I'm sorry." Rod slid into his chair and woke the PC by sliding the mouse around. "Sit."

"Thanks." Silas took a seat with the grace of a supermodel. "So I'm back on the job hunt but they gave me great references. Do you know any places that are looking?"

Rod smiled, watching Silas worry his lip. The young man was ridiculously handsome and just the type Arran wouldn't be able to resist. Should he send this lamb to the slaughter? Knowing Silas, said lamb might just waltz into the slaughterhouse and turn it on its head. "Are you willing to relocate?"

"How far?" Silas sat forward, interest piqued.

"Edinburgh. A BDSM club in there to be exact."

Silas pondered the notion for a moment, blowing on the stray curl that fell on his forehead. "Sure."

Rod reached for his phone. "Perfect."

Back at home, Rod took out the sliced beef he'd been stewing in chicken broth for a day and placed it in the oven. He wiped the counter and washed green peppers and jalapeños before he spread them on the cutting board.

The moment Caleb had mentioned yearning for his favorite sandwich, Rod knew he had to attempt to serve his lover a taste from his home country. Two evenings of research and three trips to different stores landed him with a set of ingredients and a recipe he hoped would work for his culinary experiment. He even found pickle relish at Costco, but later read that it was only for hot dogs.

Once the veggies were prepared for frying, Rod opened the ready-bought baguette dough and tossed it in the other oven. Once it was baked, he'd dunk it in the broth the meat was in and put it all together. Then, fingers crossed Caleb would like it.

He poured water into the kettle then hesitated. He and Caleb had discussed many things over the course of the past several weeks, but there were still topics untouched and stones unturned. Fishing out his phone, he texted Caleb.

'Are you a tea or coffee person?' Rod hadn't given Caleb the choice when they'd drank tea in the loft as that was the only thing he kept up there.

His phone pinged.

'Coffee all the way.'

Rod typed the reply with an appalled gasp and a smile that hurt his cheeks. 'I finally found something I don't like about you.'

'It was bound to happen eventually :P BTW I'm on my way.'

'Hurry up.'

Warmth spread in his chest, along with a spike of nerves. This evening had to be perfect. He checked the timer on the oven and leaned against the counter to scroll up to the messages from earlier in the week. He'd found himself rereading parts of their conversation to create a clear picture of what Caleb needed and what he wanted in the bedroom, as those two would not always be the same.

'How are your ribs?' He'd sent this three days after the fight, hoping Caleb would be recovering well.

'Better.'

'Your arse?'

'Not sore anymore.'

'Good.'

Then came the bittersweet text that had paved the way to this evening. 'I can't fight for now. So I'm skipping the Wednesday one.'

'Any big plans instead?'

'I was hoping you'd tell me.'

'Do you like meat sandwiches?' Rod had asked, not knowing what he was getting himself into with the damn Italian Beef.

'I'd marry one if I could.'

'I know a place.'

'I'm in.'

'My house.'

'Food only?'

'And anything else you need.' Rod had waited with bated breath for the reply, and as always, Caleb didn't disappoint.

'Pain. Since I'm skipping the fight.'

'Let's discuss.'

Rod put away his phone, remembering the rest of the conversation in detail; how Caleb wanted to experiment and accept whatever Rod came up with. He'd gone as far as not asking what they would do tonight, wanting to be surprised, putting his trust in Rod.

With a grin on his face, Rod finally opened the white tablecloth Aida had given him as a housewarming gift years ago. After spreading it on the table, he placed two plates, cutlery and a candle that had been a gift as well. Maybe next time, he'd buy wax-play-appropriate candles and make a true feast of Caleb in the middle of the room.

The preparation made him realize how unlived-in his house was and how rarely he invited anyone in anymore. He'd hosted several small kink parties back in the day, but that was before he'd closed his practice and lost the enthusiasm for the lifestyle—and life in general, come to think of it. Now he always opted to meet at a pub, even with Geordie and Patrick, his closest mates.

Declaring the table ready, he went to take a shower.

He chose a simple black button-down and jeans, ignoring the array of casual and formal suits still lingering in his wardrobe. They hung like cruel reminders of his mistakes. He should get rid of them. Today, he wanted to focus on Caleb and their time together, not his own past.

He climbed the stairs to the loft to double-check the space was perfect for Caleb's return and what Rod had planned, making sure no items lying around would spoil the surprise. The blankets lay washed, awaiting Caleb's return since he seemed to have liked them. Rod stopped in front of the cage. Caleb had been asking about it, but Rod wasn't sure he was ready to make good use of it. Rod swallowed as images flooded his mind of Caleb naked in the cage on all fours, his arse plugged, his body relaxed and eager.

He repositioned his thickening cock. *Not yet.*

Just as he was checking the time on his phone, the doorbell rang.

Ten minutes early. *How perfect.* You can't be late if you're early, as his mother used to say.

Every little thing Caleb did screamed that he belonged in Rod's life. Just as Rod's emotional response and his heart demanded that he should push harder, his mind told him it was too fast. Despite the hope brewing in him and overtaking his rational thinking, he was aware that their relationship was still well within the honeymoon phase.

Rod jogged downstairs and waited a moment to catch his breath before he swung the door open.

"Wow, you look fancy." Caleb eyed Rod not-so-subtly from head to toe.

The appreciation in his gaze sent warm tingles through Rod's chest.

Caleb stood in an unzipped purple hoodie and a black t-shirt with David Bowie's face on it.

"And you look good enough to eat." Rod waggled his eyebrows at Caleb's amused smile. Maybe soon.

With a kiss to Rod's cheek, Caleb sauntered the house. "I brought this." He handed over a bottle of wine. "I wasn't sure if you drank the red stuff, so I got these too." He lifted a six-pack of Belgian beers.

Yup, he was too perfect.

"I use wine for cooking, but I prefer beer to drink. Thanks." Rod leaned in for a quick peck on the lips.

"For cooking? Like, you're so bad at it, you have to drink while you do it?" Caleb smirked, toeing off his shoes to leave them in the corridor.

"I drink some and pour the rest into the food. But I'll let you judge my culinary skills today so you can tell me."

Caleb stopped in the middle of the dining room, his eyes on the table. "Who else is coming?"

"Only you."

"You did all this for me?" He waved at the set table and candles, his expression full of confusion, mouth slightly parted, brows furrowed.

"Of course." Rod stepped behind him, wrapped his arms around Caleb's middle and kissed his cheek. "Now, sit. I'll bring the food."

"Let me—" Caleb cleared his throat. "Let me help you at least."

"No, it will spoil the surprise."

"Oh, I love surprises." Caleb turned in Rod's arms and squeezed him tight. Rod sighed, inhaling the scent of Caleb's hair, the tension of the day draining from his body at the simple contact. "I have a few of my own." Caleb broke away, a grin on his face.

"Really?" Rod kissed Caleb again. He had to.

"I want to taste your food first." Caleb pulled out the chair and sat, elbows on the table, chin on hands, looking at Rod.

God, he was so beautiful, so ruggedly handsome with those tattoos and slight smirk. It was almost painful to look at him.

"Yes, right. Be right back." Rod nodded and swiveled on his heel.

In the kitchen, he glanced at the timer and turned it off. Two minutes remained until the beef would be done, so it was time to take it out. He left the glass roasting dish on the stove and took out the baguette. He fried up the chopped veggies until they were crispy, sliced the baguette in half and cut the halves open, before stuffing the two sandwiches with the ingredients.

On two plates, they looked similar enough to the pictures he'd seen, but he wasn't sure if he'd gotten the taste right.

Rod released a long breath and squared his shoulders. He hoped Caleb would like these. He waltzed into the dining room to find Caleb in the same position, looking at him with a glint in his eyes.

"Ta-dah," Rod said, placing a plate in front of Caleb and the other for himself.

"No way!" Caleb shot to his feet. "Did you make Italian Beef for me?"

"I tried."

"Oh, for fuck's sake, Rod, you can't do that." Caleb hugged him, squeezing hard, burying his face in Rod's neck.

"Why?"

"Or I'll catch feelings," Caleb murmured.

Oh, shit. Rod's eyes blew wide as realization hit him.

It was too late for him already.

With his arms tightly around Caleb, he wished they could stay like that forever. But what if he hoped for too much, pushed too hard, then Caleb went back to the US? His heart told him the risk of it being broken was worth pursuing Caleb with everything he had in his arsenal.

He'd have to tread carefully and not spook Caleb away before he asked him to move in, or even more... he'd had his fair share of relationships, casual or otherwise; he'd met people in and out of the kink community and all around the world. By now, he knew if he connected with someone on a visceral level. He had to take this seriously. This connection with Caleb was so much stronger than any he'd ever had before.

Slow down, slow the fuck down.

Rod slid his hands to Caleb's buttocks, squeezed them, then smacked one.

"Let's eat before it gets cold. And you can tell me what a horrible job I did making these."

"I'm sure they're fine." Caleb pulled away, avoiding Rod's gaze as he sat down to ogle his sandwich. His eyes were red-rimmed, the sight squeezing Rod's heart.

"I made duck yesterday that I can heat up, or I can order pizza in case these are—"

"Ohmygod, so good!" Caleb moaned, around a mouthful of sandwich.

"Really?"

"Oh, yeah." Caleb nodded, taking another bite. "But now I wanna try the duck too. You never told me you were such a wizard in the kitchen."

Rod chuckled. "I'm not that good, but thanks. I taught myself at uni. And my flatmate didn't like certain textures, so that gave me a nice challenge to figure out substitutes. Now I like it, it lets me relax." He bit into his own sandwich and it wasn't half bad after all.

"Can I stop by when you're relaxing like this?" Caleb took a gulp from the glass of water Rod had poured in advance.

"Sure. Or just move in and never leave." *Oops, that slipped out.* Rod paused mid-chew and saw that Caleb did the same. They looked at each other and Rod wasn't sure if it was panic or hope in Caleb's eyes.

He wanted to backtrack, but fuck that, Caleb might as well know that Rod was already balls-deep in this new relationship of theirs.

Caleb looked away first and they finished eating in silence, while Rod's deepest wishes were boiling inside him, forcing him to address them.

"Can I be honest with you?"

"Of course. I bared my soul to you and we discussed more kink stuff than I even knew existed." Caleb smirked, wiping his face with a napkin, but his eyes were watching Rod with intensity.

"I don't want to push you towards a commitment you may not be ready for, just because I am," Rod said, hoping Caleb could read the sincerity of his statement. "But when you enter my house, I want you to be mine. My *wolf*. Would you give me that?"

"I'm—" Caleb swallowed, then licked his lips. "I think I'm yours outside of it too. I mean, I want to be."

Rod's heart leapt, but something wasn't clear. "Are you?" He stood up and stopped in front of Caleb's chair, lifting his chin with his fingertips till their eyes met. "The way you just reacted to my mention of moving in says otherwise."

"That's different. I thought about us a lot over the past week and I'm ready to be in a relationship, or a kinky arrangement, whatever this is to you. But I can't move in."

"That's fair. And it's both, if you let it. You can be my boyfriend and my submissive." Rod cupped Caleb's clean-shaven cheek, caressing it with his thumb.

"I like that. I like being yours." Caleb leaned into the touch.

"You're blushing."

"This is new to me. Feeling like this." Caleb touched his chest. "It seems intense."

"It is to me, too. Now, let's be clear. I won't let you hurt something that's mine. And you have been doing that."

"The fights?" Caleb croaked.

"Yeah. Those fucking fights." The outrage steaming in Rod made its way to his voice.

"I need them."

"You skipped one today and we already agreed that I can give you pain." Rod kneeled on the rug, both of his hands on Caleb's cheeks.

"I need the money." Caleb turned his gaze away.

"Are you in debt?"

"No."

"You don't buy designer clothes... It's not drugs, is it?" As much as it pained Rod, he had to know.

"Fuck, no." Caleb took Rod's hands off his face, heaping them on his lap.

How the fuck did this conversation turn sideways so fast?

"Are you going to make me keep guessing? I can give you money."

"I don't need your charity," Caleb spat through his teeth.

"I can lend you the money then."

"No."

"Let me help you."

"You already are."

"Sorry, you don't have to tell me. I don't have any right to your secrets. I'm just worried, OK?" It hurt to say it, but it was the truth.

"Fuck you, Rod. You make me—" Caleb pushed Rod's hands away, only to grip them and squeeze, his lips forming a straight line. He wasn't angry, he looked... resigned.

Something was wrong, but not between them. "You can tell me anything, remember?"

Caleb ground his teeth then sighed. "It's my mom, OK?"

"I thought you didn't keep in contact with her."

"I don't." He closed his eyes briefly, before meeting Rod's gaze again. "I just pay for her rehab. I'm sending the money directly to the facility so I know the fee is covered. But that shit isn't cheap, man. She doesn't have health insurance, so all the meds have to be paid for, too."

Fuck. That explained a lot. Rod opened his mouth to insist on helping with that, but Caleb continued talking.

"But soon, I hope—Wait. It's as good a moment as any." Caleb stood up and retrieved his backpack that lay on the floor by the door. "I have news I wanted to tell you in person." He pulled two envelopes from the front pocket of the backpack, but tossed one back. "Read this." He handed it over and his mood lightened, a hint of a smile forming on his lips.

Rod scanned the letter quickly. "You got British citizenship?"

"Yeah." Caleb nodded.

"That means you're definitely not leaving, right?" Hope and excitement flooded Rod's veins in one second flat.

"I hope not. If I find a job and all," Caleb said, scratching his nape.

"Fantastic!" Rod lifted Caleb off the floor in a bear hug. "Fuck, yeah!" He kissed the side of Caleb's neck, his eyes prickling from the relief. *He won't leave.*

"I'm glad I waited to tell you in person," Caleb chuckled. His cheeks were pink when Rod finally put him down.

"So you won't need to fight anymore."

"Once I find a job, no." Caleb grinned.

"Oh, thank fuck!" The sheer relief was so great, tension left Rod's shoulders and he felt the air clear between them. "Could you give us two weeks of no fighting to find work you'd like? As a gift to me, your boyfriend?"

"I already have a few places lined up, actually. So yes. Definitely."

"Promise?" Rod slid a hand around Caleb's waist.

"I promise."

"Keep it, or I'll have to punish you," Rod rumbled, his hands squeezing Caleb's ass.

Caleb visibly shivered, his lips parting on a tiny gasp. "Is it weird that I love the sound of that?"

"No, it isn't."

"You making me accountable for my mistakes."

"And celebrating all your successes, too."

Caleb wiggled out of Rod's grasp to fetch the other envelope from his backpack and handed it to Rod. "This one's for you."

Rod grinned as he read the test results in front of his eyes, his mind filling with possibilities. "Bloody fantastic."

"I went to a private clinic and they were really quick—"

Rod didn't let Caleb finish, cupping his face to kiss him. Now they could fuck without protection, which opened new doors for playing.

"Right," Rod broke away, panting "I'm ready for dessert."

"What's for—"

Rod squeezed Caleb's asscheeks, watching his eyes go wide.

"Oh." Caleb's smile turned mischievous. "Good thing I'm prepared."

"You cheeky bastard." Rod chuckled, unbuttoning Caleb's jeans to find black boxer briefs. "I like your other knickers better."

"Well, someone ripped them so—"

Rod shushed Caleb with a finger on his lips. "Hold that thought." He went to his bedroom and retrieved the box that had arrived several days before, then returned to Caleb. "I ordered these last week but I was waiting for a good moment." He handed Caleb the black box. "But since we're officially a couple, I feel entitled to give you gifts."

"You don't—"

"Just open it."

Caleb placed the box on the table, removed the lid and shuffled the tissue paper aside.

"You got me jockstraps?" He laughed and lifted the three pairs in different colors: red, purple, and classic white.

"I felt bad for destroying yours and you looked so hot in it..."

"I love them. You didn't have to get them for me, but I'll wear them on every date with you." Caleb kissed Rod briefly, then shifted his gaze back to the underwear, turning it around and around.

Rod had been hesitant to buy anything for Caleb, given his aversion to being helped financially, but he was happy to see Caleb had accepted the gift. *Good.* More were to come.

"Which is your favorite?" Caleb asked.

"The purple."

With swift movements, Caleb stepped out of his boxer briefs and pulled on the new garment, adjusting the straps under his cheeks and at the small of his back.

"Decorating my dessert, I see," Rod rumbled, stepping back to take in the view.

"Just when I doubted you could want my body this much, I see it in your eyes, Rod. It's insane and I fucking love it."

"Don't ever doubt my need to have you. All of you. Now, off with that t-shirt."

Caleb shed the rest of his clothing, revealing his toned muscles and array of tattoos. Rod wanted to ask if they held meaning, but not right now.

"Turn around and hold onto the table. I've been dreaming of eating your ass," Rod growled, licking his lips.

"Here?" Caleb asked, and Rod nodded.

With an evil grin, Caleb took off in the direction of the bedroom. Adrenaline spiked in Rod and he dashed after him. Caleb managed to take only a few steps before Rod tackled him, making him squeak in surprise. They landed in a heap of limbs, but Rod twisted his body to cushion the fall for Caleb, before pinning him to the ground. "Is that how you want to play?" Rod nipped his earlobe.

"Yes," Caleb grunted, pushing his ass up to Rod's erection. "You don't have to be a proper Englishman with me."

"You just snatched my dessert from me. I gave up being proper the moment you darted off." Rod parted Caleb's legs with his knees. "Confirm your safeword."

"Red."

"What's your color now?"

"Green."

With an animalistic sound, Rod moved down his lover's body. It took every ounce of composure he had left not to ravish him, but to savor that first time. Gripping Caleb's asscheeks, he bit one of them hard enough to leave a mark. Caleb yelped, then moaned when Rod kissed the spot, then the small of his back, before spreading his cheeks.

Caleb had already welcomed Rod's cock and fingers in his needy hole, but this time, Rod could see the pucker contract as he blew on it before he licked over it. Rod's moan was muffled as he buried his face in between the pert cheeks. He flicked his tongue over the pucker, then licked in a languid motion.

The desperate noises coming from Caleb fueled Rod's movements.

Caleb thrust his hips up to meet him but Rod held him down. Then Caleb rutted against the rug. Good thing he was wearing the jockstrap, or he'd get carpet burns before Rod even got to play with his cock tonight.

Chapter Ten

Caleb

Caleb mewled into the soft rug, his eyes rolling back as Rod feasted on his ass. He grappled for purchase, hands flailing as Rod held him down, his tongue swirling, licking, sliding in just an inch, only to leave him breathless.

Pleasure singed Caleb's brain at the sheer enthusiasm Rod showed, bringing him close to coming as his cock tried to burst out of the new jockstrap. He'd have carpet burns on his thighs and face, and he would look in the mirror for days and remember this moment.

Rod lifted Caleb's hips up, never stopping his onslaught. Caleb whimpered in protest at the loss of friction to his cock, so he reached under himself, but Rod smacked his hand away.

"No touching and no coming without permission," Rod said, slapping Caleb's ass to drive the point across.

"That's torture."

"And you'll love it, trust me."

"Fuck you for making me believe that."

Rod chuckled darkly. "Now, off to the loft with you and this gorgeous arse."

Caleb looked over his shoulder to see Rod's beard was wet with saliva. With a wicked grin on his face, Rod growled just one word: "*Run.*"

Caleb darted off. A giggle bubbled out of him as he ran, taking the stairs two at a time. Rod was after him, his chuckle and heavy footsteps making Caleb's heart pound faster.

The moment Caleb stepped on the panels of the attic, Rod caught him by the waist. Still laughing, Rod turned him around and kissed the remaining breath out of him.

"God, you're irresistible," Rod murmured. "I want to make you scream tonight. Maybe even cry."

Caleb released a strangled sound as he ground his groin against Rod's jeans. "Please."

"Get on the bench, arse up. I'll be right back."

With one last peck on Caleb's lips, as if he couldn't bear to be parted from him, Rod turned on his heel and thundered down the stairs.

Caleb eyed the padded bench, then the sink inside the huge shower enclosure. He rummaged in the drawer he'd seen Rod take ointment out of before and found what he was looking for. *Even better than mints.* A drop of toothpaste on his finger helped him brush his teeth, wishing he could get his toothbrush from his backpack downstairs. *No time.* He took a leak just in case, cause knowing Rod's sadistic tendencies, he might play with his need to pee. After boning up online about all things kink, Caleb was a lot more aware of what might be lurking in Rod's wicked brain. At this point, there was little he'd read about that he wouldn't try at least once to see if it would flip his switch.

Rod's footsteps sounded at the bottom of the stairs and Caleb darted off towards the bench, planting his chest on it, sliding his feet into the stirrups on the sides, his face in the padded hole like in a massage parlor. Grinning with giddiness, the vulnerability of his position struck him and he clenched involuntarily.

"I see your back has healed nicely. How are your ribs?

"Better, but sore," Caleb answered, knowing this was not the time and place to hide any injuries—Rod had made that abundantly clear during their lengthy chats. "I'm itching for a fight."

"You want to hurt." It wasn't a question.

Caleb felt Rod's fingertips dancing up his calf, thigh and along his flank as he rounded the bench, his black leather boots entering Caleb's field of vision. "Yes. I need to release all that." He made fists and growled, remaining in place.

"Your anger? Energy?" Rod asked. His touch between Caleb's tense shoulder blades, over his howling wolf tattoo, made him shiver.

"Everything is intense. Good and bad."

"What's your safeword?" Rod asked, letting Caleb know that the fun was about to start.

"Red," Caleb said as heat pooled in his abdomen from anticipation.

"I wanted to flog your back and arse today, but I don't want you to lie on your front too long," Rod said, making Caleb grind his dick into the bench at the thought of all that sweet pain. "Maybe if you're still able to stand by the end of the evening I'll strap you to the St Andrew's cross."

"Yes, please," Caleb groaned.

Rod gripped the short hair on Caleb's nape and forced his head up. Caleb hissed and his cock stirred immediately at the sliver of pain.

"Sit up."

Caleb did as he was told, wiggling around, his mouth going slack when he saw Rod. "Whoa, you look...*fuck*, Rod..." Caleb choked out, as he took in Rod's attire.

He wore leather chaps with his ass and groin completely exposed, and a leather harness criss crossed over his chest, accentuating how big his pecs were. Caleb's mouth watered at the sight of Rod's pert nipples.

Rod glided his hand over the harness, stepping between Caleb's parted legs. "Yours would have loops so I could attach rope or a leash to it."

Caleb nodded absent-mindedly, running his hand up Rod's belly to flick his nipple.

Rod sucked in a breath and stepped closer, putting his chest inches from Caleb's face. "Suck."

Fuck, yeah. Caleb wasted no time latching onto Rod's bud, licking it, sucking, running his tongue over it. A low rumble in Rod's chest spurred him on, but a sudden sharp tug on his hair pulled him away. He hissed at the pain and was about to protest when Rod gifted him with the other nipple to give attention to. He moaned, his hands on Rod's ass, squeezing it as he sucked on the peaked bud. Rod's erection twitched against Caleb's abdomen, and he drank in his lover's response, hungrily lapping at the hard nipple.

"Enough, or I'll have to fuck you right now."

"What's wrong with that?" Caleb asked, licking his lips.

"I have other plans." Rod stepped back, his face flushed, his nipples red. "When we discussed limits, you said you're fine with restraints. Are you good with exploring that today?"

Helpless and at Rod's mercy? Sign me up!

"Yes," was all he managed to whisper.

Rod lifted a brow.

"Yes, Roderick."

"How about being stuffed? You've read about the options, right?" It was clear that Rod was making sure Caleb was on board, without ruining the surprise.

"Fuck! Yes, please." Caleb squirmed, his cock thickening even more.

An evil grin spread across Rod's face. "Perfect."

Only now did Caleb notice there were two black boxes sitting pretty on the couch. Rod picked up the smaller one.

"Your first gift."

"You already got me the jockstraps."

Rod pursed his lips, smirking, and Caleb knew he was coming up with some bullshit. "Those were for me to see you in and rip off you, so they don't count as a gift."

"That's such a lame excuse, but I'll let it slide cause you look cute trying to bullshit a bullshitter." Caleb's grin matched Rod's.

"Now open."

The inside of the black box had the same color tissue paper filling it, and he reached underneath, feeling around for the surprise. "Are these fighting gloves?" Caleb frowned, pulling out a pair.

"No, they're mitts, but they're also shaped like wolf paws. See?" Rod turned them around in Caleb's hands. "I could argue that they're for me too, since they'll prevent you from trying to touch yourself when I don't want you to."

"That's so evil!" Caleb gasped, but his throat tightened at the thoughtful gift.

"I know."

"They're beautiful." Caleb stroked the black leather with white stitching. "I can't accept them."

"Then don't. They're mine and I'll let you use them when you're here. Better?"

A master of loopholes, huh? "Yeah, OK." Caleb rolled his eyes, knowing he wouldn't win that one. He would be the best sub today for Rod, though, and earn his generosity tenfold. The funny thing was that he was sure he could do that just by being himself. What a crazy concept.

Rod took Caleb's hand and kissed the back of it like some fucking gentleman. Caleb didn't know how to react, so he remained seated and let Rod pull one of the mitts on. It fit snugly and it was generously padded on the inside, but Caleb's hand was at a slightly different angle than in a boxing glove. Then it hit him that he could easily crawl with them on. Maybe that was the plan? Heat shot to his cheeks.

"I don't know what these make you think of, but I like where your mind is going," Rod smirked, adjusting the other mitt.

Busted.

"I want to try new things with you and I trust you'll push my limits," Caleb said. "I wanna experience everything we've ever talked about."

"Perfect." Rod kissed him briefly, but pulled away only to return and deepen the kiss. *Fuck, I just can't help myself.* With a low growl, he finally let go. "Lay back."

Rod helped Caleb scoot to the edge of the bench, then pulled up steel stirrups to place Caleb's calves on, his knees bent. He lay there like he was waiting for an exam in a doctor's office, legs up and apart, ass exposed. With padded leather handcuffs, Rod secured Caleb's wrists to the steel hoops at the sides. He attached cuffs to Caleb's thighs and connected them with a spreader bar from an array of them hanging nearby.

"Try to escape," Rod said, stepping back, his eyes intense and focused.

Caleb struggled, testing the bonds.

Rod watched, then retrieved a folded rope from a drawer and wrapped it around Caleb's chest, securing him to the bench. "That's better."

Caleb wiggled again, but this time he could barely move an inch. His breathing quickened as irrational panic flooded him, immediately followed by a fresh wave of arousal.

"I have beads with your name on them. If you take them well, there's a reward waiting for you." Rod traced a finger along Caleb's inner thigh to the cuff, along the spreader bar and down the other thigh. "Are you ready?"

"Yes," Caleb panted, trying to scoot closer to the edge, to no avail. He stopped when his eyes landed on what Rod was holding.

His lover dangled a string of silicone beads the length of his forearm. The first bead was no bigger than a thumb, but they got bigger and bigger, reaching a circumference Caleb was sure wouldn't fit through his ring of muscle. He clenched at the thought as liquid arousal pooled in his abdomen. Rod placed the beads on Caleb, with the small one at his sternum and the looped end at his groin, presenting how long it was.

Caleb looked down his body and wiggled around, but he was so well-secured he couldn't even make the beads move. In the meantime, Rod reached into one of the drawers to the side.

"Be vocal, moan or talk to me, I want to know how it feels, to learn your body." With the last word, Rod slid a finger or two into Caleb. He must have lubed them already, as they glided in with ease at the start and a burn at the end.

Caleb gasped and closed his eyes, adjusting to the slight pain.

"How's that?" Rod asked, eyes on Caleb's face, his cock standing up, crooking slightly to the left. *Mouthwatering.*

Caleb loved seeing how much he affected Rod. "So good," he groaned.

"Would you rather I go slow or fast?"

"Whatever you want."

"The perfect answer."

Rod moved his fingers around, brushing against Caleb's prostate, but retreated immediately.

"You're a fucking tease... Roderick."

"We're just getting started," Rod chuckled. "My Wolf." Rod hooked a finger in the loop of the bead chain and dragged it along Caleb's body until it hung in the air; enticing and teasing. With the other hand, he applied lube to the three smallest bulbs.

The first one popped in with ease and Rod's gaze met Caleb's as he slid in the next one. Caleb moaned, seeing the look of unadulterated lust on Rod's face as he squirted more lubricant before inserting one more bulb.

"How do you feel?" he asked, his baritone sounding even lower than usual.

"Full..." Caleb licked his lips, knowing that the toy was further in than anything he'd ever inserted before. "Uh, green. I want more."

Rod nodded, then pulled on the string, popping two beads out, making Caleb moan a near-shout.

With more lube, he slid them back in with the addition of new ones—Caleb could tell by the stretch.

"Ah! Fuck!" Caleb groaned, straining against the bonds, but they kept him firmly in place.

"You can take it," Rod encouraged, pressing on Caleb's outer ring of muscle with the next bead.

In two steps, Rod was at Caleb's side, adding pressure on his pucker, his other hand caressing Caleb's cheek. "Come on."

"Nnngh! I can't."

"You're not as stretched as you claim. What's your color?" Rod asked.

Caleb paused, his head so far away he had to take stock of his body and mind.

"Tell me the truth, not what I want to hear."

There was one thing Caleb knew for sure. That he wanted more. "Green."

The moment the words left his lips, he felt Rod's lips on his and he latched onto the kiss like a lifeline. He closed his eyes as his tongue met Rod's in a needy swirl, his ass full, his body on fire, ready to come.

A tiny whimper escaped him when Rod broke away, his breathing ragged just like Caleb's.

"How about your depth?" Rod asked, his lips still hovering close. "We could check with a long tail. Or would a ribbed tentacle be better?"

"Either," Caleb groaned as he felt Rod pull on the beads, popping one out, before he pushed it back in. "Either would be good."

Caleb's erection strained in the jockstrap pouch, wetting it with precome. Rod positioned himself back between Caleb's legs and moved the fabric to the side to pull out his cock.

"Let's try again," he said, before he took Caleb's dick halfway into his mouth while pushing the big bead against Caleb's hole. He sucked on the tip, then swallowed more of the length.

Caleb wanted to close his eyes and drift away in pleasure, but instead kept them open to see his dick disappearing into Rod's mouth. He cried out Rod's name and strained, wiggling his legs only slightly, the spreader bar and stirrups holding him in place. Then he felt an impossible stretch in his ass and relief as the big bead went in and his hole closed around the string.

Rod released Caleb's dick with a wet slurp and it bounced, pointing up. Caleb's body relaxed as he focused on his lover.

"That's a good Wolf." Rod took a step back, his eyes on Caleb's hole, then took in the entirety of his bound body. "The most beautiful sight." He patted Caleb's ass cheek with a lubed hand, the sticky, wet sound amping up the sensation. "You have no idea what you do to me."

Rod's dick, standing proud, its glans glistening with precome, enticed Caleb. He licked his lips. "If I'm your Wolf, would that make you my Owner?"

"When we're here, in this room, I'd love that. Conditions remain the same. No hurting or insulting what's mine."

"Yes, I know. I agree to that. But when we do this..." he arched off the bench as much as he could, which was no more than an inch, "I want you to own me completely."

"Mmmm." Rod closed his eyes and inhaled, opening them on an exhale. "We'll talk when you're not drunk on endorphins."

"Fine. Now can I suck your dick? Please, Roderick," he whispered.

Rod's cock was so hard that his foreskin covered only the base of his crown, showing the wet tip.

Rod stepped closer, giving his cock a pump before he positioned it at Caleb's parted lips. With the other hand, he pinched Caleb's nipple hard enough for him to yelp and shoved his dick into his open mouth.

He sucked on the crown, swirling his tongue under it, feeling the foreskin. Fuck, how he loved it.

Rod took a fistful of Caleb's hair and rocked his pelvis, sliding in and out.

Oh yeah, fuck my mouth.

Caleb strained against his bonds, not to escape but to reach for more of his lover, his dick, his everything.

All too soon, Rod pulled out and Caleb whimpered for more.

"Enough." Rod wiped Caleb's mouth with his hand, then patted his cheek. "You suck my cock too well and I want to come inside you tonight."

"Now?" Caleb moved his pelvis as much as his restraints allowed.

"Yes, my cock-hungry Wolf," Rod growled. "I need to come so I can focus better on what I planned next." He dipped his finger into the pre-come that pooled on Caleb's abdomen and brought it to his lips.

Caleb moaned at the sight, and so did Rod, closing his mouth around his digit. Then he hooked it in the ring at the end of the bead string and pulled lightly.

A loud groan tore past Caleb's lips at the pressure on his anus from the inside.

"You're not allowed to come," Rod said before he slapped Caleb's cock, then took it in his mouth, pulling harder on the string.

Caleb groaned, wailed, and cursed as Rod sucked, popping the beads out, one after the other.

"I can't. I'm gonna blow! Ah!"

"Don't."

Every sensation stopped. Caleb's dick wasn't enveloped in warmth, his ass didn't feel the pull.

Silence filled the room as Caleb held his breath.

Rod squeezed the tip of Caleb's shaft, right under the crown. "Breathe."

Caleb took in air through his nose and exhaled through his mouth.

Their gazes locked when Rod pulled out the remaining beads with squeaky plop after plop.

Thanks to Caleb's knees being bent further than his hips and the spreader bar between his thighs, Rod could easily position himself at his ass. Caleb clenched at the emptiness, but Rod didn't make him suffer long, filling him with his dick. One swift glide to the hilt.

Neither of them moved, breathing deep, faces flushed.

Then Rod pulled out all the way and slammed back in, both of them crying out when their bodies slapped together over and over. Rod's grip on Caleb's hips was bruising, another powerful sensation that drove Caleb crazy, until Rod slowed down his thrusts and slathered a finger in Caleb's precome gathered on his abs.

The smirk on Rod's lips made Caleb think he'd lick it, but instead, he positioned it next to his cock, at Caleb's pucker.

Oh, fuck. Caleb nodded his approval and cried out as the finger fit past his outer ring of muscle, making his eyes prickle as his hole stretched to accommodate everything Rod gave him.

"What's your color?" Rod growled, his jaw tense as if he was as close to coming as Caleb.

A lone tear escaped Caleb's eye as he gasped out: "Green."

Only when Rod slid the finger deeper did Caleb realize that until now, it had been only the tip inside him. With slow dance-like movements of his hips, Rod glided in Caleb, making them both moan.

"No coming," Rod gritted out before he took his digit out, squeezed Caleb's cock and fucked him like he wanted to split him in half.

Not caring what sounds he made, Caleb released everything in him in sobbing screams, watching as Rod threw his head back and shot load after load into his body.

Chapter Eleven

Caleb

Deep inside, Caleb knew that Rod would make holding off his orgasm worth it. But tied up, with legs in the air, and Rod's come filling him, he was ready to blow now.

"That's my good Wolf," Rod cooed, pulling his dick out on a soft moan. His gaze dropped down and he touched Caleb's abused hole, pushing back the come that leaked out. He rummaged in a drawer and pulled out a bright-green silicone plug, then slid it into Caleb with ease.

Still strung for release, Caleb watched Rod lower the steel stirrups that held his legs in the air, leaving the spreader bar in place.

"Does anything hurt?" Rod asked, poking Caleb's thighs, inspecting his wrists.

"Only my blue balls," Caleb quipped.

Rod winked in reply. "Good."

Next, he brought a bottle of water and a tiny remote. After pressing a button, the bench whirred and lifted Caleb to a sitting position.

"You kept licking your lips and making the most beautiful sounds," Rod said, uncapping the bottle. "You must be parched."

"Yeah," Caleb croaked, only now realizing it was true. He took several sips from the bottle Rod placed at his lips. It was heavenly.

"It's time for your reward. You earned it." Rod downed half of the water remaining and reached for the second box on the couch. "I'll open it for you." He grinned, nodding at Caleb's bound hands hidden in the paw-mitts.

Caleb took a breath to mouth off, or maybe protest at another gift, but instead he scolded himself. He knew Rod was doing it from the kindness of his heart and the honesty of his kinky side, not to make him feel dependent or grateful or some shit.

Seeing the hesitant look in Rod's eyes, he wondered what could be in the box to make the man so unsure. *A tentacle dildo? Maybe a cock cage?*

Clearly as impatient as Caleb, Rod pulled out the gift.

"Oh... holy shit," Caleb breathed. "It's gorgeous."

He took in the leather mask in the shape of a wolf's head, complete with ears and a long muzzle. Thick thread connected various-sized pieces of intricately carved leather to create the masterpiece.

"So you like it?" Rod asked. "You said you're not opposed to masks and you seemed so intrigued the first time you saw my collection I thought I'd order one made for you."

"It's custom-made?" A lump formed in Caleb's throat.

"Of course. I told Arran that this one's special and—" Rod paused, leaning over to kiss Caleb's trembling lips.

Not wanting to ruin the moment with tears, Caleb held them back and hoped he could convey his gratitude in the quick kiss.

"Can I wear it now?" The thought of his face being hidden, free to cry and grimace, fascinated him.

With a nod, Rod pulled the mask over Caleb's head, securing it with a strap at the back. The scent of leather filled his nose and the snug fit brought a sense of comfort, rather than the entrapment that he'd expected. Either would be good anyway. The holes in front let Caleb see quite well, despite the limited range.

I'm strapped to the bench with legs spread, ass plugged, and face covered.

A fresh wave of arousal flooded him, and he let his head fall back, his dick pulsing. "I have no idea how you just know what I'd like before I do," Caleb said, his voice sounding muffled inside the mask. "Thank you."

"My pleasure," Rod said, his hands on Caleb's shoulders, his eyes meeting Caleb's through the holes in the leather. "Now tell me, how does your arse feel?"

"Used and raw." Caleb moved his hips to feel the plug secured inside. "I love it. But I still need to come."

"Mmhmm." Rod flicked Caleb's dick, which had softened slightly during their break. "You like your arse filled, we established that. How about your cock?" Rod's eyes glinted as he searched Caleb's face.

Caleb's mind ran over the possibilities they'd discussed before and his eyes blew wide when the answer hit him. "Oh. I want to find out."

"Are you ready to try sounding?" Rod asked, hooking thumbs into his chest harness playfully.

"That's being stabbed in the dick," Caleb said, making sure, his hole clamping around the plug at the thought.

"In so many words, yeah."

"It looks like it hurts, even in porn."

Rod's lips lifted into a wicked smirk. "It does hurt. But it can also hurt so good." His spent dick twitched once. Hanging limp with remnants of lube and come, it still looked impressive.

Interest spiked in Caleb. "Have you done it to someone before?"

"Yes. And to myself. Now I'd love to show you how it feels."

"Please," Caleb breathed, the image of Rod driving a piece of steel into his own cock filling his brain, igniting a fresh fire in his groin.

This time it was more difficult to see exactly what Rod was doing but he could tell that his lover washed his hands and was rummaging around.

With a rattle of wheels, Rod brought a rolling tray and a chair he sat on, then opened a slim drawer in the dresser and took out various sizes of long implements.

"These are surgical steel sounds," Rod said and continued explaining the difference between them and the silicone ones he'd boiled in advance, stressing the importance of sanitation.

"You planned this?" Caleb asked.

"I like being prepared."

"What if I said no?"

"Then we wouldn't be doing it."

"It's so easy with you."

"Communication makes it simple and you've been telling me for weeks how you'd like to try everything at least once." Rod kissed Caleb's knee. "I can't wait to cater to your enthusiasm. It's infectious."

Rod smiled and popped two blue gloves from a box on the rolling tray. He snapped on one, then the other and Caleb could feel his cock hardening at the very sight. The anticipation was killing him, but even worse was the unknown before him.

"Do you have any allergies? Do you get a rash from any products? Have you had a urinary tract infection lately?" Rod asked.

Caleb considered Rod's rapid-fire barrage of questions and responded with a single resounding: "No. I feel like I'm at a doctor's office." He squirmed in his seat. "It's kinda hot."

"Good. Before we start, you should know that sounding will make you sensitive and it will burn when you pee, maybe even for a few days."

"I'm fine with that." *I want to hurt for you for days.*

"Since it's your first time, it's safer not to start with a thin sound, so I'll use this one." Rod pointed to a medium girth wand. It had a ring on top and ribs along the entirety of it.

Caleb sensed a theme of the evening.

"The hollow one is good for coming through or peeing, but it's wider, so we can use it after a few sessions, if you like this one," Rod said, excitement clear in his tone. "There are so many options."

Caleb listened to Rod talk about a Prince Albert sound that would attach to a piercing, and something about Hegar dilators. In the meantime, he was cleaning the sound with tiny wipes before he wiped the crown of Caleb's dick, too.

"Urethral fucking can be good, my Wolf, but it's an acquired taste. It will hurt from the stretch, but if any of it is sharp, let me know immediately."

"OK, I will," Caleb promised, his heart pounding from the anticipation. "I will, *Owner*."

The smile the honorific brought to Rod's face put a grin on Caleb's.

"Take deep breaths and don't wiggle." Rod paused, looking at Caleb, his eyes filled with fire, his face focused. Then he stood up and rested his forehead against Caleb's leather-clad brow. "You're bloody gorgeous, bound and waiting for your pain."

Caleb bit his cheek, trying not to play the compliment down. "Thank you," he said instead. "Owner."

"You're not too hard, that's good." Rod patted Caleb's semi-deflated erection as he sat back down. "Scared?"

"Fuck you," Caleb laughed. "Maybe a little."

A squelching sound made Caleb turn to the rolling tray where Rod squirted different lube than he'd used before into a small glass plate, then grabbed a weird-ass looking syringe with three holes for fingers and sucked up the lube with it.

"This will help lubricate your urethra," Rod said in a low voice, emanating both arousal and focus.

Fuck, he's so hot like this.

He applied a dollop of the lube on the slit of Caleb's crown, then inserted the softer cone tip of the syringe in.

Caleb tensed at the unfamiliar pressure as Rod slowly injected the lube, holding his wobbly dick in the other hand. Then he remembered that Rod told him to breathe. So he did.

"You OK?" Rod asked, and Caleb nodded. "Are you ready? I need to hear your voice since I can't see your face."

"Yes," Caleb said breathlessly. "More than ready."

Rod positioned the round tip of the steel sound at Caleb's slit and glided it in.

"Oh, fuck!" Caleb yelped, struggling to keep his hips still.

"Talk to me."

"Ah!" Caleb winced, then followed it with a few deep pants. "It feels weird. I kinda wanna back away, but... also maybe not?"

"That's a natural reaction. It's an invasion, one your body is not familiar with... yet."

"OK, yeah, bring it on," Caleb squeaked.

Rod did just that, sliding the steel wand in another half an inch. Caleb's cock grew harder, then the pain kicked in and it softened again.

Rod swirled the sound just inside, the round tip rubbing against Caleb's urethral wall.

"Fuck, that hurts! So good though. Fuck fuck *fuck*." Caleb moaned, breathing fast, his face hot inside the mask as he stared at the ribbed balls of the sound disappearing into his dick. "Ah, the stretch! I don't know if I want to pee or come, but I definitely don't want you to stop."

Rod chuckled. "You're doing great. So hot. Fuck, Caleb, I'm getting hard again."

Caleb's abs contracted and he watched Rod's focused expression. Rod had one big gentle paw around Caleb's cock, while the other held the sound steady.

The maelstrom of pain coursing through Caleb's groin was wildly at odds with Rod's show of care and concern. It was fucking with Caleb's head, but somehow it was exactly what he needed—a kind of balance that he'd been searching for.

Still fondling Caleb's dick, Rod reached for something with the other hand. A click of a button later, Caleb released a squeak as the plug in his ass started to vibrate. It was delicate, but enough to stimulate his sweet spot.

"Holy shit," Caleb moaned.

"I could reach your prostate with the sound. But this one's too thin to massage it properly, so the plug will have to do this time." Rod slid out the wand completely.

Caleb strained, gasping as his cock was on fire from the inside. "It feels so weird. God, I want more."

"It's Rod, not God." Rod rolled Caleb's balls in his hand, squeezing.

Caleb wanted to laugh, but a click sounded again and the vibrations in his ass intensified, causing him to hiss and thrust his hips up.

With more lube, Rod slid the wand back in.

Pain. Pleasurable, sweet agony.

Rod fucked Caleb with the sound, then slowed down to jerk Caleb's cock instead, alternating the two actions.

"Talk to me."

"I'm close." Caleb's face was sweating inside the mask, but he was happy he was able to let the tears fall freely from the intensity of this experience. "I'm not sure if the pain or pleasure is stronger, but I'm loving both. Fuck, Roderick... Owner. Can I please come?"

Rod moved his hand up and down Caleb's dick, with less pressure than Caleb usually used on himself, but the wand inside made all the difference.

"Come now, my Wolf," Rod said, removing the steel in a slow glide, as he jerked Caleb's dick faster.

On a broken sob, Caleb let his orgasm fly. With the sound out, he shot on Rod's hand and over his own stomach, then kept coming while the vibrating plug in his ass milked him as vigorously as Rod's hand. Incoherent mewling left his lips as his dick twitched with the last drops.

His head against the bench, his eyes closed, Caleb registered the plug ceasing its dance in his over-sensitized hole. Knowing Rod was still in charge of the situation and his body, Caleb sat relaxed, listening to clatter of steel and the sound of running water before Rod's gentle paws unstrapped him from the bindings, starting with his wrists and ending with the spreader bar.

Limp and exhausted, Caleb let Rod direct him to the couch, where he sat on Rod's lap, wrapped in a blanket.

It was hard to tell how much time had passed, but Caleb was becoming more aware of the circles Rod was tracing on his back as he slowly returned from his haze.

"I really need to pee." He wiggled, feeling how raw he was in so many places.

"That's good," Rod said, lifting them both up. "It will hurt, though. I'll go with you."

"To pee?" Caleb squeaked.

"Are you shy all of a sudden?" Rod smacked Caleb's ass hard enough for the sound to echo.

Caleb snorted. "No."

They let the blanket fall to the floor and made their way to the toilet inside the glass enclosure.

Caleb steeled himself and released a stream into the bowl.

"Holy fucking shit, that hurts!" He turned his head to bite into Rod's shoulder, then back to see where he was aiming.

"Told you." Rod's chuckle was dark. *The fucking sadist is enjoying this.*

"I'm gonna remember you sliding that damn sound into me for a long, *long* time."

"Is that good?" Rod reached around from behind Caleb to gently massage his abdomen.

"Yeah. I like this pain. I like hurting because something good happened to me. The pain makes me relive it. Thank you, Owner." Caleb turned around to kiss Rod with tenderness and sated passion.

"You're welcome, my Wolf."

They washed gently but quickly under the shower, tracing each other's bodies with efficiency.

"Will you stay the night?" Rod asked, then continued immediately: "You're tired and hurting and I can't let you—"

"I'll stay," Caleb said, and saw Rod let out a breath of relief.

"Perfect. Let's go downstairs."

Caleb frowned, looking at the couch they had slept on previously. Were they going to Rod's bed?

Sure enough, they made their way straight there. Rod's bedroom was decorated with mahogany furnishings, patterned wallpaper, and an enormous bed in the middle. The warm colors, overflowing bookshelf and tiny knick-knacks in disarray on the dresser gave the whole room a welcoming vibe. It was a huge contrast to the rest of the house with its modern, minimalistic style—as if this room was Rod's sanctuary. And he welcomed Caleb into it.

"Lay down, I'll bring your stuff here," Rod said, and kissed Caleb's temple.

Caleb nodded. He wasn't sure if he'd be able to move even if the house was on fire.

Chapter Twelve

Rod

Showered, cleaned up, and rehydrated, Rod joined Caleb under the covers, wrapping his arms around him, luxuriating in the pure pleasure of having him in his bed.

He'd never invited a lover to sleep over since he'd bought the house nearly six years ago. But with Caleb, everything was different. Their intense session had been glorious. The way Caleb embraced his will to experiment and put his trust in Rod brought them closer together in a way Rod had never felt with anyone before. With every moan, every smile, and every yelped curse from Caleb's mouth, Rod wanted to tell him what he knew deep inside his heart. He'd fallen hard and he didn't want to get up. Now he made it his mission to prove to Caleb that he was worth falling for as well.

In the middle of the night, Rod rolled out of bed to go to the toilet. Caleb joined him and reached for Rod's hand as he hissed and moaned when he relieved himself. Back in the bed, he sucked Rod off before they fell asleep in indescribable bliss.

Rod woke up to the feel of Caleb's warm body in front of him. He tightened his grip, inhaling his lover's natural scent, Caleb's heartbeat strong and steady under his palm. He could get used to this quickly. Caleb was like a drug. Now Rod had had a taste, he found himself craving more and more, to the point he was going out of his mind. Now that they had entered a relationship status, Rod wanted Caleb to move in. It made sense, after all. Rod's house was empty and Caleb could have his own space, even a separate room if he didn't want to be crowded by Rod's presence. Rod would cook and they would eat curled up on the sofa, watching movies, chatting the way they did every evening on the phone, only this time it would be in person. Yes, Rod could imagine Caleb in his life with ease, and he was impatient to make his vision come true.

He'd wait a week and ask Caleb to move in, on whatever condition he'd agree upon. Spending evenings together would let them explore more kinks, take on more elaborate scenes, or ones that would require Caleb to rest longer. Rod smiled, half dreaming, half awake, willing himself not to fall asleep again. Just as he pulled his lover closer, he felt him stir.

"Rod?" Caleb's voice was groggy from sleep.

"Yeah?"

"Do you have a coffee machine?"

Rod kissed Caleb's nape. "Will a French press do?"

"Yeah."

"I'll make you some coffee then."

"I'll go with you."

"Wait, I was meaning to ask..." Rod traced a finger over the ink covering Caleb's jugular. "What does the 773 stand for?"

"Oh," Caleb touched the spot as if now remembering the tattoo was there. "It's Chicago area code. I had it inked before I left."

Rod's hand moved down his lover's arm to settle on his hip as he analyzed the rest of the tattoos scattered on Caleb's skin. "I understand you're the howling wolf but who's the angel on your ribs?" he asked.

"That's Timmy. My guardian angel," Caleb said, taking Rod's hand to place it over the ink.

"Your tats are sentimental and meaningful. I like that."

"Careful, or I'll tattoo your name on my chest."

"Pft, then I'll have to tattoo yours on mine."

"You don't have any tats. Unless they're hidden somewhere I haven't seen yet." Caleb feigned a gasp. "Maybe between your hairy asscheeks?"

Rod chuckled, then bit into Caleb's shoulder.

"Barbarian!" Caleb squeaked, then backed his ass into Rod's morning erection.

"Perhaps I've been waiting for the right tattoo idea for my first time." Rod danced his hand over Caleb's hip, then to his balls, taking them in hand.

"Feed me coffee and you can use me anyway you like." Caleb wiggled away.

"Coffee is not food."

"Pft, says who?" Caleb sat up and tapped his phone. "It's only seven, I could—" His back straightened as he read whatever was on the screen.

The glow on his face showed his expression of confusion morph into one of utter horror. Without a word, he darted out of the room, dialing a number.

Hushed, distressed cursing coming from Caleb worried Rod but he stayed in bed to give his lover privacy.

He was back within moments with a worried expression on his face. "I'm sorry, I gotta go."

"What happened?"

"I had my phone muted, cause whoever's gonna call me at night can wait, right?" He shoved his hand through his hair. "It's one in the morning in Chicago now and last night my mom... my mom..." His voice shook as he slumped on the bed.

Rod took Caleb's hands in his. "Is she OK?"

"She's alive," he croaked. "She OD'd and I'm listed as her next of kin in her rehab clinic and the hospital, so they called me, they left me voicemails. And... fuck. I need to go to Chicago. I have to buy tickets now." Caleb tugged his hands out of Rod's grasp, stumbled back but caught himself on the chest of drawers.

"OK, let's sit and get the tickets. I'm going with you," Rod said, lifting the blinds in the bedroom to let in the light and head for his laptop.

"No, you have your life here. I need to go alone."

Rod stopped in the doorway and turned back. "You don't have to do everything alone."

"Yes, I do. It's always been like that," Caleb choked out. "Lone wolf, remember?" He poked his own chest with a finger, his lips trembling.

But you're my Wolf now. "Let me come with you. I don't like you going there by yourself all distressed like this."

"Tough shit. I don't need a babysitter. I'm going. Alone." Caleb's hands shook as he grabbed his clothes off the chair in the corner of the bedroom and dressed quickly, tapping wildly on his phone between each item of clothing. "I'm gonna buy my ticket on the phone on my way to Sandra's. Uber will be here in five."

"Caleb?"

"Yeah?"

He looked pale and disheveled.

Rod wanted to hug him but he knew Caleb needed space right now. "Can you text me when you land?"

"Yeah." Caleb's gaze softened. "I'll text you." He stood still for a moment, his lips parted as if he wanted to say something. Instead, he nodded once, turned on his heel and left.

Rod collapsed on the bed, still warm where Caleb had slept. He'd respect Caleb's wishes, against his own better judgment. He wanted to be there for him even if Caleb didn't want that.

He rolled out of bed and cleaned up the plates from the night before, his head replaying Caleb's words. Every corner in the house was filled with memories of Caleb even after such a short time. He was like a fever dream that had slipped through Rod's fingers. Unable to rest, he organized the attic, folding blankets, making sure the shower was clean, all the time reeling from the anguish deep in his chest. Caleb was hurting, but Rod's hands were tied.

Or were they?

Chapter Thirteen

Caleb

After a quick ride home while spending a third of his win from the previous fight on a plane ticket, followed by a hurried packing session, Caleb was ready to catch the flight to Chicago via Dublin. His chaotic buzzing around the house woke up Sandra, and he explained to her what had happened. It hurt him to see her worried when she usually was such a ray of sunshine, especially lately.

The day before the date at Rod's house, Caleb had gone with Sandra to her doctor's appointment. He'd sat in the waiting area, his knee twitching, his brain concocting alternative routes for Sandra to have her surgery, just in case. Finally, he'd shot to his feet when Sandra had come out with a grin on her face. It had been the most wonderful evening, filled with joyful laughter as both of them had gone through the leaflets from the doctor and a bottle of wine.

"Just don't lose yourself," Sandra said, her voice bringing Caleb back to the present. She knew him and his inner darkness all too well.

"I'll try. I have to go there but it hurts me to leave you and Rod..." He sighed, plopping on the sofa.

Sandra made tea and Caleb ended up telling her about the fantastic night he'd had with Rod. After relaying the PG-ish version, he realized he'd acted like an asshole leaving so suddenly. He hadn't been thinking straight, and foolishly imagined himself on a flying death trap within hours as he raced out of there. Unfortunately, he only managed to book a flight that would take him fifteen hours with a six-hour layover in Dublin. With his hatred of flying, it was bound to be a disaster, but he didn't have much choice.

After staring at the Bears-4-U app for what felt like forever, he finally texted CuddlySadist.

'My flight is at nine tonight. I'll text you when I land.' He hit send and looked at the dry information that didn't relay what was in his heart. He hoped that the two words he added would fix it: 'Your Wolf.'

"Mom, I'm here," Caleb croaked as he walked into the hospital room, taking in his mom's face, as pale as the sheet she was covered with. She didn't stir.

Exhausted, he sat on the chair next to her, unwilling to doze off. He'd tried sleeping on the plane and managed to catch a few hours after he'd taken some calming pill Sandra had given him. The layover had ended up being hours wasted wandering around the airport to kill time before getting on the next plane. By the time he'd arrived at the hospital, it was early morning and the visitors' hours had already started.

A mixed bag of feelings shook inside Caleb's chest when he pushed away the hair plastered to his mom's forehead. He recalled her singing to him when he was little, reading him bedtime stories, and hugging him. All that had changed with Timmy's death. She'd never been the same. And neither had he.

As Caleb let his heavy lids fall, his mind brought back one of many memories that he'd done his best to forget. He dreamed of the day when he was eleven and his mom hadn't picked him up from school.

Backpack in hand, Caleb was sitting on the curb in front of the school. He'd told his teacher that he saw his mom standing by the entrance, so Ms. Maisie wouldn't have to wait with him again as mom was running late. With the number of kids running around excited to go home, Caleb had known that he'd get away with it. It happened often, but he was sure mom would pick him up or send the neighbor, or maybe one of her friends.

This time, it was a dude that Caleb hadn't seen in their house for a while, but he got into his truck anyway. It was only when he saw they were driving further from their neighborhood that Caleb realized something was wrong. Then he remembered that he was one of Mom's ex-boyfriends. The one she'd thrown plates at and accidentally hit and shattered a framed picture from her parents' wedding.

The dude kept trying to call Caleb's mom over and over, his frustration and anger hanging heavy in the cabin of the truck.

Silently crying, Caleb clutched his backpack and once again wished his father was alive. Mom didn't pick up for so long, they had to stop at a gas station. Caleb managed to steal a bag of chips to eat in the bathroom as the ex-boyfriend kept trying to call his mom.

When Caleb left the bathroom, he heard him yelling on the phone, asking mom for a ransom, screaming at her, and threatening to do horrible things to Caleb. Then he called her names as she hung up on him. He tried again, but Caleb could tell from how angry he was that she didn't pick up.

She didn't care.

The ex climbed into his truck and took off, leaving Caleb all alone. Thankfully, Caleb remembered his grandpa's phone number and the cashier lady at the station called him. Caleb stayed with his grandpa for a while, then went back home, only to move back with Pops permanently when he turned sixteen. He learned much later that his mom had been so drugged-up that time she hadn't noticed that Caleb was gone for four days.

"Caleb?" Mom's weak voice brought him awake. "Is that you?"

"Yes, Mom, I'm here." Caleb sat up abruptly, squinting against the sunlight from the window. *How long was I asleep?*

"I knew you were a good boy, even though you're a faggot."

The words stung like a slap to the face, but Caleb gritted his teeth, forcing himself to remember that he'd come to check on her. "How do you feel?"

"Like shit, what do you think?" she spat. "Can't even die in peace in this fucking place."

What? "I thought you were doing well in rehab, they sent me weekly summaries. The place looked so nice, too." *And expensive as fuck.* "I hoped you'd like it there."

"It was a pretty prison." She crossed her arms, huffing. "A fucking Zen dump run by a bunch of do-gooders."

Caleb scooted closer, reaching for her hand, but she took it away, hiding it under the covers. "I can find a different facility for you."

"Fuck facilities. Fuck you, Caleb." Her voice was full of venom as she looked him in the eye. "If Timmy was here, it would all be different."

"I know, Mom, I know." Caleb ran a hand down his face.

"But you can get me a pack of smokes. I know you have money from whoring yourself or whatever it is that you do," she mumbled, looking towards the window, away from Caleb.

"How about some chocolate, huh?" Caleb kept his voice steady. "You like chocolate."

"Yeah, OK, that too. But none of that no-milk crap."

Caleb grabbed snacks from the vending machine in the corridor and ripped his candy bar open right there to welcome the rush of sugar, chocolate, and nuts. He returned to the room to listen to mom talk about how horrible the rehab had been, but she'd flirted her way to a decent dose which ended her here. Caleb listened with horror at how the worst thing the place had done to her was refuse to give her drugs. With yoga activities, spa, and even calming time with animals, Caleb had been hoping she'd get back on her feet. He'd been a fool when it came to her. Yet again.

"You never visited me. You should have brought me something nice. It's not even that far. Do you still live at Dad's?" she asked, frowning as if she was trying to remember something.

"No, Mom. After Pops died, Aunt Felecia sold the house and I moved out." He'd visited her at the facility before he'd left for the UK and told her about his plans, but she'd either forgotten or didn't care that he left.

"Right. So you got rid of him and then shoved me in that prison so you could suck every cock in the neighborhood and I wouldn't have to see it. That's very clever of you, I'll give you that," she hissed, pulling her covers up as if she could shield herself from his sexuality. "You're an abomination, a filthy faggot."

"Fucking hell, Mom," Caleb groaned, unable to take it anymore. "Why do you have to say it like that?"

He'd explained to her many times what being bisexual meant, but she'd told him once he sucked one cock, he was tainted forever. He called her a hypocrite so she'd thrown a mug and then a knife at him. Today, he was not in the mood to straighten her with facts.

"Don't worry, soon I won't bother you anymore," she mumbled, turning her face away with a grimace. "I have a plan. Watch me."

Caleb shook his head. "Just rest. I'll be right back." His bladder reminded him he hadn't taken a leak since the plane landed.

In the corridor bathroom, he splashed his face with water then braced his hands on the sink to look at his tired face in the mirror. "She's your mother," he said to his reflection. "Be nice." Her addiction and depression had started after Timmy's death and they both knew that had been Caleb's fault. He couldn't blame her for resenting him.

Resting his back on the cold, tiled wall, he pulled out his phone. He reread the texts Rod had sent him since they'd parted, saying that he'd be thinking of him, that Caleb was strong and amazing. Caleb wasn't in the headspace to reply, but he added a heart reaction to each sentence so Rod would know he appreciated them more than he was capable of saying in a message. The newest text reminded him to eat and drink water. Caleb smiled. As if Rod knew that the economy class meal and a stale candy bar had been the only things Caleb's stomach had seen. Maybe he should get some chips and a Coke from the vending machine and more chocolate for mom.

Caleb nodded at his reflection, straightened his back and left the bathroom.

"Hey man, you just missed your uncle," the nurse said, his big hand fixing the name tag on his scrubs. *Zack.*

"Who?" Caleb frowned.

Zack pointed at a guy whose back disappeared behind the door at the very end of the long hallway. "Uncle Chad, your mom's brother. He's in the system here listed as family." He pointed to the monitor at the nurse's station behind him. "I just brought her water, she looked happy that he visited."

"My mom doesn't have a brother..." Caleb's voice trailed off.

Like a set of horror flashes, the words his mother had said to him came back. *I won't bother you anymore.* "What the fuck?" he whispered and ran towards the room, the nurse on his heels.

With a squeak of soles, he halted in the doorway, his stomach dropping to his knees. Mom's mouth was open, her eyes rolled back, and a syringe sticking out of her arm.

"You fucking bitch!" Caleb yelled running to her side. "Mom! Wake the fuck up, mom!" He shook her by the shoulders as the nurse tried to drag him away.

His mind flashed back to the time he'd yelled those same words when he was ten, the first time she'd OD'd after Timmy's death. He'd called the ambulance then. But this time, as he held her icy hand, he retreated to a numb state of nothingness.

"Sir, move away!" someone yelled next to him, as alarms blared in the background. Zack escorted him out of the room and into a chair, talking to him. Caleb didn't hear a word. All sounds blurred together; the alarm, the yelling, and the nurse's words of comfort. Someone in a white coat ran past them and into mom's room.

Minutes passed, and the alarm stopped, leaving only the one blaring in Caleb's head. A doctor came out of the room to tell Caleb what he already knew. She was gone. His mom was dead.

Caleb didn't sob, but he felt tears streaming down his face.

"Do you want me to call someone?" Zack's kind face was still in his field of vision, blurry and unfamiliar.

Caleb shook his head.

Zack's soft tone explained what would happen next, but Caleb looked at his hands, barely registering the words. Finally, he managed to stand up and wobble to the bathroom. In a stall, he sat on a closed lid and buried his face in his hands. His mind overloaded, his heart palpitated, and his breath was impossible to keep even.

Think of a happy memory.

His grandpa's advice came to him in a rush of comfort.

It used to be a memory of a Christmas he'd spent with Pops and his friends. They'd been a bunch of people from all walks of life; Laura, a woman who had grown children who couldn't visit and her condition didn't allow her to travel, Frank, a man with no children at all, living with his male best friend, and Sally, a teenager like Caleb who was stuck in the foster system but came to spend Christmas with them. It was a lovely memory, but at this moment it was foreshadowed by one even stronger.

Rod.

Caleb breathed out slowly, remembering Rod's arms around him as he'd pulled him close, a soft blanket around them. Rod had whispered to him and they laughed, snuggling together. *Safe. Content. Happy.*
Loved.

Caleb sat up straight and smacked himself in the face, once, twice. *You fucking idiot.*

Hands trembling but sure, he took out his phone and typed.

'I can't do this alone.'
'I wish you'd come with me.'
'I was so stupid.'
'I'm sorry I made you stay behind.'
'I need you.'
'I'm sorry I said I don't.'

He sent the messages one after the other, probably with typos, but he didn't care.

He locked his phone, not expecting a reply. It was the afternoon in the UK so Rod was probably at work. A ping startled him and he nearly dropped the device before unlocking it.

A message from CuddlySadist: 'Where are you?'
'At the hospital.'
'Which one?'

Since Rod was so far away, it didn't matter, but Caleb indulged his boyfriend anyway. The conversation was keeping him distracted for a moment at least.

'Advocate Lutheran General.'

'Meet me in the lobby in 20.'

Caleb snorted, wiping his face. 'Minutes or hours?'

'Min.'

Caleb shook his head as the meaning of the messages barely registered. Was Rod sending someone he knew in Chicago? Caleb didn't want to see strangers now, but he washed his face and took the elevator downstairs anyway.

He sat on one of the chairs alongside a row of windows. The sun was warming his nape as he stared at the patterns on the tiles in a stupor, hugging his backpack to his chest.

Someone sat next to him and put a hand on his back. Caleb flinched and was about to tell them to fuck off, but he recognized the touch.

He looked to the side, his eyes prickling, his chest constricting.

"Rod? How?" he whispered, hardly believing his eyes.

Rod opened his arms. "Come here."

Caleb slumped into Rod's chest, letting the waterfall streak down his face. "But I told you to stay. I was such an ass to you." He sniffed. "And you said that you wouldn't come with me."

"I didn't. I just flew to Chicago to try deep dish pizza," Rod said, and kissed Caleb's temple.

"That's ridiculous." Caleb sob-snorted, looking up at his lover's face. A mere day had passed but he missed those eyes, that face, and that enormous heart. "And did you?"

"Yeah. At a restaurant by the airport."

Caleb grimaced. "And?"

"It was definitely better than the boxed one from Tesco," Rod admitted, resting his cheek on Caleb's head.

Caleb snorted and the sound ended in a sob.

"What happened, my love?" Rod asked, smoothing Caleb's hair before he cupped his face in his big hands.

Caleb looked down, burying his face in Rod's chest. "She's dead," he mumbled into Rod's shirt, inhaling as much of the man's scent as he could. "My mom is dead."

A breath caught in Rod's throat and his hand stroked Caleb's back. "I'm so sorry," he said, and Caleb could hear the sadness in his tone. It was for Caleb. He was grieving with him, even though he'd never met his mom.

Without letting go of his boyfriend, Caleb shuffled onto his lap. It felt ridiculous and out of place in public, but he needed the comfort more than he cared about propriety. When Caleb's tears ran dry and Rod's soothing strokes on his back brought some semblance of solace, he lifted his head to see he'd soaked the collar of Rod's polo shirt.

"Where are you staying?" Rod asked, repositioning Caleb so he could see his face. "With your family?"

"No. I was supposed to crash at Natasha's, but I came straight here and didn't even text her yet."

"Will you go with me? I have a room at a hotel by O'Hare."

"I don't—" Caleb swallowed and looked at Rod, his boyfriend's expression warning him off saying something stupid. No playing strong. No self-deprecating comments. Caleb felt like telling Rod that he didn't want to be a burden, but he knew Rod hadn't come all this way for Caleb to act like an ungrateful little shit. Besides, he wished for nothing more than to have Rod with him, close enough to touch at all times. He refused to admit how fragile he was right now, like he could fall apart and start crying again at any moment.

Even though he'd always found it hard to accept any form of help, he knew Rod would never make him feel guilty. "Yeah, I'd love that."

Chapter Fourteen

Rod

Still wrapped around Caleb, Rod listened to the gruesome story of how his boyfriend's mother had ended her life. Caleb's voice—strong but shaky—relayed the information with no more tears left to spill, and Rod's heart broke for the man who deserved so much more than a life of constant anguish. He wanted to shield Caleb from all the pain in the world, except for what he could give him in the bedroom. But he knew that was impossible, so he was glad Caleb let him be here today, holding him close, lips on his temple.

"Sir? Are you Caleb Doron?" a tall woman in scrubs asked as she approached with a clipboard in hand.

"Yes," Caleb croaked, wiping his face as he turned on Rod's lap to face her.

"Could you come with me, please?"

Caleb stood up and reached for Rod. His red-rimmed glare dared her to tell him to go alone. Rod squeezed Caleb's hand and they followed the nurse to a station.

Rod watched as Caleb absorbed the information about the hospital procedure and funeral arrangements. He looked exhausted, but his gaze was sharp as he nodded, having a grasp on what to do next. Caleb told the nurse that he didn't need the hospital to hold the body for long as he had the funeral home already picked, and once he called them, they'd collect his mom quickly.

On their way out, Caleb squeezed Rod's hand and kissed him on the cheek. "Thank you," he said.

"Thanks for letting me be here. It looks like you already have a plan."

"I helped Great Aunt Felecia arrange Grandpa's funeral. Well, I ended up in charge of everything, so now I've got it all figured out, I guess." Caleb's voice was steady as he continued talking about arrangements.

They walked towards the exit and Rod nodded along, thinking it might be good for Caleb to focus on the organizational side. He hoped that by now Caleb was ready to lean on him if necessary.

"The cremation and funeral ceremony shouldn't be more than four grand since Mom wanted to be buried in the family plot with her parents," Caleb continued as they exited the hospital.

"Do you—"

"Before you say anything, I have enough money from my last fight." He gave Rod a warning glare, daring him to comment. "And now I won't have to send it to the rehab center anymore..." He cleared his throat. "I can take a bus from here and—"

"I'm driving you." Rod stepped in front of Caleb and cupped his face until their gazes met. "I'm driving you everywhere while we're here. That's not up for discussion."

Caleb's lips turned up on one side. "Did you just pull out your dom card on me?"

Rod squished Caleb's face in his hands. "Yes."

Confusion crossed Caleb's face before he relaxed and smiled softly. "Let's go, then."

They sat in the gray Ford sedan Rod had rented at the airport. Rod was amazed how, despite being in distress, Caleb was pushing to start the process right away, giving him directions on where to go.

"Shit, how the fuck did you learn to drive on this side of the road?" Caleb asked, waving at the steering wheel. "You make it look so effortless, too."

Rod shrugged. "On trips to Europe and here over the years."

"A well-traveled man, huh? I'm jealous."

Rod opened his mouth to say he'd take Caleb anywhere, around the world if need be, and they could see everything together. "You have your whole life ahead of you to travel," he said instead.

They stopped at an internet cafe where Caleb printed a Cremation Authorization Form and stopped at a Notary Public office next door to notarize it.

"Illinois has a mandatory wait period of 24 hours before a cremation can be performed, so I want to get on it right away," he explained.

Back in the car, Caleb called the funeral director and agreed to them obtaining the death certificate directly and told him he was on his way to drop off the Cremation Authorization Form. With a grave expression, but unstoppable determination, Caleb tackled the emotionally draining tasks. Rod could see they were taking a toll on his boyfriend, as he was going paler by the minute. He breathed a sigh of relief when he was finally able to deliver Caleb safely back to the hotel.

When they entered the room, Rod offered to order food, but by the time he picked up the menu to call, Caleb was asleep on the bed fully clothed. Rod covered them both with a blanket and pulled Caleb to his chest. He could use a nap as well.

It was late afternoon when they awoke and Rod ordered room service, not willing to drag Caleb anywhere, even to a restaurant. He woke him gently, rubbing his back until Caleb opened his eyes.

"Wake up, food's waiting for you," Rod said, hoping the smell of fresh coffee would serve its purpose. It would do them both good if they acclimatized to the time zone and shook off the jet lag as quickly as possible.

"I'm not hungry," Caleb grumbled, but his eyes were fully awake as he sat up.

"You have to eat. At least try some soup or bits from the platter." Rod had ordered a cheese and meat board, hoping small bites would be easier for Caleb to tackle. "How about I feed you?"

"I'm not a child."

"You're not. But you're tired." *And mine to take care of.*

"I need to send the funeral announcement to my family and whoever I can think of. I should have a few of mom's old friends following me on social media, too." Caleb unplugged his phone from the charger and plopped on the end of the hotel bed. "I'll call my great aunt but I think I can get away with sending texts and messages to the rest."

Caleb's great-aunt spoke loudly and it was impossible not to hear what she said, even over the phone. After the initial wailing and blaming Caleb for his mother's death, she promised to spread the message to the rest of the family. After the call, Caleb sighed and opened his social media apps.

Rod hated seeing his man so accustomed to verbal abuse from his family that he didn't even react to the harsh words.

Determined to keep Caleb from starving, Rod hauled the platter to the middle of the bed. He took a bite of a piece of rolled-up meat, then offered it to Caleb. "Come on, open."

Caleb looked at him, eyes haunted, but he parted his lips.

Bite by bite, Rod fed his boyfriend as he sent the funeral announcement to family and posted it on social media.

"I'm done. But I'm not replying to condolence messages and comments." Caleb tossed his phone aside.

"How about a movie with commercials," Rod pointed to the telly on the wall, "and cuddling in bed?"

Caleb stayed silent for a moment, looking at Rod. "Why are you so good to me?"

"Because I—" It was the wrong time to say the big words for the first time. It just was. "Because I care."

"I don't deserve this," Caleb said in a flat tone, his gaze on his phone.

"Hey," Rod said sharply to get his boyfriend's attention. "You deserve the world." *And I intend to give it to you.* "You're *my* Wolf, and no one can offend what's mine. Not even you. I won't allow it and you know this. Now take it back and apologize."

"I won't." Caleb thrust his chin up.

Under different circumstances, Rod would beat an apology out of Caleb, edging him until he cried out and promised never to belittle himself. Today, he needed something else. Rod rolled over Caleb, pinning him on the bed. "Or I'll squeeze you until you surrender."

Caleb's eyes fluttered closed. "You can squeeze me like this forever." Caleb's breaths were shallow with Rod's heavy body on top of him.

Rod kissed Caleb's cheek then propped himself on his elbows to see his man take a deep breath and open his eyes.

"I like you on top of me," he whispered.

"Me too," Rod smirked, loving the sight of Caleb's tiny smile. He kissed that smile, tender and soft and Caleb wrapped his arms around him.

"I need a shower." Caleb grimaced, wiggling from under Rod.

"I'll help you."

When morning came, Rod cracked one eye open to see Caleb's messy hair as the man lay plastered to Rod's side, face on his pec. He'd been tossing and turning, crying in his sleep. Each time Rod had hugged him hard, squeezing them close together till Caleb calmed down enough to fall back to sleep.

They started the day with Rod driving Caleb from place to place to make final arrangements for the funeral. The young man looked like a zombie with bags under his eyes, but he soldiered on, from picking the urn to arranging for the nearest date, just a day away. The time passed on, with more preparations and Caleb answering phone calls from distant family who wouldn't be coming.

"Mom had no siblings," Caleb explained as they drove to the cemetery the following day. "Grandma died when I was little and Grandpa just last year, so there's no immediate family left. Grandpa's sister, Felecia was the closest, but since she'd never gotten along with Mom, I don't know her well. She purchased Grandpa's house when he needed more money for Mom's rehab and let him live there with me until she sold it last year. Oh, here she is." Caleb pointed to a short, thin woman with teased hair. "There's a parking space over there."

Oak Woods was a large lawn cemetery with plaques surrounded by grass. Only the wind blowing the flower petals on the ground and people shuffling around created any noise on the somber day.

They dressed in their regular clothes. Caleb said most of their wardrobe was black anyway so there was no point buying a suit he'd never wear again just for one day. Rod wore his regular outfit of polo and jeans, while Caleb covered his t-shirt with a button-down.

The black fabric was a stark contrast to Caleb holding the white marble urn to his chest as relatives and friends started to appear next to him.

"I'm glad you came," Caleb told them, but Rod saw he was only being polite. "This is Rod." He nodded, his hands full. "Rod, this is Aunt Felecia and her daughters, Daria and Lena."

Rod offered a wave to the trio, who glared daggers at him as if he was the reason they were here.

Caleb exchanged only cursory hellos with the handful of people gathered, introducing them as his mom's friends, until a tall blond woman with short hair approached him. She hugged him around the urn, and by the way Caleb welcomed her touch, Rod had an idea of who she was.

"This is Natasha." Caleb turned to Rod.

"I've heard a lot about you," Natasha said, clasping Rod's hand. Her eyes scanned Rod before settling on his face with a warning glare as she squeezed his hand hard.

Message received, Rod nodded, and her expression relaxed. He was the last person who would let Caleb get hurt and he hoped Caleb would realize that he had people who cared for him deeply. Even in the home country that he'd decided to leave.

"Can we get going?" Aunt Felecia poked Caleb's arm. "We don't have all day."

"Yes, let's go," Caleb said through his teeth.

He led the procession to the grave where Caleb's grandparents had been buried. There, he released the urn to the funeral home people who placed it on a shelf inside the open grave. As no one offered to make a speech, one of Caleb's mom's friends started praying and several people joined.

Rod hated the judgmental glances at his hand clasped in Caleb's, and how his mom's friends' condolences sounded stiff and insincere when they approached Caleb before leaving. Within moments, only a few people were left and Caleb held onto Rod's hand like a lifeline, his eyes never leaving the open grave.

"My condolences," Caleb's aunt said to him as she approached, her crunched nose defying her words. "I'm not really that surprised. Your mother was heading towards disaster for years now. I hope you'll do more with your life than her. Fred always spoke so highly of you, God rest his soul."

"He spoke fondly of you," Caleb said to his great aunt. "So I never understood why you two weren't close."

"There are some things this family doesn't tolerate and you two were like peas in a pod, I suppose." She glanced at Rod, then back to Caleb. "Take care, boy." With those words, she walked off, her daughters at her heels.

Caleb frowned. "What was that supposed to mean?"

"I don't know, my love." Rod kissed Caleb's knuckles.

"Well, I'm ready to leave." Caleb turned to the grave. "Bye, Mom. Take care of Timmy wherever you two are now."

Chapter Fifteen

Rod

"How are you feeling?" Rod asked as they sat in his rental car at the cemetery.

"Like a boulder has been lifted off my chest." Caleb looked ahead through the windshield. "I know it's a shit thing to say, she was my mother. But I feel like she can't hurt me anymore, you know?"

Rod reached for Caleb's hand and squeezed it. "Do you want to go back to the hotel or somewhere else?"

"Adler Planetarium."

The answer took Rod aback. "You want to go to a planetarium now?"

"No, just the skyline walk. You'll see."

Not about to argue with a grieving man, Rod nodded and turned on the engine. "Will you put it in the car's GPS?"

"Sure. But I'll tell you where to go. Just drive."

Lake Michigan was vast enough to be mistaken for a sea. The wavy surface shone in the early afternoon sun as they drove towards it. Once on a pier, Rod saw the round roof of the planetarium in front of them.

"Just park on the curb, we're not going inside so we don't need tickets," Caleb said, already unbuckling.

Rod followed Caleb off the sidewalk and to a grassy downward slope towards the lake. Caleb sat on the grass, his gaze in the distance. Rod joined him and lost himself for a moment in Caleb's profile. Rays of sun danced on his boyfriend's face, kissing his naturally tanned skin and the slightly crooked nose that made him even more beautiful.

"It's the best view of the skyline," Caleb said, reaching for Rod's hand and pulling it onto his lap.

Rod forced his gaze to the buildings peppered along the lake's shore, some older and smaller, some tall and characteristic, like the John Hancock building with the two antennas he'd seen on postcards at the airport.

"Magnificent." It was a truly spectacular view.

The lake was humming with waves, soothing as much as the depths of it were dangerous.

"I came here whenever I could, once a friend told me about this place. It's how I saw Chicago most of my life. I lived here, but I was so far away from the excitement of downtown, or rich family neighborhoods like Winnetka. We used to drive there with friends to look at houses decorated for Christmas. They looked like they were from a movie." He smiled, resting his head on Rod's shoulder. "So I could see the city, but not touch it, not live in it."

"Where did you live?"

"I grew up on the South Side, a complete opposite of the glamor you see in movies."

"Will you show me?" Rod asked, and put his cheek on top of Caleb's head.

"We can drive through it, but Grandpa's house is already sold and mom was always renting, so I have no family left there. I feel like I have no family here at all. Not after today."

Rod wrapped an arm over Caleb's shoulders. "You have Natasha. I can tell she cares about you even if you're not together anymore."

"Yeah. She's from the South Side too. Even after her gym and MMA school became popular, she stayed. She's helping so many young people now. A few of the guys we hung out with made it out of South Side; Jake works in a restaurant, Chad in a casino, but Martin was shot trying to rob a 7-Eleven last year." He snuggled up to Rod, his voice growing sad again. "They're all great people, but I need to find my own thing, just like they did. Well, except for Martin."

"I'm glad your decisions led you to me. It's selfish but true."

"Yeah, me too." Caleb patted Rod's thigh. "Let's go see my old digs."

The drive through the South Side unveiled large old houses with high windows, but lacking the TLC they so desperately needed. This was a part of America rarely shown on TV. Rod drove slowly, waiting for Caleb's instructions.

"That's my grandpa's house." Caleb pointed at a bungalow with white steps and a porch in front. "Was his house, that is."

"Do you want me to park somewhere?"

"Nah, keep driving, it belongs to someone else now, anyway."

Rod felt the nostalgia waft off Caleb, but it was tainted with the many mixed memories he'd told Rod about. It was clear from his stiff posture that he wanted to leave.

"Where do you want to go now?" Rod asked, passing by a derelict house with broken lawn chairs in the front yard.

"Portillos."

"A what?"

"Just drive towards the hospital, I'll tell you where to go. From there it will be like a ten-minute drive to your hotel." Caleb turned to him with a smirk. "You need to taste an authentic Italian Beef Sandwich."

Rod chuckled. "Can't wait."

During the drive, Caleb remained quiet but Rod's brain was busy. He knew that Caleb was grieving, and he was determined to see his boyfriend through it to have him eventually smiling again. Now that Caleb had flown back to his home country, Rod couldn't help but wonder if he'd want to leave again. Even though the question weighed heavily on Rod, he refused to pressure his boyfriend for answers.

They parked on Dempster Plaza in front of a red brick building with a huge sign "Portillo's Hot Dogs" and smaller letters: "Beef - Burgers - Salads".

As they neared the glass entrance, Rod looked up at the enormous painting right above it portraying workers with barrels and an old blue pickup truck. He was hoping for a true show of Americana, but when they entered, the interior surpassed his expectations altogether. Rod took in the classic red-and-white tablecloths and wooden decor, topped with old coca-cola signs painted on the brick walls. But the life-size old beer truck full of barrels suspended from the ceiling overshadowed all of that. It was truly an "only in America" kind of place.

They approached the service window and Caleb ordered two Italian Beef sandwiches, a Coke for himself and water for Rod. It didn't escape Rod's notice that his drink had more ice in it than actual water. As they sat at one of the tables with their food, Caleb's mood lifted, as if the sheer anticipation of the taste made him feel better.

Rod was glad that Caleb was feeling well enough to eat.

Hands around his sandwich, Caleb paused and gave Rod an expectant look. "Go on. I need to see your face when you take your first bite." He waved at the plate in front of Rod.

First, Rod made a show of taking a sip of his icy water before he bit into his food, his gaze on Caleb's.

Oh. My. God.

Rod moaned. Even if a sandwich wasn't his idea of the perfect dinner, this one was fantastic. "Oh, fuck, that's so good," he said. Seeing Caleb smile, he pointed an accusatory finger at him. "But you have some explaining to do, mister."

"What?" Caleb sat back, confused.

"It tastes nothing like the one I made you," Rod said in the most serious tone he could muster, before he broke into a smile, putting the sandwich down. "You said my sandwich was good."

"It was! Just nothing like the actual Italian Beef," Caleb explained, chuckling softly.

"Ugh, that's awful." Rod buried his face in his hands, laughing.

"You made the effort and it was more than anyone had ever done for me. Besides, it was romantic as fuck, come on." Caleb tugged on Rod's hands. "Giving you an experience, even one as simple as this, makes me feel like less of a complete failure."

"Stop that, Caleb." Rod's smile was gone and he lowered his hands to look at his boyfriend. "Not just saying that, but get it out of your head. I wish you could see yourself the way I see you."

Caleb shrugged one shoulder, looking down. "I'm just a hefty bag of issues."

Rod leaned over the table and took Caleb's hands in his. "Do you know why I closed my practice?"

"No, you never told me."

"Because I didn't want you to know how I failed. How I fucked up so bad there was no going back for me, my patient, or his family."

Caleb swallowed, his eyes wide. "What? What happened?"

The ache in Rod's chest intensified at what he was about to divulge. It wasn't a story he shared easily, but Caleb had a right to know what had fucked him up so badly.

"Adam was my patient for four years. He had a wife and a beautiful toddler. He struggled with depression but we were working through it, or so I thought." Rod held onto Caleb's hands, the touch grounding him in the present as his mind reached for the darkness from his past. "One night he woke me with a phone call to tell me he lost his job that day. He was saying negative things about himself, about being useless, unable to fend for his family... I knew he sounded more distressed than during our weekly sessions. As I was talking to him, I got dressed and started driving. Along the way, the connection broke, and I couldn't reach him again. He didn't pick up when I tried to return the call. Even when I stopped in front of his building, he still didn't answer. His flat was on the fourth floor and—" Rod swallowed, remembering all too vividly what had happened next. "And he was still alive when I ran to the patch of grass in front of the building. You see, the jump didn't kill him, but when he landed on his legs, they went..." The image of a broken Adam illuminated by the street lamp haunted Rod to this day. "At that point, he had only moments left to live. The window to his kitchen was still open, his wife and child asleep, unaware their life was about to change." Tears trickled down Rod's cheeks, disappearing into his beard. "I held his hand and he made me promise I'd check in on his wife and Anna, his daughter. I kept that promise, but I should have been able to save him in the first place." His voice sounded haunted, even to himself.

"Rod, I'm so sorry." Caleb reached over to cup Rod's face, thumbing his tears away.

"That was three years ago. I closed my practice immediately. What was the point if I was unable to help Adam?" He reached for the icy water and took a long gulp that didn't soothe his anguish.

"It wasn't your fault, Rod."

"Yes, it was."

"From what you said, Adam was a troubled man and you tried to help him for a long time."

"Apparently not well enough."

Caleb stood up, scraping his chair against the floor, and unceremoniously parked his ass on Rod's lap. "I don't believe it." Caleb smoothed Rod's beard, offering him comfort. "I know you haven't gone all shrink on me, but you're easy to talk to, to open up to, I'm sure you were fantastic at your job. You don't do anything half-assed, I know that."

Rod sniffled, kissing the inside of Caleb's palm. "I haven't known happiness since then. I only realized that after our first date at the bear picnic. You lit up my world within weeks. Everything changed."

"You give me too much credit." Caleb rested his forehead against Rod's.

"No, I don't. And you're not allowed to tell me to diminish your impact on my life, or my general well-being," Rod said in a serious tone, before he kissed the tip of Caleb's nose.

"I know what can improve the last one even more," Caleb said, smoothing Rod's beard.

"What?"

"A real Chicago-style hot dog." Caleb smirked and stood up.

Rod snorted. He hadn't even finished his sandwich yet. "Prove it. And bring ketchup this time."

"For a hot dog? You nuts?" Caleb gasped with a hand on his chest, as if Rod had offended his core values.

"Why? Everyone puts ketchup on their hot dog."

"Shhh," Caleb put a finger over Rod's lips as he glanced around. "Not in Chicago. Dude, lower your voice with that blasphemy. Sheesh," he murmured, shaking his head.

Chapter Sixteen

Rod

On their way to the hotel, they stopped at a CVS Pharmacy. By the time Rod found everything he wanted to buy for himself, Caleb had already paid for his shopping and was waiting for him outside. With a receipt so long one could write a novel on it, Rod packed his ass into the car.

"I need to hurt," Caleb said, emerging bare-assed from the bathroom, toweling off his short hair.

Rod shot up from his seat on the bed, his body already dry after a shower, but still naked. He cupped Caleb's face, wanting to kiss it all over. "Oh, my love," he said, his heart aching. "Maybe you could relax and I'll make you feel good, hm? Forget responsibilities for a moment."

"I need to let it all go. Feeling good doesn't help me do that. A fight would. Something intense. But I'd rather you work your magic on me, if you're game." Caleb turned his face to nuzzle the inside of Rod's hand.

"Oh, I'm game, but are you sure you want that today?" Rod smoothed his hands over Caleb's shoulders, watching goosebumps break out in their wake.

"Sex? With you? You're so all-consuming, I forget everything else when we fuck. I need that right now, a complete, filthy brainwash. I wish you could put the mittens and mask on me." He closed his eyes and released a shaky breath. "I could forget I'm human. Just your Wolf..." His eyes opened, boring into Rod's. "Your fucktoy."

Breath caught in Rod's throat as his arousal spiked. "Bloody hell, Caleb. You make me hard just thinking about you on your knees on a leash, ready to be fucked." Rod repositioned himself but it didn't ease the ache in his growing erection. "I don't have any toys with me, but on a scale from one to ten, how intense do you want it to be?"

"I dunno." Caleb let his forehead fall on Rod's pec. "I don't want to think. I... Rod? Owner..." he whispered before he lifted his head up to speak louder. "Make me cry. Please."

Rod sealed their lips together, his heart beating faster for the man he embraced. The kiss was lazy until Caleb held Rod's bottom lip in his teeth, meeting his gaze with a challenging stare. Rod got the message. "Ok, I'll make you hurt until you come."

Until you fall apart in my arms. "Lay back and close your eyes. Breathe deeply so I can hear it."

Caleb plopped on the middle of the bed, tossing the small towel next to him. With his hands behind his head and his eyes closed, he looked magnificent: from his shapely legs peppered with tiny tattoos, to his flaccid cock lolling against his thigh, to his sharply-defined abs, and the chest that rose and fell with every breath. A body worth worshiping, and Rod had a plan on how to give Caleb exactly what he needed while making him writhe in pleasure.

With one last glance at his gorgeous man, Rod went on a hunt. He started by rummaging in the hotel's closet, looking for items he could use. Between the iron and laundry bags lay a set of fresh towels wrapped with a thick, terry ribbon. *That'll do.*

Next, he went to the bathroom. The bag Caleb had brought from the pharmacy was on the counter and an opened douche box and a razor were next to it. *So that's what took him so long.* In a decorative bowl by the sink lay a small sewing kit, and a shower cap. Rod pondered the possibilities, but these items were of no use to him today.

He'd have to do it the classic way: using his tongue, hands and cock. With that thought, he reached for the bottle of lube he'd bought at the pharmacy and smiled, eyeing its phallic shape. Caleb's drop, his need for pain, was bound to come sooner or later and Rod wanted to be ready. He was glad he knew his man so well by now.

The bed dipped under his weight as he crawled over to Caleb, grabbed his ankles and prompted him to bend his legs up, folding him in half. "Hold your legs like this."

Caleb obeyed, pretzelling himself by hooking his arms under his muscled thighs, putting his hole on display. *So flexible.*

Rod climbed between Caleb's spread legs, letting their cocks slide against each other. Caleb moaned and Rod captured his lips in a quick kiss before he dangled the strip of terry cloth from his finger. "Close your eyes."

Caleb's eyes fluttered shut, his body surrendering to Rod with ease he cherished with every fiber of his being.

"Do you want to know what I'm going to do to you?" Rod secured the blindfold over his lover's eyes.

Caleb shook his head. "No. Do whatever it takes. Use me. Make me cry. Anything."

"Does not knowing turn you on?"

"Yes. And it scares me too, gives me that adrenaline rush. It's like anticipating a blow in a fight. But with you, I'm always the winner in the end."

Whenever Caleb said something like that, Rod wanted to fall to his knees and tell him that he couldn't live without him, that he was so insanely in love with him it hurt his soul to keep that information from spilling from his lips. But deep inside, he hoped Caleb could feel it through his touch.

"Good, you'll be my fucktoy tonight. Don't move until I tell you to, understood?"

Caleb nodded, his half-hard erection twitching on his belly. "Yes, Owner."

The words in Caleb's calm, obedient tone pumped blood to Rod's cock so fast he had to take a deep breath before he proceeded.

"Up," he said, tapping Caleb's hip. Caleb complied straight away, lifting his arse so Rod could slide a pillow underneath.

His lips met the cool flesh of Caleb's thigh, and he traveled towards his groin, moaning as the dark hair caressed his nose along the way. Rod buried his face in the crook where his leg met his groin. The hair that had been trimmed during all of their encounters was now shaved completely, probably with the razor Rod had found in the bathroom.

"You don't have to shave for me, I love every inch of your body anyway I can have it." Rod inhaled the clean scent of Caleb's skin. "But I appreciate a smooth sac," he said, before licking the delicate skin and sucking one ball into his mouth.

He'd been hairy since puberty and self-conscious about it for most of his life. Not all of his lovers appreciated the carpet on his chest or even his hairy arms, and he'd never judge anyone on their body shape or fuzz. The fact that Caleb was insanely hot was a bonus, but not a driving force behind his attraction to him.

Rod paid attention to Caleb's sac then dove under it. With the flat of his tongue, he swiped over Caleb's hole. Fueled by his lover's moans, he ate him out with languid strokes, sliding his tongue in, taking note of the texture of his pucker, and the smoothness around it. He returned to suck the delicate skin of Caleb's scrotum, then up the underside of his cock before he lapped at his hole once more.

Dutifully, Caleb held his legs spread, not moving bar his muscles twitching, his hole gripping Rod's tongue. Caleb's moans of pleasure turned into groans of frustration as Rod purposefully neglected his lover's cock. He wanted Caleb to wait for his orgasm, to come when he wouldn't be able to hold it any longer.

The sound of lube being opened made Caleb roll his hips as much as his position allowed, and Rod smacked one asscheek so hard that a red imprint of his hand started to form immediately.

Caleb sucked in a breath through his teeth then moaned.

"Patience," Rod said, landing a slap on the other cheek, making Caleb's butt wiggle. "Your hole is twitching for attention." He squirted lube over his palm, letting it spill over the edge. A huge perk of hotel sex was not needing to wash the sheets in the aftermath. With that thought, he poured a generous amount over Caleb's pucker before he slid one finger inside with ease.

A groan left Caleb and his cock dribbled precome, connecting the glistening head and his abdomen with slick string. Sliding out, Rod moved to lie alongside Caleb. He kissed him as two of his fingers glided over Caleb's pucker, before dipping in just as Rod's tongue slid past Caleb's lips.

His lover's ass clamped over his digits, so he added a third, pumping them, spreading, stretching. With one last peck to Caleb's lips, Rod returned his face to his crotch, this time taking the knob of his cock into his mouth. As he sucked on it, he forced a fourth finger in.

Caleb gasped, throwing his head back, his eyes hidden behind the blindfold.

"You're still so tight, but someday you'll be able to take my fist," Rod rumbled, licking the underside of his lover's cock.

Caleb moaned, pushing down on Rod's hand until his knuckles punched the outer ring of muscle. "Yes," he panted. "I'm ready now. I swear."

Bloody hell. Rod's legs went weak at the imagery of his fist inside Caleb.

"Shhh," he said. "Fucktoys don't talk. Unless they want to safeword. Then you can speak or tap any part of my body twice. Other than that, no touching me or yourself. Nod if you understand."

Caleb did.

Gently but firmly, Rod pushed his fingers in deeper, the widest part of his hand pressing on Caleb's outer ring of muscle. With a squirt of lube, he pumped faster, creating a smoother glide with his slippery hand. Caleb's soft mewls sounded distant, as if he was high on the experience. *Good.*

Rod moved up the bed, fingering Caleb as he kissed him gently, swallowing his needy whimpers.

"That's my good fucktoy," Rod whispered. He wished he could see Caleb's eyes as they rolled back in pleasure, but the sight deprivation would help Caleb focus better on the here and now. Seeing Caleb's cheeks flush even more, Rod continued: "Your needy hole is clamping on my fingers. Now loosen your fucksleeve for your owner. Breathe, and welcome my hand."

Rod thrust rhythmically, in and out by just an inch, wrenching tiny mewls from his lover. Then Caleb relaxed and Rod's hand slipped fully in, Caleb's hole clamping around his wrist.

A low, animalistic growl tore from Caleb and pulled Rod in for a scorching, sloppy kiss.

Fuck, yeah. Rod drank in the broken sobs as he moved his hand around infinitesimally.

"That's my good Wolf," he cooed. "My wild animal, my warm hole to be filled." He growled, his cock rock hard at the way Caleb reacted to the dirty words—writhing, moaning, crying. "You're my gorgeous pain slut, my lover, my boyfriend." *My life.*

With one more kiss, Rod moved down Caleb's body to take a peaked nipple into his mouth. He sucked and rolled it between his teeth, making his lover arch and clamp around his hand.

"Nnggh…" Caleb was struggling to keep quiet, his breathing uneven, his body nearly feverish.

"I know," Rod said, his voice low with lust. "But you can hold on longer."

He was between Caleb's legs again, kissing the inside of a muscled thigh, watching his hand gloriously stretching his lover. He had to close his eyes and breathe for a second so as not to come at the very sight. "No talking, but you can howl." Rod took Caleb's cock into his mouth and sucked, pulling on his fist to add pressure from the inside. Fuck, he tasted good, and Rod swallowed the precome on his tongue, inhaling the scent of the hotel's eucalyptus body wash.

A loud moan escaped Caleb, ending on a hitched sob, as Rod worked his hand inside, his mouth giving Caleb's cock a thorough suck. He let go for a moment to speak.

"I want to swallow your load, give me everything you have." With that, Rod sucked in earnest, pulling his hand out slightly, stretching Caleb's ass.

With a mumbled curse, Caleb started coming, shooting deep into Rod's throat. Rod swallowed, welcoming the tangy taste and the twitch of his lover's cock in his mouth. Pulling his hand all the way out, he triggered a fresh wave of come out of Caleb. As he lapped it up, Caleb thrashed around on the bed, forcing Rod to pin his torso to the mattress with his forearm.

His tongue still swirling around Caleb's deflating erection, he traced his used hole with slippery fingertips until Caleb hissed at the sharp pain taunting his post-orgasmic flesh.

"Don't move. We're not done yet," Rod ordered, wiping his hand on the towel Caleb had dried his head with before.

Caleb nodded, his lips parted, his legs still in the air.

Rod positioned himself next to the bed and pulled on the cover to slide Caleb to the edge of it. His gorgeous Wolf remained pliant, holding himself by the calves, his head hanging off the side of the bed, his long throat exposed.

"Open." Rod slapped Caleb's cheek and watched it turn pink as his lover parted his lips.

Rod smacked his cock over Caleb's face and took satisfaction in the way Caleb fought to stay still, only his tongue searching out his prize.

Finally granting it, Rod seated the crown on the roof of his lover's mouth before gliding in. Caleb's throat spasmed as he tried not to gag, then relaxed, swallowing Rod's entire length.

"Remember you can tap out anytime," Rod said and Caleb nodded, his mouth full.

Rod grazed his nails from Caleb's chest to his throat before wrapping his hand around it. He squeezed only enough to feel his cock moving as he rocked his hips, but Caleb's moan reverberated through his shaft, spurring him on. He squeezed harder, watching Caleb strain for air, his dick hardening as precome formed in its tip. He held his breath, his throat struggling but his body unmoving. Rod loosened his grip and retreated, letting Caleb gulp in a lungful of air just in time for Rod to shove his cock back in.

With the hand that had been inside Caleb, he reached over his body to slap his sensitive cock which was already showing its willingness to rejoin the party. Caleb yelped, sucking harder, making Rod wish he could see his tear-filled eyes. Rod delivered several more smacks in rapid succession, drinking in Caleb's mewls around his cock, his throat working overtime. His cries were of mixed pain and pleasure as every one of his muscled strained to remain still.

"You're such an insatiable pain slut. The most beautiful fucktoy I've ever seen." Rod slapped his lover's abused hole, still on display with Caleb's legs in the air.

Caleb wailed, thrusting his hips up as much as his position allowed, earning more rough treatment.

Rod pulled out, letting Caleb gulp lungfuls of air as he twisted both of his nipples in his fingers. He kneeled to remove Caleb's blindfold, seeing his eyes unfocused, his face blotched-pink and gorgeous.

"What's your color?"

"Green," Caleb mumbled.

"I didn't hear you."

"Green, Owner!" Caleb said, loud and clear, his gaze on Rod.

Caleb's swollen lips begged to be used as he licked them, and Rod indulged him with a languid, wet kiss before he stood up again.

"Straighten your legs. Hands to the sides."

Without a word, Caleb maneuvered accordingly, hanging his head off the bed, and opening his mouth.

One smooth glide, and Rod buried himself deep again. He rocked his hips, fucking his lover's mouth, bruising the back of his throat. Caleb drooled and whimpered, his fists gripping the sheets, but not reaching out. Rod wrapped his hand around Caleb's throat and squeezed, watching as Caleb's cock twitched. He was so perfect.

And all mine.

Rod's balls drew up and he tensed, before shooting his load down Caleb's throat. Under his palm, he felt his lover's Adam's apple bob as he swallowed, his hips humping the air.

Rod pulled out, but at the sight of Caleb shuffling to catch his cock again, drool around his mouth, bruises the shape of fingertips forming on his throat, he spurted one more load. This time, his come hit Caleb's face and jaw and Rod spread it all over with his hand. Then, he kneeled to lick it off Caleb's face before he kissed him slow and tender.

He maneuvered Caleb's limp body to the middle of the bed and placed kisses over Caleb's eyes, tasting the salty tears he'd helped to form.

"Thank you," Caleb whispered, his eyelids fluttering closed. He tried to get up, but his blissed-out expression suggested he didn't want to.

"Rest. I'll help you wash later," Rod said, covering Caleb with a fresh sheet from the closet.

He washed his hands and splashed his face. The mirror above the sink showed utter contentment in his dark-oak gaze, his disheveled hair and crooked smile. It was hard to believe, but he'd found a piece of his soul in Caleb, a piece that he'd never known existed. Now, he'd do anything not to lose it.

The sight of Caleb napping on the bed, his swollen lips parted, his face still smeared with come, was a picture that sealed itself in Rod's memory. If he could satisfy his lover's desires while at the same time giving him the pain both of them enjoyed for the rest of his existence, he'd consider it a life well-lived.

With a damp cloth, he wiped Caleb's face, then put a glass of water to his lips. Caleb took two sips with his eyes still closed, before he pulled Rod onto the bed, plastering his body to Rod's side.

Minutes passed as they lay sticky and unwilling to get up, with only the faint sounds of hotel staff and guests in the corridor a reminder that they weren't alone in the world.

"I'm going back to the UK once this is all over," Caleb said against Rod's pec, breaking the silence. His voice was raspy, letting Rod know how used his throat must be. He made a mental note to add honey to the room service order he was planning to make soon. Tea with honey would help. And cuddles.

"I was afraid to ask." Rod smoothed back his lover's sweaty, come-soaked hair.

"Thanks for giving me the space, but as much as I love Chicago, there's nothing here for me."

Rod didn't hide his sigh of relief. "I was scared to lose you like this. That you'd want to stay."

"For a moment, I thought so too. But coming here only sealed my decision to go back to the UK." He lifted his head off Rod's chest. "And to you. If you still want all the baggage that comes with me."

"I do. It's a part of you. And I—" Rod brushed his lips over Caleb's temple. "And all parts of you are important to me."

"Let's buy return tickets quick. Then we can shower." Caleb's grin lit up the room as he sat up, the sheet pooling at his waist.

"I'll draw you a bath if you let me pay for them." Rod nuzzled Caleb's throat where bruises from his fingertips had started to form. "I mean, it's only fair since I'm the one really wanting you in Bristol."

"I'm not going back just for you," Caleb said, then scooted closer, wincing in the process. "But you're a big part of the reason."

"You know, I'd move here if you asked." The sincerity with which Rod said it shocked him, and by the look on Caleb's face, it shocked his lover too.

"What?" Caleb squeaked, leaning back to take a gander at Rod. "You have your life in England."

"It's all meaningless." It became abundantly clear shortly after meeting Caleb. Rod sneaked a hand around his boyfriend's waist, his entire being reacting like Caleb was a magnet whose pull he couldn't ignore. "My house is empty without you there." It was the truth. Since Caleb's first visit, Rod had noticed how much joy the man had brought to it.

"Suppose you could marry me and get US citizenship." Caleb nudged Rod in the ribs with his elbow.

"Only for citizenship, huh?" Rod bit Caleb's earlobe lightly.

"Ouch!" Caleb averted his gaze, but his cheeks turned pink.

Rod's heart swelled, but he didn't want to let his imagination soar as he was liable to drop to one knee right then and there. "OK," he rasped and cleared his throat. "Let's get that flight so we'll know how much time we have left in Chicago. Maybe you can show me some views."

Caleb's grin was wicked. "Views, huh? Right then, we're taking the L to downtown tomorrow."

The nearest direct flight was in two days: O'Hare to Bristol via Frankfurt. Rod couldn't wait to hold Caleb's hand for nine hours in a flying can.

Chapter Seventeen

Rod

Rod couldn't stop smiling as he watched Caleb get dressed in the morning, rattling off all the places they should visit and all the ones they wouldn't be able to squeeze into a one-day tour. Seeing him so lively made Rod realize how Caleb's light had been dimmed until now. His mom's situation must have been weighing on him much more than he'd let on.

"We'll park and ride," Caleb said, the moment they sat in the rental. "We can leave the car at 5800 N. Cumberland Avenue and take the blue line from there. Should be about a forty-minute ride to Jackson." Caleb poked the sat nav to input the address.

After leaving the rental, Rod let Caleb direct him to the train that was similar to London's underground, except it was above it.

"It's called the 'L' for 'elevated railway,'" Caleb explained, as they rattled in the loud train all the way to the heart of Chicago.

The commotion and crowds of downtown reminded Rod of Manhattan's morning rush, except the smell was a lot more pleasant than the stench of New York City, which had shocked him the first time he'd visited it.

"Not sure if you're a fan of musicals, but this sign is quite famous." Caleb pointed to a theater building with a huge vertical neon sign that spelled the name of the city. "It's the Chicago Theatre. I've never been, though." He looked thoughtful as he glanced up, reaching for Rod's hand. "I don't know if I'd be into theater plays, but I like musicals turned into movies."

"We'll have to go one day." Rod kissed his boyfriend's temple. He could imagine them attending any play and musical there was from London to Manchester if Caleb would want to experience the variety.

"Sure, why not," Caleb said, but his grin betrayed his enthusiasm.

"Live musicals are unforgettable. My music tastes are a bit eclectic. Somewhere between Madonna and Nirvana, so there's always something I'll like."

"I love that." Caleb swung their clasped hands, his face turned up slightly to catch the sun streaming between the tall buildings.

Rod had never seen him so carefree, devoid of his usual inner anger. Maybe it was the fact that he was in his home city, the gruesome closure he got with his mom, or the sex from the day before. Probably all of them at once. Looking at Caleb like this, Rod promised himself he'd make that radiant smile appear more often on his boyfriend's face.

"How about you?" he asked.

"David Bowie and Elton John are my faves, but I wouldn't say no to The Doors on a rainy day," Caleb replied. "Oh, or Adele. I usually listen on my headphones, but I'd love to blast loud tunes in my own home someday."

"It's a good feeling for sure," Rod confirmed. "My house is always open to you and to blasting music... Well, maybe on weekends—my neighbors work from home."

"Careful, or I'll take you up on that offer."

Please do. There was nothing Rod wanted more than to have Caleb feel free and comfortable in his space.

Caleb looked ahead, maneuvering them between buildings. "Come, you have to see Chicago Pedway."

Leading the way, Caleb took Rod through a network of underground tunnels. "The locals use these for daily commutes, especially during the cold winters," he said. Eventually, they emerged above ground near the City Hall with its classic architecture and huge columns.

"It has a rooftop garden," Caleb said, when they passed it by without sparing a second glance at the building. As they plowed on, Rod could feel Caleb's excitement as he continued to show him his favorite parts of the city. "Now it's time for the Riverwalk." Caleb nearly skipped. The joyful energy wafting off him proved to be insanely infectious as Rod felt it in his chest. Or maybe it was something else?

Caleb led them down a set of stairs next to a red-iron bridge and they ended up on a pathway alongside the river. Rod admired the way Caleb's hair gleamed in the afternoon sun. The place was packed with so many people that nobody paid them any attention, letting them get lost in the crowds, making the romantic destination so much more intimate. It was just him and Caleb; nobody else existed.

Rod wrapped his hand around Caleb's waist, needing to feel him close, and they strolled like they had not a care in the world. Rod soaked up the surrealism of the moment as he listened to Caleb's tour of the surrounding area. His voice grew louder as a boat passed by, and he pointed to several buildings, talking about the Marina Towers, the Britannica Building, and the Willis Tower—which locals still called Sears Tower after its previous name.

They toyed with the idea of a river cruise, but decided against it, instead opting to take a few stops on the L to the Magnificent Mile. The bustling commercial district brimmed with wealthy locals and tourists, packing the street and the upscale shops that lined either side. The diversity of downtown led them along parks, boutiques, and even a tiny old church hidden amongst tall, modern buildings. Joy filled Rod as he listened to Caleb talk about shenanigans he'd gotten into with his friends on a night out, crashing parties they couldn't afford entry fees to.

"It's beautiful here," Rod said, relishing the afternoon breeze on his face.

"This is how tourists experience it. You saw where I grew up. This," he waved to the tall, glass buildings, "is Gotham City from Nolan's Batman. It's the city full of blues, the place where the river turns green on St. Patrick's day, but, unless you're filthy rich, it's all a romanticized dream. Like everywhere I guess. I romanticized the idea of the UK and Bristol in my head, too."

"The grass is always greener, huh?" Rod asked, as he himself had wondered many times whether he should look for happiness in a new place.

"That too. But I also wanted to see the city Pops told me so much about." Caleb sighed, a small, nostalgic smile gracing his lips. "I told you about my grandpa's friend, right?"

"Yeah, you did. What's the story there?" Rod asked as they passed a fancy restaurant, then another. He took note of how Caleb didn't spare them even a glance, not interested in the white tablecloths and waiters bringing champagne to people who no doubt treated them poorly.

"He mentioned Henry quite often," Caleb continued. "He would say things like 'Henry would love this book,' or 'I wish I could show this to Henry.' But from what I knew then, they just sent each other postcards for Christmas and birthdays." He looked to the sky for a moment and repositioned their linked hands, intertwining their fingers together. "After he died, I was packing his stuff and found a carved box under his bed. It had two letters from Henry and decades' worth of postcards from him. At first, I refused to read any of it. It was private, you know? But I couldn't stop thinking about the letters and finally caved. In the first one, Henry said that he was sorry that Lucy, my grandma," he clarified, "burned the collection of letters they exchanged over the years, saying they were too old to be so obsessed with each other. In the other letter, Henry said that his biggest heartbreak had been my Pops leaving the UK, but he'd found someone to share a life with and was happy. Both letters were written in the mid-seventies and the rest of their correspondence after that date was only postcards. When they started sending them, they'd cover the whole damn card with writing. It was kinda sad seeing how the messages on them got shorter and shorter as time went by. There was never a return address but Pops must have replied to them as they kept coming, right?"

"Did they ever talk on the phone?" Rod looked at Caleb intently. He was mesmerized at how Caleb was opening up to him, freely sharing parts of his life. With every new tidbit of the story, Rod found himself becoming more and more invested.

"Not that I'm aware of, no. I figured it would be great to find his friend or his family since I was going to Bristol anyway."

"Did you check the Bristol Archives catalog?"

"Don't tell me it's that easy." Caleb turned to Rod, disbelief on his face.

"Might not be." Rod chuckled. "You need to have some information beyond a name."

"Well, this is where I'm fucked. His name is—or was—Henry Smith."

"I can help you look when we get back." Rod smiled at the thought of Caleb returning to England with him.

Caleb kissed Rod's cheek. It was just a quick peck, but it filled Rod's chest with warmth.

They continued their stroll to the picturesque Millennium Park, stopping at the Cloud Gate. The modern sculpture was dubbed "The Bean" for its shape reflected the city's skyline and the surrounding green space. Tourists gathered to take pictures of it from afar but most walked underneath the belly of the bean. Caleb tugged Rod's hand and that's where they headed. "Look up." Caleb laid his head on Rod's shoulder, holding his phone upside down.

Rod craned his head up and grinned at their misshapen reflection in the surface of the sculpture. Caleb's hair was kissed by the breeze, and his eyes crinkled at the corners, showing a man who strove for happiness even under the worst of circumstances.

"This one should go in a frame," Caleb said, looking at the picture on his phone.

Rod kissed his boyfriend's temple, pulling him close as they continued walking.

"I googled events in the city this morning," Caleb said, checking his phone, "and there's a free blues concert about to start here. Come on."

They speed-walked to a clearing with a small stage at the very end of it. People of all ages, including toddlers, sat on blankets on the grass in front of it. Picking a spot, they joined the crowd waiting for the band.

Caleb wrapped his arms around Rod's waist as theIcmusicians started playing, the smooth guitar carrying on the wind in the open space. Rod looked up against the sun at the tall buildings surrounding them and decided it was a truly magnificent city indeed, but half of its magic was thanks to having Caleb as his tour guide.

Rod listened to the harmonica solo but his eyes were on his boyfriend, his heart singing knowing that they'd be flying back to Bristol together. It was hard for him to stop himself from imagining the possibilities; more dates, mind-blowing sex, Caleb moving in...

With his head tilted, Caleb leaned on Rod as he looked over the stage, somewhere in the distance.

"Are you OK? You spaced out for a moment," Rod asked, wrapping an arm around Caleb's waist.

"Yeah." Caleb ran his fingers over Rod's thigh. "I've been thinking about what happened to you and Adam. No, let me finish," he said when Rod opened his mouth to stop him. "You told me how you loved being a therapist and helping people. I mean, I'm sure you're doing a great job at the center now, but you have a specific skill set that you could use as a therapist."

"What?" Confused, Rod repositioned to face Caleb. "What are you talking about?"

"Kink." Caleb clapped Rod's thigh as if the single word explained everything.

"Caleb, love," Rod said, placing his hand over his boyfriend's. "You're not making any sense."

"Think about it. I'm sure—" He paused to reposition himself, clearly excited about whatever he was about to say. "No, I actually know for a fact, that some people in the Bristol kink community have a therapist. What they don't have is someone to discuss their issues that include kinks, and the dynamic of their BDSM relationships, because a vanilla person wouldn't understand that. They can try, but it's not the same."

"Right." Rod nodded, urging Caleb to continue.

"Now, imagine how you could help individuals and couples with counseling if you applied your knowledge of the kink community and being a dom during the sessions. They could tell you their problems freely, knowing you'd not only understand but could actually help them." Caleb squeezed Rod's hand, looking at him, waiting for a reply.

Rod sighed, shaking his head. "I don't think I can do it again." The very idea filled him with dread.

"Giving up, I see." Caleb puffed his cheeks, crossing his honed arms over his chest.

Rod smirked. "I know what you're trying to do here, Caleb."

"Well, good. The way I see it, by staying away and not using your skills, you're robbing the community of vital help they need and can't get anywhere else—not in the way you could give them."

"Fuck," Rod mumbled under his breath as Caleb's idea took root in his mind. "The way you're saying it makes sense, but—"

"Try?" Caleb's big, dark-oak eyes urged him to reconsider.

Fuck, it was impossible to resist.

Caleb sighed, reaching for Rod's hand. "One of the books on your nightstand was full of scribbled notes inside. I liked the passage on the bookmarked page about facing your demon, embracing your mistakes, and moving forward." He smirked, meeting Rod's gaze in a challenge.

The little shit was sneakier than Rod gave him credit for.

"I don't want to rent a sterile office again," Rod said, recognizing when he was beaten at his own game.

Caleb's lips turned up in a cheeky grin. "I have an idea for that, too."

"You really have thought this through, huh?"

"Oh, yeah." Caleb repositioned to sit cross-legged in front of Rod, his expression full of excitement. "So listen, your conservatory has heating but you use it as an extra storage room. Let me help you clean it out. I can install new floors, a fresh coat of paint, and we can hang some soft kinky art. Imagine a sofa there, a couple of chairs, even a kettle that you're so fond of. Think about it. It's perfect. It has a separate entrance from the garden, so people won't have to go through the house, but it would also give them a homey feel, as opposed to a room in an office building that you hated before."

"You missed your calling as a barrister." Rod smiled, reaching for Caleb's hand. "And I didn't know you knew how to do renovations."

"Just basic stuff. I worked so many odd jobs, I learned a few things here and there." Caleb shrugged, leaning forward.

"If I agreed to that—"

"Yes! So, I'll obviously need a helper." Caleb waggled his eyebrows. "Preferably big, strong, and able to lift heavy shit."

"I could do that." Rod chuckled, pulling Caleb between his open legs, ready to apply his own agenda to this idea. "So, how about you move in for the duration of the renovation to save on commuting?"

"Sneaky."

"I'll play dirty if I have to." Rod kissed Caleb's temple as his boyfriend rested his back against Rod's chest.

"You really want me in your house that bad, huh?"

"No, I want you in my bed, in my arms, every night."

"That does sound amazing." Caleb nodded.

"Well, then?" Rod asked, reaching out for Caleb.

"Deal."

Rod grinned, the happiness in him bubbling like freshly opened champagne, filling him with excitement. Listening to the band concluding the concert, and enjoying the afternoon breeze on his cheeks,

Rod concocted plans of making sweet and tender love to his boyfriend at the hotel tonight.

"Now let's go pack, we fly home in the morning," Rod said, standing up and pulling Caleb with him.

Caleb sighed, taking a wide glance at the city as he took Rod's hand. "Yeah, home. To Bristol."

Chapter Eighteen

Caleb

Caleb returned to Bristol and couldn't find his footing. After the mentally and emotionally draining week in Chicago, he woke up from the bubble he had existed in with Rod. It had been a temporary realm where he'd allowed himself to lean on this wonderful man so much, he was now afraid he'd break him.

Reality hit him when, after the long flight, he collapsed into the single bed in a tiny room at Sandra's house. Exhausted, he slept for the entire day until Sandra knocked to see if he was feeling OK. Accepting the tea she'd made, he texted Rod, saying he'd caught the flu. After all the crowds they'd been in contact with during their time in Chicago and on their journey back to the UK, this seemed entirely plausible. He knew he wasn't sick, but he couldn't deal with Rod's caring and supportive attitude. He felt like a burden. After spending a week in his hometown with Rod, his entire body and mind craved him and yearned for his presence. Not wanting to be clingy, Caleb wrapped himself in blankets and stayed at home for days, sinking deeper into the reality of his life.

His mother was dead.

He had no proper job.

He was a complete mess.

Evenings passed by watching reruns of cooking and drag shows with Sandra. Rod sent him well wishes and lovely messages that hurt Caleb even more. He knew it was a shitty move to lie to Rod after all he'd done to help, but Rod's patience and kindness were overwhelming. Caleb was waiting for him to snap and dump him, tell him he was too much, too problematic, too needy.

"I see what you're doing," Sandra said, slurping the noodles Caleb had freshly prepared.

They sat on the couch in front of the TV, as was Caleb's custom for the last week or so, ready to watch something Caleb could ignore and think of his life instead.

"Oh yeah? What is that?" Caleb blew on the hot soup, trying to catch the floating piece of carrot with his spoon.

"You care for him and you don't want to fuck it up," Sandra said matter-of-factly, a smug expression on her face.

"No shit, Sherlock. Tell me something I don't know." Caleb grimaced, burning his tongue on the fucking soup. He placed the bowl on the table and took a sip of water. Dammit. "Care is not even a word I'd use..."

"Oh?" Sandra sat straighter, her interest piqued.

"I haven't told him." Caleb sighed, running a hand over his face. "When we were strolling in Chicago, I realized that I love him. Pure and simple. And it's stronger than anything I've ever felt before. I didn't have the guts to say the big words to him then and I don't have the courage now. "

"Right." Sandra tapped her chin with a pink fingernail. "And your solution is to ignore him and hope he'll go away?"

"No, I don't want him to leave me."

"Ah, of course. So that's why you're ignoring his phone calls? That makes *total* sense," Sandra said with zero chill, rolling her eyes for good measure. "I'll support whatever you decide, but you looked so happy when you were with him. It hurts me to see you trying to fuck it up."

"Why would he want this?" Caleb spread his hands, leaning back on the sofa with a huff.

"Bruh. This," she waved at the entirety of Caleb's body, "is some unwashed bum I don't know. I haven't seen my friend for a week." She sighed dramatically. "But Caleb? That ballsy dude who moved countries on a whim and actually made it work? That dude is dope."

"I don't have a job," Caleb mumbled.

"Then move your talented arse and get one. I know you applied to a gazillion places cause you leave your shit open on my laptop. So, attend some interviews you have lined up and see what happens."

Caleb opened his mouth to argue.

"I get that it's not easy," Sandra interrupted him. "But take a good look at yourself. How far you've already come. If you don't reach for what you want, it will never be within your grasp. That's what you've been telling me since we met."

"Fuck you for being always right, Sandy." Caleb stuck his tongue out like a child and grinned, knowing that it was time to pull his head out of his ass. "I'll get a job, then I'll contact Rod to tell him." Yes. That was a solid plan.

Caleb had to admit that he looked quite decent in the salmon button-down he borrowed from Sandra's stack of clothes prepared for donation. The interview at the fancy-ass cafe the day before had been a complete bust. The moment the snobby dude's eyes landed on Caleb's neck tattoos he'd known it was over and it had only gone downhill from there.

He hadn't been picky when he'd sent out his applications and he'd take any stable job at this point. But in the long run, he'd like to work doing something he enjoyed.

Now, on his way to the next job interview, Caleb re-tucked the shirt into his skinny jeans and stopped to take a big breath. Releasing it, he looked up at the neon sign above the door: "Baskerville's Tattoo Parlor". He was sure he wouldn't get the job here. It was a long shot, but definitely worth a try.

The doorbell chimed when Caleb entered, repositioning his backpack on his shoulder.

Hip-hop music streamed from the speakers at a volume that merged with the buzz of the tattoo machines. The place had painted portraits in frames right below the ceiling, smaller sketches pinned to the wall, and pieces of art attached to any surface that would hold them. The pictures varied from faces of famous people, cartoon characters, monsters and killers from horror movies, to various tribal swirls.

This place was awesome, and he was already getting the interview jitters. Annoyed, he opened the collar of his shirt. It was too tight and he wasn't used to wearing these kinds of things. He untucked and unbuttoned it in hopes it would help. It didn't, but now he felt less stiff, showing off the printed t-shirt underneath.

Caleb approached the tiny reception desk and his eyes drifted to the three stations on his left. A skinny woman with bright red hair in a bun sat on a stool and was bent over, tattooing something on the calf of a big guy in a heavy-metal t-shirt. The remaining two stations were occupied by women getting matching sparrow tattoos on their forearms from two dudes sitting with their backs to Caleb.

Mesmerized, he almost missed the colorful curtain at the back move before a tall, muscled guy emerged from behind it. "You must be Caleb," he said, his low voice booming even over the buzz and the music. The braid of his black beard reached his upper chest, bouncing over the warm brown skin where his shirt was open. His friendly smile put Caleb at ease immediately.

"Yeah, that's me." Caleb shook the hand offered and followed the man to a round acrylic table on the right. Portfolios with gorgeous, detailed tattoos and sketches lay scattered over the surface.

"I'm Louis, we spoke on the phone," the guy said, placing a steaming mug on a sliver of table peeking out between the folders.

"That smells nice," Caleb said as the aroma reached his nose.

"Green tea. Want some?" Louis asked, his gaze taking in Caleb. The relaxed way he sat and the slight crinkle to his eyes from his smile told Caleb that Louis was not judging him, merely observing.

"No, thanks. I, uh—"

"Have you ever tattooed before?" Louis asked, crossing his alligator boots at his ankles.

"Well, once at a party some guy had a homemade machine and I did this bit on my calf." Caleb lifted the edge of his jeans to show the ink there.

"That's a blob."

"I was drunk."

"You're not selling yourself well, mate." Louis shook his head, sending his short dreadlocks bouncing around his face. "Listen, I'll be honest with you." He leaned forward, resting his elbows on his parted knees. "I can teach you how to use a tat machine, but not how to art, OK? I value variety and we need artists with different styles, but also people who'd fit in with us. Someone who's chill but who could draw, for example, something like that." He pointed to the t-shirt Caleb was wearing. "We got plenty of clients asking for modern cartoony stuff with an edge."

Caleb tried not to grin. "That's mine. I mean, my friend made me this t-shirt with my art. I have a folder full of those with me." Caleb pulled out the prints from his backpack to place them on the table. His heart pounded with dread and anticipation as he sat quietly waiting for the verdict.

Long fingers flipped the pages, as Louis frowned, analyzing Caleb's art before he lifted his head. "Bloody hell, mate, you drew this?"

"Yeah." Caleb nodded.

Louis whistled low. "Well, shit. I dig the kink theme in the last ones, too." He tapped a finger at the sketches inspired by Rod's attic and the BDSM research he'd been doing.

"New obsession, I guess." Caleb shrugged, but inside, he desperately hoped he was on the right track.

"Even if you've never really tattooed before, I can arrange you some pig's skin to practice on and you could learn, but um..." He ran his tongue over his upper teeth before he nodded, agreeing on something that was in his head. "Listen, mate, I'll be straight with you. We cater to the kink community a lot and we get our share of exhibitionists, OK? Various genders. Would you be cool with that?"

Caleb nodded. "Yeah, no problem." Decorating bodies of kinksters who'd then display his art sounded like the best job in the world.

"We need someone who won't shy away from tattooing an arsehole if that's what the client asks for." Louis leveled an expectant gaze on Caleb, waiting for his reaction.

"No shit, really?" Caleb grinned, amused.

"Oh, yeah."

"I don't mind. I'm totally your man."

Louis chuckled and clapped his hands on his thighs as if he'd made a decision. "OK, let's talk details, then."

Fuck, yeah!

He got the job.

On the walk to Sandra's, he thought how absolutely perfect the timing was. He was itching for a release, for pain, for a fight. Or better yet, for Rod's brand of sweet torture.

Grinning from ear to ear, he pulled out his phone to text Rod and ask for them to meet when he saw a message from his friend, Mat. He was the guy who made it possible for Caleb to join the underground fighting ring.

He'd sent a condolence message after Mom's funeral but they hadn't talked after that.

'Hey! I'm in Bristol this week. Are you free to meet up?'

'Yeah. When?'

'Tonight OK? Maybe the ring? I'd love to see you fight. I've heard good things about your mad skills.'

Shit. That had not been Caleb's plan. He'd promised Rod he wouldn't fight, especially if he'd gotten a job. But for one, he hadn't earned a dime from tattooing yet, and two, he itched for a fight. He craved the pain and adrenaline. Meeting Rod after over a week of semi-silence and asking him to make Caleb hurt as their first date back might not be the most romantic of ideas. Caleb needed to try harder, to prove to Rod how much he loved him before he told him the big words.

Caleb's fingers flew as he typed a reply. 'The ring sounds great.'

When Caleb arrived at Sandra's she wasn't home, so he was able to grab his fighting clothes and head out without worrying her.

He saw Mat from afar as he approached the night's venue. His friend wore a perfectly tailored suit and sucked on a cig, puffing circles into the air. With a smile on his face, Caleb approached the entrance to an underground parking lot belonging to a hotel which had closed during the pandemic. The 'For Sale' signs suggested that the coast was clear for their event tonight.

"Caleb! So good to see you in person. Finally!" Mat pulled Caleb into a quick hug, patting his back.

"Yeah, great to see you too."

Mat wasn't much taller than Caleb, which meant they both barely reached the armpits of the Zielinski twins when they approached the bouncers guarding the entrance. Mat's straight blond hair styled in a short, modern cut floated on the wind as he exchanged information with the bulky guys. He threw in a word or two that Caleb didn't understand but suspected was Polish, the language the three shared.

Mat's accent showed that he was born and bred in the UK but sometimes a harder consonant slipped, especially when talking to his friends.

A moment later, they all bumped fists and entered the venue.

This was a mistake.

Stepping into the ring, Caleb realized that the punches were not what he wanted. As the week in Chicago played through his mind, including his mom's last words to him, he got distracted. His movements became sloppy, and he took several punches that he could have avoided.

He nearly lost. But his expert left hook at the end saved him from defeat. His eye would be black and he hoped his kidneys were fine, but he won.

"You OK, mate?" Mat asked after the fight as they sat outside on the curb to get away from the noise.

The sun had nearly set and Mat's lit cig was the only glow apart from the street lamps.

"Yeah, I'm fine," Caleb said, stretching his arms above his head. The win didn't feel good. Neither did his body. Or his conscience.

"You got me some money, thanks." Mat patted him on the back.

"You bet on me?"

"'Course I did. Let me buy you a beer with my win and we can chat."

They stayed until the last fighters and spectators left and the twins could join them. Mat had told him that the three of them had grown up together in London, except the inseparable siblings grew a lot bigger.

"Do you have a place you could recommend?" Mat asked as they headed to the cab Mat had ordered.

Caleb's knee-jerk reaction was to say The Lion's Mane, but it was his and Rod's place and he didn't want to stain it with the guilt he felt after taking part in the fight.

"Let's go to my friend's favorite place. I'll text her to join us."

Miami Dream was a beach bar by the river with a unique atmosphere. The five of them sat on the swings outside, Sandra's feet in the sand brought to make the pub's patio look like a beach.

The twins were immediately enamored by Sandra, chatting with her about movies and complimenting her hair. Both Mark and Mickey had closed-cropped mohawks, tattoos, and black t-shirts with torn-off sleeves. Mark's had a flaming skull on it while Mickey's pictured the famous mouse in red shorts. Their large presence turned the heads of the mixed-gender evening crowd, but they only had eyes for Sandra.

Caleb's conversation with Mat flowed well until Caleb heard a familiar voice behind him. A shiver ran down his spine as he stiffened.

Rod.

Flanked by two other guys, Rod frowned, then a shadow of disappointment crossed his face the moment he noticed the fresh bruises on Caleb.

Busted.

"Can we join?" Rod asked approaching them.

Caleb felt his boyfriend's gaze on him and saw Sandra's eyes dart between them as she mouthed: "Oh, shit."

"Yeah, sure." Caleb waved them over, telling Rod that Mat was the friend he'd told him about, and Rod introduced Geordie and Patrick.

Rod's friends ordered drinks and broke into a conversation with Mat, while Rod stayed silent, tension clear in his shoulders. His eyes stayed glued to Caleb's beaten face on the other side of the table until he finally stood up.

"We need to talk," Rod said in a voice that brooked no argument.

Caleb winced, then reached for his backpack on the sand.

On his way out, Rod leaned in to whisper into Geordie's ear and the man handed something to Rod under the table.

Caleb sighed, dreading trying to explain to Rod how stupid he'd been tonight. "Let's take a walk," he said to Rod, but looked at Sandra who was sitting on Mark's lap as Mickey massaged her bare feet.

"Go," she waved Caleb off. "I'll be fine," she mouthed, smiling at something Mark whispered in her ear. "See you at home."

Chapter Nineteen

Rod

Not wanting to crowd Caleb, Rod didn't put up a fight when his boyfriend rejected the offer of going to Rod's place after they landed. He was aware Caleb needed space, but returning to the empty house only strengthened his belief that he'd never be happy in it without Caleb by his side.

The first night was hard, as the memories of falling asleep with his lover in his arms were still fresh. After a week of Caleb having the flu and sending only vague messages, Rod was afraid Caleb was backing into his negative mindset and slipping through his fingers. He promised himself he'd let Caleb be for a week longer before confronting him. The only saving grace was Sandra who found him on the Bears-4-U app and texted him that Caleb was fine.

Refusing to wallow in his headache over Caleb's silence, Rod accepted the invitation from Geordie and Patrick under one condition: they couldn't go to The Lion's Mane. He needed a break from obsessing over Caleb, even just to clear his mind before they could meet again and discuss if they were still on the same page when it came to their relationship. Back in Chicago, Caleb had been very enthusiastic about it and the renovations in Rod's house. But Rod had seen people grieving in many different ways and staying positive when Rod was around might have been Caleb's way. That didn't necessarily mean that what he'd said then hadn't been true, but Rod had to be emotionally prepared in case Caleb changed his mind.

Wearing a simple black polo and black cargo trousers stuffed into his boots, Rod met his friends by the Cascade Steps at Bristol city center. During the day, the place was always brimming with locals and families, dipping their toes in the fountain stairs, looking at the boats on the river. At night, it was a meeting spot for those who wanted to spend their evening in one of the restaurants or pubs along the river.

He waved to his friends as they weaved their way in a crowd dressed for a party. Between skirts, heels and sleek clothing on people of all genders, Rod felt gray and boring. His style hadn't changed for over a decade, but he was comfortable with that.

While Geordie chatted a mile a minute, Patrick was onto Rod with a side glance and a whispered, "What's wrong?"

Rod shook his head, not willing to discuss what wasn't yet an issue. It might be his brain overthinking Caleb's silence as their time together had been too good to be true.

The moment they'd neared a beach-style pub, the roar in Rod's head grew louder. He saw Caleb laughing with the bouncers from the fighting ring, Sandra and some dude in a suit that Rod didn't know. It would all be fine if not for the telltale bruise forming on Caleb's face. Rod knew immediately where Caleb had spent the evening and he confirmed it with the guilty-as-fuck expression on his face when his eyes landed on Rod.

The introductions came and went but all Rod could hear was Caleb's voice promising he'd never fight again, and definitely not without Rod with him or a solid reason. He'd either slipped up or was sending a harsh message that Rod had no claim on him anymore.

Unable to sit still any longer, Rod directed his gaze at Caleb on the other side of the table. "We need to talk."

Pushing to his feet, he asked Geordie for a packet of lube before he headed outside. Depending on the outcome of the night, it might prove useful. He waited for Caleb to say his goodbyes and marched out, hoping Caleb would follow.

Once far enough from the pub to talk, Rod sat on a bench facing the river. The broken lantern nearby and the bushes on both sides of the bench gave the spot the privacy of near darkness. The wooden boards creaked when Caleb sat on them with a heavy sigh, dropping his backpack between his feet.

"I know I promised," Caleb said, his voice gruff. "I'm sorry."

Was it because he regretted what he'd done or because it was deliberate and he wanted them to be over with a bang? Was Caleb trying to prove a point by hurting himself? Was he trying to assert his independence? He knew how protective Rod felt towards him so Rod wasn't sure if Caleb was acting out, or if it had just been a mistake.

"Are you still mine?" Rod's words pierced the eerie tension between them as he leaned forward, bracing his elbows on his knees.

The breeze from the river blew in his face, not cooling the intensity of the feelings swirling in him. He wasn't sure if he was more angry or disappointed, but he was certain that he wanted Caleb to feel his emotions on his body tonight. If he'd let him.

"What?" Caleb squeaked, putting a hand on Rod's arm. "Of course I am. Rod, look at me," he choked out.

"You promised," Rod whispered, turning to see Caleb's face.

His eyes were glassy and his lips formed a firm line as he swallowed hard. "I know."

"You broke a promise and you hurt what's mine. You have to be punished for it." Rod's gaze bore into Caleb, waiting for him to protest. "Do you agree?"

"Yes." Caleb nodded vigorously.

The relief that flooded Rod made him dizzy. They were still a couple. And everything would be fine after Caleb learned his lesson tonight.

"Do you want to change anything from your list of hard limits?"

"No." Caleb straightened, quickly understanding that their scene was on and the rules they'd drawn were now in motion.

"Then you won't know what your punishment will be. Depending on how sorry you prove you are, I will decide if I'll allow you to come."

"That—" Caleb swallowed, repositioning himself on the bench. Fuck, he was already aroused. "That sounds reasonable," Caleb said as a blush crept up his cheeks.

Rod's chuckle was dark and carried in the open space. "You're the same brand of mad as me."

Caleb smirked, holding Rod's gaze, confirming his statement. Rod was unable to talk about Caleb's reasoning behind tonight's fight, he had to calm down from the initial raging need in him first. By the fiery look in Caleb's eyes, he wasn't the only one.

"Stand up and face the river," he ordered and smiled when Caleb obeyed immediately.

Rod tugged his lover's joggers down to his knees in a rough motion. Caleb gasped but stayed in place, waiting.

Oh, this will be fun.

Caleb was wearing one of the jockstraps Rod had bought him and the bright red fabric worked like a Matador's cape on a sex-starved Rod.

"You need punishment, but I just want to fuck you first," Rod said, squeezing Caleb's asscheeks hard before pulling them apart. "Grab your ankles."

Caleb hesitated, his posture tensing for a moment, before he bent over and did as he'd been told. Rod's cock stiffened at the wordless obedience and the glorious view of Caleb's ass before him.

"I don't think you deserve lube, but I'll use it cause I don't want to put your hole out of commission. I'll need it later tonight." It took an enormous amount of self-restraint not to lick his lover's taint, not to bury his face in between those gorgeous cheeks he'd missed so much. Caleb hadn't earned it. Yet.

"Reach between your legs, palm up." Rod bit on the edge of the packet he'd taken from the ever-prepared Geordie, and ripped it open. There was no squirting sound when he emptied the lube on Caleb's fingers, only the silence of anticipation. "Prepare yourself for me."

Caleb shivered, his bare thighs breaking out in goosebumps. "What? Here?" Caleb's voice was barely a whisper.

"You heard me."

At first, Caleb's fingers trembled when he slathered his pucker, but when he slid a finger in, he moaned and quickly added another. Under the cover of semi-darkness, Rod watched his lover fingering himself in a public area, stifling groans as he prepared his hole.

God, he's so fucking sexy.

The remnants from the packet were enough for Rod to coat his raging erection, ready to sink into the heat of Caleb's ass.

"Enough." Rod removed Caleb's fingers and pulled him down.

Losing his balance, Caleb yelped, then cried out when the crown of Rod's cock slid past the first ring of muscle. His breathing became loud, punctuated by whimpers as Rod glided all the way in until Caleb was sitting on his lap.

He should invest in those packets or a small bottle to carry with him at all times. He was too horny around Caleb not to. Tonight, he was much more than that. He was furious.

Caleb groaned, rolling his hips.

Rod wrapped one hand around Caleb's waist and clamped the other over his mouth. "Quiet. You don't want people to hear you. We'll get fined or arrested," Rod whispered, hoping the night patrol was too busy with drunk partygoers to answer a call about people fucking on a bench.

Caleb nodded but otherwise didn't move.

Rod thrust his hips upward and Caleb groaned into his palm.

"I will take my hand away, but you have to stay quiet. Understood?"

Caleb nodded again.

Rod lifted the front of Caleb's t-shirt and stuffed it into his mouth. That way, the fabric rode up at the back so he had a better view of Caleb's buttocks. Gripping his lover's hips in both hands, he lifted him halfway off his cock, only to slam him down again, biting his lip to stop himself moaning at the sight and feel of the gorgeous ass. He spread his legs wider to thrust up as he guided Caleb up and down.

The night breeze and distant pub noises didn't drown Caleb's breath as it punched the air between the quietest of whimpers. His triceps strained as he held onto Rod's thighs, taking all of what Rod was giving him.

"Your hole is so greedy. I love when it squeezes me in a hug even when I'm angry with you," Rod growled low, watching his cock disappear into his lover.

Caleb arched his back, the honed lines of his body making him look like a dancer in the throes of a performance.

"Ah, gonna come," he groaned, gasping.

"No, you won't." Rod grunted on a vicious thrust.

"What?" Caleb croaked.

"That would be a reward and you don't deserve one."

"Fuck you."

"Mmmhmm. I'm not done reminding you who owns you," Rod growled, tightening his grip on Caleb's hips.

"Yes, fuck... so good," Caleb moaned. "Remind me. Punish me. Please, Owner... Ah!"

Rod's balls drew up at the words and he held Caleb in place, seated on his cock as he shot a load deep into his lover. Caleb tried to move, whimpering for release, but Rod held him firmly, wrapping his arms around his waist.

Biting Caleb's shoulder through the fabric of his t-shirt, Rod kept coming, his dick pulsing, filling Caleb up.

Spent, Rod nuzzled the place he bit as a clear plan for the rest of the evening formed in his head.

"We're just starting," Rod said, reaching around to squeeze Caleb's balls through the jockstrap, making him gasp. "Remember your safeword cause I'll ignore everything else you say. Feel free to be vocal once we get to my house and know that a sharp tongue would only fuel me more. How do they say it in America? Fuck around and find out?"

"You fucking sadist." Caleb clenched his tunnel, milking one last drop from Rod.

"Now, off," Rod smacked Caleb's ass so hard it echoed in the night. "And clench. I'm ordering a cab."

Caleb glared over his shoulder as he pulled his joggers up and bent over slowly to pick up his backpack.

Rod didn't hide his amusement, grinning over his phone as he scheduled their ride, thinking of how uncomfortable it was going to be for Caleb not to spill his come once in the car.

Footsteps close by made them look up. A drunk man in his twenties stopped in front of them, his eyes blowing wide as he took them in. Despite the darkness, it must have been clear what they'd been up to. "Fucking fairies," he mumbled.

"Oh, I get it," Caleb said, louder than necessary for the bloke to hear. "You're jealous 'cause you can't take a cock up the ass like a real man!" Caleb crossed his arms, giving the horrified guy the brattiest expression Rod had ever seen on his lover.

Rod's hearty laughter startled the young man even more and he picked up his pace until he started running away.

Chapter Twenty

Caleb

"Strip."

The clear and simple order from Rod hit Caleb like a slap. One that he'd been waiting for and welcomed with glee. Rod's gaze bore into him as he crossed his arms over his massive chest, daring Caleb to defy him.

Caleb thrust his chin up stubbornly but they both knew it was just a front. Yes, he'd broken his promise to Rod and he was aware that his punishment wouldn't be pleasant, but he wanted to hurt at Rod's hand so fucking much. He had a feeling Rod had been treating him like a delicate vase but now maybe he'd release what he'd been holding back. Caleb would welcome that, of course, but there was no way he'd be doing it with a pliant attitude. Whatever Rod had planned, Caleb trusted he'd honor the hard limits they'd set and respect Caleb's safeword. That didn't mean, however, that he had any idea what Rod had up his sleeve. Now, he was trembling with excitement to find out.

Clenching his ass not to spill Rod's come, he stepped out of his sneakers, wriggled out of his sweats, and jockstrap before he pulled his t-shirt off. He did it without finesse, but quickly and efficiently, tossing all his clothes into a pile on a chair.

"Lay on the bench, arse up." Rod's baritone pierced the silence of the attic.

Caleb complied, placing his face in the hole at the end of the table, his body flat. He breathed slowly, closing his eyes to enjoy Rod's touch as he covered Caleb's hands with mitts, then secured him to the bench with ankle and wrist cuffs. His legs were only slightly parted, making him wonder what Rod would do with him next.

The sound of heavy footsteps and water running on the other side of the room told Caleb that Rod was busy preparing his punishment.

Caleb felt Rod's paws knead his ass, as a low, approving rumble emanated from his chest. Something slim and hard touched his buttocks and Caleb immediately tried to imagine what it was.

"It's a rattan cane," Rod said as if reading Caleb's mind. "You know what to say if you want me to ease up or stop."

"I do."

At first, Rod patted the thin stick delicately over Caleb's buttocks and upper thighs, changing positions as if checking for the best angle. Just when Caleb was getting used to the mild sensation, his body relaxing, Rod spoke.

"This will sting."

"I don't thi—"

Thwack.

The cane landed hard across Caleb's mid-ass.

"Ouch fucking asshole motherfucker!" Caleb yelled as a burning, ringing pain exploded on his skin. It definitely got his attention.

Rod let out a throaty chuckle. The rich sound of his evil laughter made him sound like a sexy villain, and Caleb immediately imagined Rod as a leather-clad baddie in a big-budget porn movie.

"That was one. Let's say we start with ten, what do you think?"

"I think you're enjoying this." Caleb squirmed, the pain sending wake-up signals to his dick.

"You have no idea. Hmm..." Rod ghosted his fingers along the cane-landing zone. "Fifteen it is then."

"What?"

"Count," Rod ordered.

Thwack.

"Ouch!" Caleb yelped. The fucker didn't give him time to prepare. "Two! Now let's finish at ten!"

"Are you safewording?"

"Fuck you," Caleb spat but the malice in his words didn't reach his chest. The comfort of knowing that he could let go like that and Rod would understand was refreshing.

"Sure thing, my love."

Thwack.

"Three!" The tip of the cane landed squarely on the fleshy part of his asscheek. This one felt like it would leave a mark and Caleb couldn't wait to see it later.

With the fourth and fifth, Caleb noticed that Rod never hit the same spot twice, alternating between his buttocks and upper thighs. When the sixth flash landed, Caleb let himself get lost in the pain. Tears dropped to the wooden floor underneath him and he forgot about the world outside and focused on counting.

By the time he reached fifteen, he was sobbing and his ass was on fire. Yet his cock was half-hard.

"Such beautiful, red train tracks," Rod said, patting Caleb's butt gently. Even that touch hurt the caned skin.

He released Caleb's limbs but the freedom didn't convince Caleb to sit. To Rod's clear amusement, he remained on his stomach, resting his chin on his hands.

Rod dropped a stool in front of Caleb's face and sat on it; his parted legs showcasing his thick erection.

With a finger, he scooped one tear that was about to drop and put it in his mouth. Clearly satisfied, he nodded. "Now that I know you're hurting, we can talk. I'm so fucking mad, my Wolf. Why did you do it?"

"Mat was in town and he wanted to see me fight," Caleb replied, his stomach cramping at the idiotic eagerness he'd had to go back into the ring.

"So it's Mat's fault? You're innocent in this?" Rod lifted a thick eyebrow.

"No, no, it's not!" Caleb backtracked. "Fuck. I wanted it."

"What did you want?"

"The pain."

"I can give you that. Hurt you in a safe way. I can tear you apart and stitch you back together, remember? You fucking promised." The fact that Rod's tone remained calm was more upsetting than if he yelled and lashed out. Then again, he had a lot better ways to show Caleb how angry he was.

"I know," Caleb's voice hitched with a sob.

"So, what was the real reason?"

Caleb sighed, taking in Rod's ruggedly handsome face, his thick, impeccably-styled beard and kind, mahogany eyes. This man deserved so much more than Caleb could give him, but he had to accept that it wasn't for him to decide for Rod. And he clearly, for some insane reason, wanted him.

"You already took care of me in Chicago; you shoveled all my shit for a week. When we came back, I didn't want you to get tired of me. I'm too much sometimes and—"

"Are you telling me I can't handle you?"

Fuck. "No! No, that's not what I meant!"

"Because I'm here for all of you. The good, the bad, the fantastic, and the hard times." Rod leaned forward, their faces now inches apart. "You should know this by now. But since you don't, I'll make sure you remember it after today."

"Yes, Roderick," Caleb breathed. "Make me remember."

"Stand up."

Caleb rolled off the bench to avoid sitting on his ass, aware of Rod's hawk-like gaze on him. Arms at his sides, he stood in front of Rod.

His lover's big hands cupped his cheeks, swiping the drying tears away with his thumbs. "You're crying and yet you're hard. I've been doing a poor job of this punishment." Rod looked down, and reached to squeeze Caleb's sac. He held it so firmly, Caleb struggled not to stand on tiptoes to ease the grip.

"No, it fucking hurt. It really did. I promise!" Caleb clenched his cheeks, feeling the welts pull on his skin.

"But you liked it too much." Rod smirked. "Are you ready for more?"

Caleb swallowed and released a breath when Rod let go of his balls. "Yes."

"Do you want to know what's next?"

"Will it hurt?" Caleb asked, even though he knew the answer.

"In many ways."

What's that supposed to mean?

Rod's smile was like Mona Lisa's, impossible to decipher, but Caleb was certain his lover's evil brain had concocted something painfully beautiful.

"Then that's enough. I don't want to know more."

"Will your cock to soften." Rod nodded at Caleb's erection and turned to the dresser to rummage in it.

Caleb looked at Rod's ass and his broad shoulders, making his situation even worse. "I can't just—"

"Then try harder."

Caleb closed his eyes and breathed steadily, focusing on the fear of the unknown before him.

"Very good." Rod glanced from Caleb's dick to the implements cradled in his paws before he picked one and showed it to Caleb.

"What the fuck—" Caleb's eyes widened. "Oh, no."

"Oh, yes. Legs wide."

Even semi-flaccid, Caleb's cock was not tiny and the cage Rod held didn't look like it was gonna fit. It was shiny and beautiful, though, made of metal rings and with a tiny padlock on top.

Caleb desperately tried not to get aroused as Rod fitted his dick in the cage, squeezing his balls into the tight ring before he closed the padlock with a delicate click.

Sliding the key into his pocket, Rod took a step back and looked at Caleb.

"Fuck, you're so beautiful. And now, at least you won't get hard during your punishment. Well, you can try." He chuckled, petting Caleb's crown through the space. He scooped the drop of pre-come from it and licked it off his finger.

Caleb's treacherous dick tried to stiffen at the sight, but the cage restricted it. He stifled a groan just as Rod brought over the wolf mask. Caleb welcomed the smell of the leather and the weight on his head, only now noticing that the bottom collar of it had a metal ring attached at the nape. Rod pulled on it and it brought Caleb's head back.

"Mmm, my naughty Wolf," Rod said, meeting Caleb's gaze through the holes in the mask. "Kneel on all fours."

Caleb lowered himself to the floor to assume the position and tilted his head to the side to follow Rod's movements. His lover held a large steel hook that ended in a ball at the crooked end and a loop at the other.

"What the fuck is that?"

"Relax. It's an anal hook."

"Fucking hell," Caleb breathed. He didn't have time to wonder what it was for as Rod slathered a tiny amount of lube on the ball and disappeared from Caleb's field of vision. Caleb felt the cool steel breach his ass and he welcomed the intrusion with a moan. Rod moved it around before sliding it deep enough to burn. With little lube and mostly just Rod's come in there, the sensation wasn't the most comfortable. Then again, as punishments went, it wasn't bad either.

"Chin up, back straight."

Caleb complied and heard a click at his nape and mid-back.

"Lower your head," Rod said, amusement in his tone.

There was resistance on the mask and around Caleb's neck when he tried to look down, then he felt the hook in his ass pull deep in him.

Caleb hissed. "Wha— what did you do?" he asked, lifting his head up.

"I connected your mask and the hook with a spreader bar."

"Now be a good Wolf and crawl to the cage," Rod said, smacking Caleb's asscheek.

Fresh pain exploded on the raw skin and Caleb sucked in air with a hiss. "How am I supposed to—"

"Mouth off and see what happens." Rod approached the cage and opened the gate. "In, naughty Wolf."

Caleb gritted his teeth and very carefully crawled into the cage. His knees were thankful for the rubber-covered mattress that was there but it wouldn't help him more than that as he had no way of sitting or laying down. At the realization of how weirdly restrained he was on top of the mask and mitts, a wave of humiliation mixed with lust washed over him. His ass hurt like a motherfucker from the cane, his cock was in a cage and so was he. Yet, he was so fucking aroused, it was uncomfortable under the circumstances.

A click of a lock startled him and he stiffly turned around to see Rod closing a padlock on the gate before he crouched in front of Caleb's face.

"Color?" He asked, his eyes roaming over Caleb's form, as he rearranged his erection.

Caleb lifted his chin up, easing the strain inside his ass in the process. "Green."

"Lovely," Rod said with uber-cheer. "Now think about what you've done."

"Where are you going?" Caleb squeaked as panic struck him.

"I'll be back."

"When?"

"When I'm ready with the next stage of your punishment," Rod replied in a cheery tone.

"But—"

"Careful."

"Fucking sadist," Caleb mumbled as Rod's hearty chuckle faded along with his footsteps down the stairs.

Chapter Twenty-One

Rod

Grinning like a Cheshire cat, Rod jogged down the stairs and into the kitchen. As eager as he was for the next stage of the punishment, he wanted to take his time.

He knew how impatient Caleb was, so waiting in restraints would mess with his head more than any pain would. Fucking Caleb on the bench earlier had proven to be the best impromptu strategy. If Rod hadn't had that release, there's no way he would have been able to resist pounding Caleb's ass once it was covered in cane marks. And even if he had, he'd have had to at least wank at the sight of his lover in Wolf gear and a hook inside him.

A glass of water helped him cool down and he raided the kitchen in search of healthy snacks. He wasn't prepared for guests but his fridge was always a treasure trove. He took his time cutting cheese and meats then added grapes to the platter before covering it with foil wrap. It would wait for aftercare snacking. Maybe Caleb would let him feed him in bed again?

Moving onto the task he'd come downstairs for, Rod felt the evil grin on his face when he reached out for the ginger root that had been sitting on the fridge door for several days. The juices should be ripe and just perfect for what he had in mind. He was supposed to make a carrot ginger soup a few days prior, but now he had much better plans for the latter vegetable.

With a small, sharp knife, he carved a shape as close to an elongated butt plug as he managed. The proper base would keep it from getting sucked into his Wolf. When finished, it was smooth, with no rough patches or edges, and ready to be used.

Rod ventured to the attic with the ginger root plug on a platter like the most succulent dish, not an instrument of torture.

Seeing Caleb on his knees in the cage in the same position he'd left him filled Rod with pride and caused his cock to stiffen.

Bloody hell, he's perfect.

Rod left the plate on the sofa next to the cage and fished a key from his pocket. The click of the padlock opening made Caleb shuffle closer to the gate.

"Where the fuck have you been?" Caleb asked in a frustrated tone.

"If you hadn't earned this plug before, your sharp tongue definitely has now." Rod lifted the carved ginger root, presenting it to his sub.

Caleb looked down at it, sucked in air as he pulled on the hook inside him, then thrust his chin up again. "What is this?"

"You didn't want to know. Did you change your mind?"

"No," Caleb clipped.

"Now, come here." Rod grinned, moving to the side to let Caleb out.

With careful movements, Caleb shuffled onto the wooden floor, his cock spilling precome onto the panels. The very sight called for Rod to lick it through the cage and watch Caleb's pained expression as his dick tried to harden.

Instead, he patted Caleb's gorgeously-caned ass until his lover hissed at him like a cat.

"Chin up," Rod said and with a click of the carabiner at Caleb's nape, he unclipped the spreader bar. "Let go of the hook for me, Wolf."

Caleb grunted and the metal slid out, but Rod had to pull to get the ball at its end out with a wet plop. Rod watched Caleb's hole clench on air, and he longed for the moment he would sink his cock into the hot fucksleeve again.

He hadn't added much lube before on purpose. The less of it there was, the better the effect of the ginger root.

"Do you have anything to say to me?" Rod asked, making sure Caleb remembered he could stop him at any time. The fact that he hadn't wanted to know about the punishment was proof of how much trust he put in Rod.

"No, Owner." Caleb hung his head and thrust his ass back.

"That's right, keep your hole loose," Rod said, placing one hand on Caleb's red cheek and positioning the vegan buttplug with the other. He pushed it in with some resistance, but Caleb dutifully took it all.

Once the root was inside, Rod walked Caleb to the St Andrew's cross on the far side of the room. Enjoying how Caleb let him maneuver him, he strapped his arms up and his legs to the sides using the cuffs attached to the padded X.

"My asshole tingles. Rod? What's happening?" Caleb wiggled in his leather shackles.

"It's ginger root," Rod said, squeezing Caleb's buttock. "You're feeling the juices now. The sensation will build up for about half an hour."

"Ah! Fuck, it burns too. Like, it's warm and shit. What the actual fuck?"

"Just say the word and I'll take it out."

Caleb shook his head. "I want to complete my punishment, Owner."

Rod touched his forehead to Caleb's leather-clad one. "What's your color?"

"Uh, fuck." Caleb grunted, wiggling his ass. "I'd say yellow but I don't want to slow down. I want to suffer for you. For breaking my promise and for what that did to our relationship. And, um... I'm excited to find out how it feels. Shit, fuck!" He thrashed again. "Even if it fucking hurts."

Rod danced his fingertips down Caleb's back to his crack, tapping the root before he smacked Caleb's red ass.

"You're bloody amazing, my Wolf." Rod kissed his shoulder. "I'll let you enjoy this punishment. You're allowed to make noise but keep the plug in until I come back for it."

Caleb nodded, thrusting his caged cock into the air as he clenched his cheeks.

The sounds of Caleb struggling after willingly giving himself to the punishment filled Rod with pride as he walked to the other side of the loft.

In the huge glass enclosure doubling as a bathroom, he approached the sink and trimmed his beard in the mirror above it. After stripping, he welcomed the heat of the shower water on his strung body, relaxing under the spray, humming a melody from a show he'd finished binging the day before.

Minutes passed and Rod could tell that the juices had started working on Caleb's ass as his wails grew louder. Once Rod deemed his Wolf had howled enough, he unstrapped him.

His lover fell into his arms and dutifully bent over for Rod to retrieve the ginger root. After taking off the wolf mask, Rod kissed Caleb's tears and guided him into the tiled stall. The slim cock-shaped shower head attachment would be perfect to help Caleb clean up before they went to bed.

Rod woke up before eight, but let Caleb sleep longer, knowing the man needed it. He went upstairs to tidy the attic, then to the kitchen to make tea.

All the while, he thought about how much he loved seeing Caleb in the wolf gear, and concocted plans on accessorizing his lover's kink outfit more. A leather jockstrap would go well with a tail plug, but a chest harness with hoops was definitely his next purchase. Yes, wearing all that Caleb would look perfect hanging in the suspension harness Rod had in a chest in the loft.

Once awake, Caleb walked into the kitchen stark naked, with sleepy eyes and a messy bedhead. It was the best view Rod had ever dreamed of seeing in his house.

Rod leaned in for a kiss and loved how Caleb's muscular arms wrapped around his waist.

"You brushed your teeth," Rod noted, pulling away. "Is that why you have a toothbrush in your backpack? I saw it after the fight and you seem to always carry it with you."

"It's an old habit," Caleb said, accepting tea as he leaned against the counter. "Back when Mom used to have bad days or have someone over when I came home from school, I would go to a friend's for a sleepover. I started carrying a few things with me since then."

"That explains the change of socks too."

They had a light breakfast and returned to bed for the softest morning fucking, after which Rod applied soothing lotion on Caleb's bum.

"What are you thinking about?" Rod asked when Caleb fell silent. He lay on his front on the covers, his bubble-butt on display.

"One moment I can't believe yesterday happened. But then, I know deep down I was hoping for it." Caleb propped his head on his hand to look at Rod.

"For what?"

"For you to snap. It took a lot and you did it with finesse. You always got your shit together."

Rod snorted, propping himself up on the pillows. "You got it all wrong, Caleb. I'm a complete mess without you. And seeing you needlessly hurt yourself for no reason made me go ballistic. Once I got a taste of having you, I couldn't—" He scratched his beard then repositioned himself again as Caleb lay his head on his chest. "I didn't have my shit together when you waltzed into my life. Despite my practice and my nonexistent love life, I could pretend everything was OK. But after you spent a night in my bed, in my arms, I couldn't do that anymore. It was as if you filled all the cracks of my broken existence and glued the parts that didn't hold. Now, it would fall apart without you." Rod kissed Caleb's hair and realized his lover's shoulders shook. "Caleb?"

A quiet sob sounded before Caleb lifted his head off Rod's pec. His tear-filled eyes met Rod's. "I love you so fucking much it hurts."

"Bloody hell." Rod pulled Caleb up for a kiss. "I love you too, my Wolf."

Rod smiled and their lips met again as he tasted salty happiness. Caleb straddled Rod and braced his hands on Rod's pecs, giving Rod a clear visual of how he'd look riding Rod's cock.

"I feel light in here." Caleb tapped his own sternum. "The whole punishment thing helped me with guilt." He slid his fingers through Rod's chest hair. "It seems like we're square. Well, sort of." He grinned. "Cause I enjoyed most of it."

"What was the part that you didn't?" Rod slid his hands up Caleb's thighs to rest on his hips.

"The waiting. The ginger root hurt in a weird-ass way and was humiliating, but in the end, it did what it was supposed to do. It cleared my mind completely. It was quite brilliant, I'll give you that," Caleb said, tracing circles around Rod's nipples with his thumbs. "But being alone for so long was awful. I was losing my patience and I couldn't even wank while waiting."

"That was the point." Rod smirked. "And you took it all with so much grace."

"I want to be your Wolf, your boyfriend, someone worth those titles. Not a child with issues. But you somehow let me be all of those."

"Our inner child, our past self, lives inside all of us," Rod said, understanding Caleb's words more than the man could know. "But even if you're not him anymore, he needs your attention. He's a part of you and how you got here, but he's not you. You don't have to be that perfect being you imagine, that social-media-worthy picture of you. Embrace your entire self, because every piece of you is precious. It is to me."

"Is that what you did with your inner child?" Caleb traced the scar above Rod's eyebrow with a gentle fingertip.

"Every time I think I did, I find something from the past that can still hurt me." Rod sighed, dancing his fingers on Caleb's back all the way down to his tanned hide. "That evil voice in our heads is the demon we have to fight. But we can't defeat it completely. We'd be too confident then, and stop striving to improve, thinking we've reached our potential. But if a tiny bit of that voice remains, it pushes us forward, makes us try again and again. And you," Rod squeezed Caleb's ass, "are definitely a fighter."

"Hmm, yeah, OK. But does that mean that you'll open your practice again?"

Rod shook his head in disbelief. The little shit had turned it all on him. "I don't know, Caleb."

"Ha!" Caleb poked a finger at Rod's chest "See, you can't live in a bubble outside of your own advice."

"You're right." Rod sighed, admitting defeat. "I actually gave your idea some thought and I think it's pretty solid. I should give it a shot."

Caleb's eyes blew wide. "And let me renovate your extension?"

"Only if you agree that the work comes with accommodation," Rod said, swallowing hard as he waited for Caleb's reaction. He wanted to straight-up offer Caleb to move in, but he knew Caleb's pride would get in the way. It was the most economically sound decision, though.

"Did you just ask me to move in with you?" Caleb's voice was neutral, not revealing his inclination.

"Well, yeah." Rod pinched the bridge of his nose.

"As a roommate?" Caleb quirked a brow. "Who would occasionally fuck me?"

The brat was fucking with his head. Rod snorted. "Yeah."

"I'm in."

"Really?" Rod sat straighter, excitement driving his body.

"I'm paying half of the bills, no questions asked." Caleb crossed his hands over his chest.

"But—"

"Dude, like, don't even start."

"I want to tan your hide for this."

Caleb smirked. "Punish me all you want, but that's my fucking hard limit."

"God, how I love you," Rod breathed as warmth spread in his chest.

Caleb blinked. "I'm not sure I'll ever get used to hearing that," he whispered.

"I'll say it so many times, you will."

Caleb threw himself at Rod, kissed him senseless and growled: "I've never loved anyone so fucking much in my life. It fucking hurts, man."

Rod exhaled. "But you like to hurt."

"Yeah. When my body hurts."

"Your heart is safe with me."

"I hope so. Now tear my body to pieces again," Caleb rolled his hips, his cock hardening. "And then stitch me back up."

"With pleasure," Rod rumbled, ready to start.

"But first, I'll tell you about the awesome job I got."

"What?"

Chapter Twenty-Two

Caleb

One month later.

Caleb set the paintbrush into the tray on the floor to wipe his sweaty forehead with his arm. He looked at his work and deemed that the sea-blue walls would be calming and go well with the furniture they'd picked.

"God, you look so hot like this." Rod's baritone filled the extension room as he leaned on the doorframe with two open beers. With a bare chest covered in lush hair, massive, muscled arms, and wearing only low-slung shorts, Rod was Caleb's ultimate fantasy.

Except he was real and he was allowed to touch him.

Caleb walked over to kiss his boyfriend and take his beer. "I'm done with this coat—one more and we can bring in the sofa and chairs," he said, then took a swig, enjoying the lager cooling his throat.

The entire week after Caleb's memorable punishment had been one big cuddle-fest. They'd fucked, snuggled, cooked, and watched TV, picking favorites the other hadn't seen before.

Caleb had moved in within days after that, bringing his meager belongings to the guest room. Rod had cleaned it out for Caleb to have a place to draw, but he usually ended up with a pad on the sofa anyway.

His job at the tattoo parlor consisted of sweeping the floor and watching other artists create masterpieces on human skin, but this week he started practicing basic script and tribals on pig skin. The flexible hours let him work on Rod's extension, and with mutual hard labor, the musty conservatory was on its way to becoming a full-fledged office. Soon, Rod would be able to consult with his new clients here.

For now, the three people from the local BDSM community who'd jumped at the opportunity to have a dom therapist had had their sessions in the attic. The feedback they'd given was that the BDSM equipment there put them at ease, reminding them that Rod understood many things that were a huge part of their lives.

To keep the kink atmosphere in the new office, Caleb ordered prints of Tom of Finland's leather erotic sketches to frame and cock-shaped coat hooks for the entrance.

Rod traced Caleb's bare, sweaty back with a finger then squeezed his buttock. "How's your arse?"

"Ready." Caleb thrust into the touch.

"Show me."

Caleb handed the beer over and slid his shorts off. Positioning himself on all fours, he showed the plug that had been keeping him on edge for the last hour. Rod tapped it and Caleb moaned as the motion put pressure on his prostate.

"You made me wait enough, Owner," Caleb said, eager to have his lover inside him.

A low growl suggested that Rod approved of the idea. A clink sounded when Rod put the beers away and Caleb felt his hands kneading his ass cheeks. He really had a thing for Caleb's glutes.

"Push it out," Rod said, gripping the base of the plug.

Caleb did and squirmed at the emptiness as Rod barely traced the rim with a finger. Fucking tease.

Caleb looked over his shoulder to see Rod shedding his shorts and kneeling behind Caleb. On one long thrust, Rod was seated inside, stretching Caleb the way he loved it most. They both groaned as Rod flattened Caleb to the ground with his massive body and rolled his hips, driving Caleb wild.

The smell of paint and beer around them was the peak domesticity Caleb had never even dreamed could be on the cards for him. But it was the lovable brute on top of him that made it all absolutely perfect.

"It's my birthday next week," Rod growled into Caleb's ear, keeping him from wiggling to get friction. "I know what gift I want from you."

A series of kinky ideas flashed through Caleb's mind, from that electro-stim kit they'd planned on trying out, to going to the London BDSM club Rod had praised so much.

"What is it?" he asked, trying to thrust back.

Rod lifted himself enough to reach around for Caleb's cock. He stroked it as he moved his hips in a languorous dance. "I want you to fuck me, Caleb," Rod whispered into Caleb's ear. "I want your cock deep inside me as you come."

"Oh, fuck!" Caleb moaned as the idea brought him to the brink.

"Then I want you to tattoo your name on my chest, over my heart." Rod licked Caleb's neck, his dick punching Caleb's prostate just right. "Cause that's where you belong."

With a broken wail, Caleb came into Rod's fist, spilling onto the wooden floor before he collapsed among cans of paint with a big bear on top of him.

Caleb loved the tattoo idea so much, he didn't dare tell Rod that it would require shaving his chest for it. Matching name tats sounded perfect.

They remained panting for a moment longer before Rod rolled them over.

"You need a break," he said, kissing Caleb's sweaty shoulder. "I made Cottage Pie."

"That's the one with beef?" Caleb asked, feeling ravenous already.

"Yup."

Within an hour, they were showered, full of minced meat, and ready to watch TV.

"Caleb? Are you fine if I don't go to The Lion's Mane tomorrow with you?" Rod asked, carrying mugs of tea from the kitchen.

"Yeah, sure. Everything OK?"

"Oh yes, I just got a text from Tom and he asked for a last-minute session."

Tom was one of Rod's new patients. He'd heard about the opportunity from Rod's friend, Geordie, and after a messy breakup with his dom, he reached out.

The couch dipped when Rod sat and placed the tea on the table in front of them. "I wanted to see Simon and Jimmy react when they find out about the exhibition, but you'll tell me all about it."

"Of course. Jimmy is busy but Simon will be there. It won't take me long and I'll be back when you're done, so we can go to Sandra's like we promised."

"Great. I'll text Tom now." Rod reached for his phone and started typing.

Caleb's and Rod's first meeting, as well as their first official bear picnic date, had been at The Lion's Mane pub. Since then, they'd visited often, each time commenting on the watercolor paintings. In time, they'd struck up a conversation about them with the owners—brothers Simon and Jimmy. Caleb had met Simon that fateful evening with Sandra when he'd helped toss out the white supremacist. The brothers had spoken of their great-grandparents with fondness, relaying the tales they'd heard about the refugees from inland Europe they'd helped during WWII. One evening Caleb put two and two together, and realized that their home was where Pop's parents stayed before he was born. To make sure he was right, the brothers dug out old photo albums and Caleb had found his great-grandpa and pregnant great-grandma on one of them, and with his Pops as an infant on another.

The information only sealed Caleb's idea of reciprocating kindness to the people who'd helped his family so much. Even though Alice, the lady who painted them, was dead, her art should get the recognition it deserved.

Both owners were keen on Caleb's idea of displaying the watercolors to the public but had no clue where to start. Caleb offered his help and as one thing led to another, Caleb's persistence paid off. After emailing every potential place in the city that could host an exhibition with paintings by an unsung war hero of the people, Bristol Museum & Art Gallery finally agreed. Tomorrow would be the day Caleb would get to tell the brothers that thousands would see their great-grandma's paintings and that they would have the proper media coverage and fanfare they deserved.

"All done," Rod said, putting his phone away. "I'm so excited about the exhibition, you did a hell of a job organizing it."

"The organizing part is still ahead but I know how to fight for things worth fighting for." Caleb nudged Rod's knee with his own.

Rod grinned and handed Caleb his tea. "Me too, especially for you to watch British shows you haven't seen yet. Now stop rolling your eyes and pick one, I know you secretly like them."

Caleb eyed the selection of movies and series he'd hauled to the table to decide what they should watch next.

"This box says *Sherlock* but it's not a frilly-clothes drama." They'd been going through Rod's collection of Blu Rays on and off for weeks, alternating with Caleb's favorite classics. He was still shooketh to his core that Rod had never seen the *American Pie* movies.

"It's a modern take on it," Rod said, reaching across for a blanket to throw over them.

"And it's in London! I'm sold." Caleb scanned the description in the booklet inside. He was going to finally see the city next week and he'd sunk into the information hole that was the internet to read as much as he could about it to enjoy even the historical sites. Well, and he was also looking forward to visiting The Golden Handcuffs wearing his wolf gear...

"I can't wait for your opinion of it." Rod reached for the box set and stood up to put the disc in. "We should start watching it from the unaired pilot." Rod grinned, glancing at Caleb.

"Your smile makes me suspicious." Caleb crossed his arms and leaned back on the couch.

"I have fond memories of watching *Merlin* with my uni flatmate back when. You might meet him when we visit the club in London." Rod slid the disc in and took the remote before returning to sit. "Then *Sherlock* came out and it was a completely new box of awesome."

"OK, OK, just play it already."

30 min later.

"Wait... Are they gay? You didn't tell me that!" Caleb gasped, sitting at the edge of his seat, watching a lanky detective in a swishy coat make googly eyes at his new roommate.

Rod chuckled, patting Caleb's knee. "Just watch."

"Come on, you didn't tell me this was gonna be gay. How did I miss this series? Wait, are they getting together at the end? Rod!" Caleb shoved at Rod's shoulder but the man continued chuckling. There was an evil glint in his eyes. Rod fed off keeping Caleb on his toes even when doing the most mundane of things, turning them into little adventures. Caleb straddled his lover and had to taste that smile.

"Mmm, I like what this show does to you already." Rod pressed pause before he grabbed Caleb's butt.

"It's not the show, it's you. Although I can't say John and Sherlock aren't hot. And dayum, have you seen Lestrade?" Caleb wolf-whistled then laughed when Rod nibbled on his collarbone.

Caleb was on a mission.

He'd emailed Simon beforehand so they knew he was coming. The pub was already open in the early afternoon but only a couple older locals sat watching reruns of *Doctor Who* on the TV above the bar while sipping tea. Caleb had fallen in love with the English idea of a pub. Here, it was a place to meet with friends and family during the day, have lunch, or even organize Christmas dinner. Most pubs had playgrounds outside for families with children and some had rooms above it to rent for the night.

Caleb waved to the men on the other side of the pub and sat on a stool by the bar. His next shift at the tattoo parlor was the following day and Rod was with a client now, so he had time to spare. He didn't have to wait long as the Wild West-worthy doors to the kitchen swung open to reveal Simon with two servings of fish and chips balanced on each forearm.

"Hey, Caleb! You're early. I'll be with you in a sec." He rounded the bar and headed past Caleb.

"Let me help you with these." Caleb took one packed plate from Simon and carried it to the table at the far end.

"Uncle, this is Caleb," Simon said to one of the men.

He was clean-shaven and wearing a tailored suit that could belong in *Peaky Blinders*. "He's the one who's trying to have Nana Alice's art on display."

"Hi, nice to meet you," Caleb said, shaking hands with the older man.

"I'm Henry, his great-uncle actually, but he likes to make me sound young so I don't mind." Henry chuckled, then motioned to the man beside to him. "And this is Hashim."

"I'm his best friend. Or the only one that's still alive." He laugh-wheezed and Henry joined him, sharing the dark-humor inside joke.

"Come, sit and tell us about your idea," Henry said, patting the chair next to him.

"Actually, that's why I came here today." Caleb turned to Simon. "I finally got a confirmation from one of the places I was talking to. This is really happening." He grinned, seeing Simon's eyes go wide.

"What? Who? Bloody hell, I'm buzzing here." Simon plopped on a chair, then stood up, before Henry tugged his hand to sit him back down.

"I couldn't believe it when they agreed." Caleb paused for dramatic effect, enjoying the three pairs of eyes on him. "Bristol Museum."

"You're pulling my leg!" Simon slapped his thigh. "Come on!"

"I'm dead serious. They said they not only loved the art, but your family's story and that it deserved to be told. It will be displayed in the gallery but it will take a few months to schedule and organize."

"Did you hear that?" Simon turned to his great-uncle.

Only then Caleb noticed that the older man's eyes turned glassy with emotion. "Mother would be so happy," he said, swiping a stray tear that rolled down his cheek. "You went to all this trouble... You're a good young man."

Caleb smiled, knowing it was all worth it if it made this man cry. "I wish my Pops could see it. He was the one who told me about how his parents sought shelter and found an amazing family who helped them," Caleb said, and seeing how everyone was listening, he continued. "He was born here but left for the US in his twenties. All the stories about his childhood in Bristol were what brought me here in the first place. I just wish I found his best friend too.

He missed him all his life but never reconnected with him in person before he died last year."

"What was your grandfather's name?" Henry asked, exchanging a glance with Hashim.

"Frederick Doron," Caleb replied, looking between the two older men. "Why?"

Henry covered his mouth with a hand to stifle a sob.

What is happening? Caleb panicked. "I'm sorry, I—"

"My Fred was your grandpa," Henry said, as Hashim wrapped an arm over his shoulder in comfort.

"Uhhh, what?" Caleb stuttered out.

"Mother and Father had two sons, but my brother was never interested in running the pub, so they knew they'd leave it to me." Henry leaned forward, releasing a sigh. "I loved this place, but told them I'd never have kids to pass the business onto. Thankfully, my brother had and so did his children." He patted Simon's shoulder. "So I could leave it to Simon and Jimmy."

"I'm sorry, but what does that have to do—"

"Let the old man tell a story," Henry interrupted Caleb's question and they all chuckled before he continued. "Since I was a teenager, I thought I'd be manning the pub with my best friend, the boy I grew up with, the one who stole my heart..." He sighed, then looked straight at Caleb. "But society didn't approve of us, and neither did his parents. So they had him married and with a child by the time he turned twenty-two. His heart was always too big to disappoint his parents, but when they declared they were leaving for the USA and taking him and his new family with him, he refused. He came to me crying that evening and—" Henry swallowed, shaking his head, gazing into the distance through the window. "It was a pipe dream—the two of us together. Always had been. So I told him to go. He had a family, and a new life that waited for him in America. But I never forgot him."

Caleb was processing the information, sitting paralyzed. *Pops knew true love. No wonder he mentioned Henry so often.* "Thank you for being there for him. For telling me. I uh, I suspected... but Pops never told me—"

"That he was a friend of Molly's?" Henry supplied, smirking.

"A what?"

"He was gay, or bisexual most likely," Henry said, turning his kind eyes to Caleb. "He was a good man and I loved him with all my heart. We were just never meant to be."

It was Caleb's turn to cry. He suspected Pops had had a relationship with his best friend back then but having it confirmed was a different story. He'd never had the guts to ask Pops why he'd never remarried but now he regretted not talking to him openly. Thinking back, Caleb was sure that his grandpa hadn't been lonely. Deep down, he knew that Grandpa's friends were queer, and it explained why the bunch of them vibed so well despite coming from different walks of life.

Caleb let the tears fall, but he smiled through them. He was crying for so many reasons: the revelation itself, the regret for not talking to his grandpa about it, and the knowledge that Pops had had someone who loved him when he was young.

Caleb felt a pat on his hand on the table. It was Henry.

The man offered Caleb a soft smile. "You know that Fred was the only person I was allowed to cheat on my husband with," Henry said, leaning back on the chair.

"Oh?" Caleb swiped his tears away, wanting to hear stories of the past.

"My Tom knew that Fred was my first love. Even though he was far away, he always stayed close to my heart."

"You were married?" Caleb asked.

"We had nearly forty years together, Tom and I. But we tied the knot on the twentieth of March 2014, the month it was finally legal to do so in the UK." He smiled. "I had a great life and I hope so did Fred. He sent us a bauble every Christmas, you know. We kept all of them and hung them on the family tree every year. I kept his letters and postcards, too."

"He never forgot you either. And cherished your letters." Caleb sniffled. "Thank you for telling me."

"Thank you for organizing the exhibition. My mother would have loved it. And it means so much to all of us." Henry pulled Caleb into a hug.

Caleb let go of his tears, soaking the older man's suit. Crying in Henry's comforting embrace felt like connecting to his Pops. As if through his childhood love, a part of him was still alive.

Six months later. The day of the exhibition.

Caleb squeezed Rod's hand as they walked towards Bristol Museum, the building that would forever remind him of their Banksy-themed date. Tonight, however, it was time to celebrate another artist, Alice Smith.

The moment Caleb found out that the date for the opening of the exhibition fell on the weekend of Rod's and his anniversary, he knew he had to make the best of it. It had been a year since the day they'd met and Rod had stitched his forehead.

They arrived an hour before the lines would open to meet with the Smith family inside, ahead of the public storming the place. Caleb pulled them to a stop, pushing Rod against the wall.

"I remember you standing in this spot on our date," Caleb said, sliding his hands up the crisp white shirt covering Rod's chest. The open collar teased the enticing view of his chest hair and the charcoal suit accentuated his bulky frame to perfection. Caleb had never been a fan of suits, but seeing Rod in one made him reconsider his stance. He wore one as well. Rod helped him pick the style, but it was Caleb who fell in love with the purple three-piece. He figured it would be good to own one suit for special occasions. Like today.

"It feels like a lifetime ago and makes me realize how lucky we are to have found each other." He took Rod's hands in his and looked up, getting lost in Rod's mahogany eyes. "And for it to happen in a time and place where we don't have to hide."

"I thank the stars every day," Rod said, kissing Caleb's temple, then his lips briefly. "I love you."

Caleb closed his eyes, basking in the sound of those words. "I love you so fucking much," he whispered, reaching into his pocket to touch the tiny ring box resting there. Caleb already wore Rod's collar around his neck to honor their kink relationship, but if this evening went well, he would put a ring on Rod's finger to seal their future in the eyes of society as well.

"Mmm, music to my ears," Rod said, nuzzling Caleb's neck, his beard scratching in the most delicious way.

"You fixed my life. You fixed me," Caleb breathed, his heart full of happiness and jitters all at once.

"Nah, I just stitched up what was already there. And I love every single piece of you, Caleb."

THE END

If you enjoyed the story and would like to leave a review, you can do so on Amazon, Goodreads, Bookbub, or any social media or blog. I appreciate every kind word and review! <3 As a self-published author without the support of a publishing house, I rely on reader's reviews which help bring attention to the book and let new readers make an informed decision before purchasing it.

If you'd like to read stories slightly interwoven with this one, check out my Pursuit of Love series. You can even glimpse young Rod in The Lonely Date (part of The Blindfold Date Duology).

You can check out my other books on my Amazon author profile: author.to/KCCarmine

Thank you for reading!

Also By

If you'd like to check out my free stories, you can download them on BookFunnel: https://books.bookfunnel.com/carminefree

The Flower Arrangement
Heartbroken after a bitter divorce, Brendan finds solace in running his beloved flower shop. Wary of being hurt again, he vows to think twice before jumping into a new relationship. Then he meets flamboyant hairstylist Hugh, a man with skilled hands and a cheeky smile who tests Brendan's resolve.

Hugh has at long last realised his dream of having his own salon, but the glow of his success is hampered by the shadow of his loneliness. When brawny, six-foot-three Brendan appears wielding a bouquet of exquisite flowers, Hugh feels that shadow begin to fade. Brendan's kind eyes, chequered shirt, and dad-next-door appeal dare Hugh to break his no-dating-clients rule.

Sparks fly as their desire for each other grows. Passion and laughter help heal old wounds, but only time will tell if it is enough to build a lasting relationship.

A standalone story of second chances, idiots in love, and steamy jacuzzi scenes.

MM Contemporary Romance Novella (Pursuit of Love Series, book 1 – standalone)

Get yours on Kindle Unlimited, eBook, or paperback: mybook.to/TheFlower

The Blindfold Date

A new dating app. Rules: both parties sit at a table with blindfolds on. Each can ask three questions to the other. If they don't like the answers, they can leave. If both parties enjoy the conversation, they take the blindfold off. What can go wrong? Nothing. Unless after taking off the blindfold, you realise the other person is the last guy you expected to see.

This is exactly how Ernesto—an autistic video game programmer with a secret dominant streak, meets Brian—an easy-going ex-football player with a burgeoning desire to submit. And giving in to the demands of this lean, geeky Dom may be just what Brian needs.

A standalone MM book from the contemporary Pursuit of Love series. TW: D/S dynamics, mention of past abuse.

MM Contemporary Romance (Pursuit of Love Series, Book 2 – standalone)

Get yours on Kindle Unlimited, eBook, or paperback: mybook.to/TheBlindfoldDate

The Lonely Date

Brian has always dreamt of a professional football career. Years of dedication and hard work have brought that goal within arm's reach, but now he's facing a new battle—with his sexuality he can no longer repress. Coming out—or even experimenting—would endanger his prospective career. After a devastating accident, Brian finds himself being led through doors he was reluctant to open before.

E has always struggled with intimacy. As a gay geek on the spectrum, his love life has consisted of a series of haphazard and unrewarding anonymous encounters. After a hopeless crush on a fellow student, E faces a tough decision: step out of his comfort zone and reach for what he wants, or face a life alone.

A prequel to "The Blindfold Date," "The Lonely Date" meets Brian and Ernesto at a pivotal moment 12 years earlier as students at the same university.

MM Contemporary Romance Novella (Pursuit of Love Series, book 1.5)

Get yours on eBook, or paperback: mybook.to/TheLonelyDate

The Blindfold Date and The Lonely date are now available as **The Blindfold Date Duology** on KU, eBook, and paperback: mybook.to/BlindfoldDuology

The Sinner's Penance
Even disguised as a priest, Mat can't resist a man kneeling at his feet, begging to be punished.

Being a bodyguard for London's Polish Mafia had its benefits. Fast money, fast cars, and an endless stream of hot men fuelled Mateusz's insatiable lust for life. But when he takes out the son of a rival Mafia boss, he is forced to flee to a remote island in the West of England. Posing as a priest, Mateusz hopes he found the perfect disguise. Until a handsome stranger shows up to confession, begging for punishment. Can Mateusz rein in his ferocious carnal desires? Or will his cover be blown to smithereens?

As a newcomer to the island, Peyton's social life is limited to a dram at the local pub. Everything changes when he attends a mass on a Sunday and his gaze lands on the man he can't have. The one in a cassock.

Tropes/Themes: mafia, insta-lu$t, roleplaying, priest k!nk, wax play, flagellat!on, D/S, hurt/comfort, morally grey characters, bla$phemous use of religious artifacts, MM, HEA.

MM Contemporary Romance (Pursuit of Love Series, book 3 – standalone)

Get yours on Kindle Unlimited, eBook or paperback: mybook.to/SinnersPenance

The Golden Handcuffs

Tired and brokenhearted, he wanted a fresh start. When faced with an opportunity to work at a BD$M club, he embraced it, despite zero knowledge of what the work would entail. He definitely didn't expect to fall for tall and broody Dom.

MM Contemporary Romance (Pursuit of Love Series, book 4 – standalone)

Get yours: mybook.to/GoldenHandcuffs

Whispers in the Woods

MM Paranormal Novella (BPO Series)

When a gigantic forest creature saves Tomek from a falling tree, he feels an intense desire to know more about the young man the creature turns into. As Tomek and Robert's friendship blooms, the bigotry permeating society puts their relationship to question, while Tomek's heart fills with doubt and his head with denial about his sexuality. Will he be able to face his friend and admit his feelings? A new adult, queer tale of love in extraordinary times — full of emotion, reflection, and second chances.

Themes and tropes: pan + gay MCs, shifter romance, fighting bigotry, friends to lovers, Eastern European setting.

Get yours on Kindle Unlimited, eBook, or paperback: mybook.to/WhispersInTheWoods

About Author

K. C. Carmine is a Polish-born writer, currently living in England. She loves writing about people falling in love with a focus on characters and their journey to HEA. As a member of the queer community, it is important to her that her writing reflects the diversity of voices around her. While she is a lover of romance, she also enjoys horror, paranormal and mystery stories. When she's not writing, she likes travelling, playing the guitar, video games, and reading.

Check out my free short stories on BookFunnel: books.bookfunnel.com/carminefree
All my books: author.to/KCCarmine
Follow/reach out to me on social media: kccarmine.carrd.co/
Add my books to your TBR on Goodreads: www.goodreads.com/kccarmine

Printed in Great Britain
by Amazon